OATH OF POSSESSION

A DARK MAFIA ROMANCE

DEVIANT DOMS
BOOK 6

JANE HENRY

Copyright © 2022 by Jane Henry

All rights reserved.

No part of this book may be reproduced in any form or by any electronic or mechanical means, including information storage and retrieval systems, without written permission from the author, except for the use of brief quotations in a book review.

Cover art by Popkitty Designs

SYNOPSIS

Vivia Montavio is a traitor, and it's my job to see to her punishment and interrogation.

What a tragedy.

She's the hottest little number I've ever seen with that defiant little chin and eyes that spark with wit and boldness. I love a good challenge.

We're left with little choice when the truth outs.

So I take her far, far away to *La Cabina,* a rustic cabin in the middle of nowhere.

To…interrogate her.

Discover the truth.

But when I uncover more than I anticipated, she's not the only guilty one.

Because now that we're alone, I'll take whatever I want.

The truth.

Her innocence.

Everything.

She's in danger, but there's only one way to protect her now:

Claim her as mine.

Keep her captive.

Possess her.

And there's no one left to protect her from me.

CHAPTER ONE

DARIO

OF ALL THE jobs I've been given as capo in the Rossi family... something tells me, this one's gonna be my favorite.

I look in the rearview mirror at the furious, stunning redhead who looks as if she could tear me to pieces with her bare teeth, and give her a wink. I don't give a fuck about the guy sitting next to her, who's brooding like a pouty toddler, staring out at the hazy sketch of the Boston waterfront as it whizzes by the tinted window.

"Gonna 'fess up now?" I ask congenially, tossing the offer to either of them that might take the bait. They won't, though. Half wish I smoked so I could light one up just to add to the whole nonchalant vibe.

I shrug my shoulders. "Might be easier than when I've got you two suspended in chains in the family dungeon."

"Fuck off," she says in a half-whisper. She tries to hide the way her lips tremble, but I don't miss it. I wonder what exactly she's afraid of. She hasn't seen a fraction of what I'm capable of, so I don't know if there's more she fears than me.

But she knows I haven't made up the dungeon, and likely knows she's absolutely heading there.

I don't know much about Vivia Montavio except that she's a Montavio—which is almost enough to know. Youngest sister of the Montavio brothers, cousin to my fellow mob brothers the Rossis. Sergio Montavio, the eldest surviving Montavio after the death of his brother Nicolo, mentioned he had a younger sister. He even went so far as to casually mention I might like to meet her someday, but that was a few years back. And leave it to the asshole not to tell me she was a fuckin' knockout. I've only caught glimpses of her, but it was enough. I look forward to a more casual perusal, I smirk to myself.

Of course, she's off-limits now that she's a prisoner.

Though maybe…

My phone rings just as I pull up the traffic on GPS.

Romeo. My Don, the leader of the Rossi family.

"Yeah, brother?"

"You're gridlocked from where you are to the tunnel, then it's a fuckin' parking lot until you practically get here. You're looking at three hours minimum to get home."

I curse under my breath. The typical drive's only thirty to forty minutes without traffic but leave it to the Boston highway system to complicate shit.

"Got another plan, boss?" He don't want me sitting in traffic with cuffed captives likely to cause a scene, not to mention we'd be like sitting ducks on the highway if anyone decided to pull something funny on us. I have no idea who these two were involved with.

"Yeah. Take them off the highway, someplace private. Keep them quiet, keep them covered. Let me know if you get even an inkling you've got a tail."

Jesus. A tail?

I glance in my rearview mirrors, but with this traffic, it's impossible to tell if we've been followed.

"Mario and Gloria following?"

Mario, the youngest Rossi brother, and his woman Gloria helped me bag these two, and I expected they'd come as backup. Probably just as well if they didn't, though. If it comes down to a high-speed chase, having two cars to keep safe is bullshit. This ain't my first rodeo.

"No, I figured you could handle my spoiled little cousin and her henchman. Gave Mario and Gloria the night off."

A warning bell dings in the dark recesses of my mind, but I ignore it. I don't have much of a choice here. Got two prisoners I need to get to safety, a possible tail, and nothing short of a private jet to The Castle's getting me outta here anytime soon. If I had just the girl, I wouldn't even question nabbing a motorcycle from somewhere—hell, my brother-in-crime Mario's got connections on every street corner. But with two of them, I'm shit out of luck.

Romeo's voice is tight, controlled. He's concerned, goddammit. "Keep them safe until the traffic clears, see if you can get some answers in the meantime."

"Will do, brother."

"Stay in touch, Dario."

He disconnects the call. I know what that means. He wants a location on my phone and me to answer a call from him on the second ring, no more.

I take a quick left, scan the roads, then pull illegally down a one-way street. Vivia gasps behind me when the horns of oncoming traffic scream at me. I easily take my tires on half the curb, bang a right, knock out a mailbox that splinters like tinder, then hightail it outta there.

"You know that was illegal," she breathes from the back. Her voice is resigned, with a slight tremor.

I give her a look in the rearview mirror that says no shit, Sherlock.

"As if you should talk about illegal," I mutter under my breath. "Save the lecture, princess."

She wrinkles her nose. "Princess is the most pedantic, insulting term of endearment ever."

"Ah," I say, my tone dripping with sarcasm. "You thought that was a term of endearment. Nah, babe, that was condescension. See, I know how to use those pricy words, too."

Her eyes flash at me before she gives me a bleak, tight-lipped glare and looks out the window. She doesn't bother to respond. I'm surprised to realize I'm a little disappointed.

I wanted to hear her voice again.

It's on the tip of my tongue to ask the asshole she's with if he's gonna fill us in on what we can expect with a police raid, but his eyes are cold and merciless, and I already know from experience he won't say shit without the threat of torture and pain.

If that's how we have to play it, then okay, though I'd much rather tie up and torture the girl.

"You gonna fill me in about who you are and what your plan was?"

I don't miss the furtive glance Vivia sends toward him.

"Yeah, why don't you fill us in," she mutters.

Interesting. As if she didn't know what he was up to, or is this part of the game?

I drive down the now-empty road in the opposite direction of where I should be going, and tap my phone on the dash. "Call one."

I've got Orlando saved to speed dial, and never use names in my contacts. He answers on the first ring

"Hey, brother," he says warmly. I catch Vivia's eyes light up with recognition before she shutters them again. She has a past with the Rossis I need to dig into, and soon. "Hear you've got one of my favorite cousins in your possession."

Possession. I fucking wish.

"Yeah," I say, my voice tight. "Got some trouble, though. I've got two in my possession, highway's gridlocked, Romeo wants me to take them someplace off the grid until I can get them back to The Castle."

"You being followed?" he asks.

I look again out the window. It's easier to tell now that we're out of the main line of traffic. "No."

The guy behind me chuckles, a bone-chilling laugh that makes me want to haul him over the back of this seat and break his neck. When I get him out of this car, he'll answer for that. I grit my teeth and take another turn. Glance back in the rearview mirrors. Still nothing.

"Take 'em to Eatalia," he says. "Closed early, staff's gone home. I'll text you the lock code to get in."

When Orlando and I first met, it was behind bars, serving time. The day he flew the coop thanks to Romeo's connections, he told me to call him when I got out, told me he'd get me a better job than grand theft auto. When I got out, he was the first person I called and he took me straight to Eatalia, his restaurant in the North End.

"Aw, gettin' all nostalgic on me," I say, grinning despite the fact that I've got hostages, we could be followed, and I've got a shit ton of interrogation ahead of me. Orlando's the brother I never had.

He snorts. "Sentimental my ass. We've got a meat locker that locks from the outside there, it's where I keep all the fresh imports and butcher deliveries."

"Classic. Thanks, bro."

I hang up the phone and bang a right. We're only a few blocks away from his restaurant. I look in the mirrors again to see no one's following us, but the asshole's staring at me in the rearview mirror. He shakes his head, as if warning me.

"What the fuck are you smiling about?" I ask him. Jesus, I'm gonna sober him the hell up when we park.

He looks out the window and doesn't respond. I hazard a glance at Vivia, surprised to see there's alarm written on her face, fear she's barely containing. He looks over at her and shoots her a twisted smile, but she only shakes her head. What the hell is going on with these two?

I'll wait to ask them until we're safely inside.

I blow out a breath as I find the side alley entrance to Orlando's restaurant. The lot's empty, which is both good and bad. Bad, because it means our car will stand out like a sore thumb. Good, because it means we won't have an audience. But my sixth sense is triggered, and something tells me shit's gonna go down soon.

I take him out first, drag him by the arm, and don't give a shit his head whacks the door on his way out. That's for being an asshole. He curses but follows. I shove him up against the car and reach for her.

I'm more careful with her. I ease her out of the car and make sure she doesn't bang her head or knees on the way out. Her douchebag friend notices.

He narrows his eyes at me. "Gonna have a tough time interrogating her if it fucks with your sensibilities to manhandle her."

I've had enough of his bullshit. I turn and deliver a hard, quick blow to his gut, a warning.

"You shut the fuck up and stay out of this."

He comes up wheezing but still grinning. "She's a fuckin' Montavio. I wouldn't use kid gloves touching her if I were you."

I deck him again, a swift right hook to the jaw that makes Vivia cry out and recoil, but the motherfucker's only amused, bloodied lips pulled against white teeth in a sickening smile like a fucking sociopath. Maybe he is one.

When I look back at her, her eyes shine as if filled with unshed tears. Does she feel hopeless? Hate that I hit him? Or did she have something going on with this asshole? I note everything then get my ass to work. I've got a job to do.

We enter the back door after I put in the code, and I lead them both to the back of the kitchen near the meat locker. I don't even wanna know what—or who—Orlando's put in that damn thing. There's a reason it was the first place he told me to go.

I think of steaks and sides of bacon and pork tenderloin and try not to let my imagination get the best of me. Hell, if we're lucky, we'll end up not even having to use that thing. The douchebag will cry like a baby when he knows what he's up against, and Vivia will totally cave.

So I tell myself.

I sit them both on stools in front of me and check my phone. Orlando's got surveillance cameras up on the walls near his office. Parking lot's still empty. No calls from my brothers.

I pull up a stool across from them, lean forward so my arms are on my knees, and begin. "So," I say, nodding slowly at one then the other. "Who wants to go first?"

The man snorts. "I had nothing to do with it. Vivia's the one who set everything up. For Christ's sake, I'm a dead man walking if you guys thought I had anything to do with it. I never would've touched a hair on anyone's head!" In the bright overhead light, I can see his eyes are bloodshot and his voice ragged. He's a damn user is what he is, and it ain't just drugs he's used. The hurt expression on Vivia's face says it all.

I shake my head and grab one of Orlando's butcher knives. Grab a lemon from a bowl on the counter and demonstrate just how sharp this knife is by cutting a slice of lemon so thin you could see right through it.

"It would be really awesome if you two cooperate," I suggest. "So let's start from the beginning," I say, shrugging out of my suit coat and draping it across a chair. I lean over the back of one of the chairs and meet Vivia's eyes first. "You're Vivia Montavio. You a natural redhead, lovely?"

She has a shit poker face and looks like she's gonna wet her pants.

"No," she whispers.

"Ahh. What's your natural hair color?"

She swallows and doesn't answer. She doesn't trust me. Good, that's a start.

I push away from the chair and stalk over to her. Here, in the bright light, I can see that her eyes are a light gray, like the morning sky over the water after an early rain. I could float away deep into the recesses of eyes like that and not touch ground.

I drag my eyes to her neck, and note when she swallows, how she's nearly panting. When I reach her, I put my hand at her hairline, a gentle tracing of my finger to her scalp, and look to her partner. He's watching us with interest but doesn't look like he wants to murder me. If that were me in that chair and some asshole mobster touched my woman, I'd burst a motherfuckin' blood vessel trying to get at him.

"No reaction," I say out loud, shaking my head at him. "You don't care if I touch her?" He rolls his eyes and shakes his head. I lift my second hand to her hair and gently drag it along the edge of the wig she wears. She sits still, eyeing me but not moving a muscle or blinking. I know shit about wigs, but it's thankfully easy to take it off. Shoulder-length, honey-colored hair tumbles down.

She looks… younger.

Illegal.

And I fucking want this woman.

I swallow hard and toss the wig to the counter.

"Now that's better," I tell her, running my fingers through her tangled mane. "Good job, sweetheart."

Her eyes widen unexpectedly, as if I surprised her. Her pretty, heart-shaped mouth parts, and I don't know if it's my imagination, but she leans her head against my hand. I try again. "You did so good, didn't you?"

She releases a stifled gasp. I'm not sure why.

Interesting.

If I don't take control right here, right now, I'm gonna strip this woman and fuck her over that marble counter, job and onlooker and status be damned. I've hardly touched a woman since I got out of jail and didn't realize just how hungry I've been. And there's something about a woman like her that ticks every fucking box in my book.

She's a Montavio.

My captive.

And I have a job to do.

I pull away from her as if burnt and face the man sitting next to her.

"Thought you two were together?"

He snorts. "You thought wrong."

She flinches as if struck. Guess that was news to her. For some reason, his callous nature and her surprise infuriates me. I grab him by the front of his shirt and lift him, chair and all.

"Does she know that?" I ask in a deadly growl.

"She does now." I drop him and he flinches. Good.

I want to beat his scrawny ass, but I have to stay focused.

"Which one of you tried to hurt Marialena Rossi? Which one of you was behind that attempted hit?"

Vivia gives a strangled cry. The guy in front of me doesn't bat an eyelash, and he jerks his head at her. "Who do you think did? I don't even know who Marialena fucking is."

"Marialena?" Vivia whispers. "What?"

Looks like I've got some filling in to do.

I stand in front of them, cross my arms on my chest, and shake my head. "Let's start at the beginning." I want to watch every reaction, see what's news to them and what isn't. "My name's Dario DeRocco. I'm a sworn brother of the Rossi family, which probably comes as no surprise to either of you. Head Capo for Romeo Rossi."

No surprise. They knew that much.

"You two were caught by one of our detectives as the very same people who put a hit on the youngest Rossi sister, Marialena. She has a very perceptive bodyguard who'd lay down his life for her, who discovered the attempt on her life just in time to save her, but not without scaring the shit out of her and seriously pissing off her oldest brother Romeo."

Vivia's eyes fill with tears, and she shakes her head.

"I had no idea," she whispers. "I didn't know. You have to believe me. I'd never hurt one of my cousins. Never."

She doesn't look like someone who's lying, but then again, they never do. I can't let her pretty looks and pleading soften me.

"Then why no surprise when I apprehended you?"

She looks away and bites her lip. What the fuck is she hiding from me? Yeah, I thought so.

I jerk her chin so she looks back at me. She flinches at the look I give her.

"I thought—I thought you worked with Sergio."

"I do." Sergio, the eldest Montavio and Don of the Montavio mob, is one of our closest associates.

She slams her lips together and looks away, shaking her head.

I turn to him. "You. Tell me."

"I have nothing to tell you," he says, shaking his head. "It was all her idea. She was behind the whole thing."

"What? No!" she screams, shaking her head. "He's lying!"

I want to beat this man to within an inch of his life. Not only is he not willing to protect her, he's willing to let her take the hit for what he's done.

"I'm gonna beat the living shit out of you," I tell him, advancing toward him. "You a fuckin' pussy trying to put this on her? What kind of a fucking asshole lets someone else take the blame?" My eyes go blurry with rage as adrenaline pumps through my veins. I've got him by the shirt, lifting him straight off the floor when he begins to cry like the pussy he is and my phone rings again. Romeo.

Shit.

I drop him again, hard, raise my hand, and give him a solid backhand across his face. He screams like a little girl, and I curse under my breath while I answer the phone. I didn't hit him hard enough.

"Yeah."

"Get out. Now. They're coming after you. Mario and Gloria will be behind you as backup. Go, go, go!"

I don't ask him who or what, don't ask a single damn thing. I drag the two of them out the way we came and toss him in the back of the car. I take the extra second I hope I don't regret to put her in the front passenger seat instead of behind me and floor it.

CHAPTER TWO

Vivia

I SIT in the passenger seat. Stunned.

I don't know what happened. I hardly know how I got here.

One minute, I was meeting up with the guy I thought I loved. He was acting… suspicious, yeah. But he said something about one of my brothers. My brothers finding out I had an illicit affair is one of my greatest fears, one that had me shaking at the thought of what that would mean. The consequences would be disastrous. Painful. Devastating.

The next thing I know, I saw my cousin Mario and a woman I'd never seen before. And this guy driving the car, apparently one of the Rossi family's made men… This huge, larger than life, seriously intimidating guy sitting in the driver's seat handcuffed me and took me out of the club.

I'm in so much trouble I don't even know where to begin. As a Montavio family sister, I'm not even allowed to talk to men unsupervised and never have been. It was always chaperones, and bodyguards, and "you're not allowed to talk to that kind." I've known since a very young age that I was going to be married off because the Don of an Italian mob has no greater bargaining chip than his virgin daughter.

Gag.

I told my mom when I was six that I had decided to become a nun. I knew the sisters from the small parochial boarding school I went to. I fantasized about being untouchable, never attached to anyone but God, living among others just like me where no man could ever touch or abuse me.

I was proud of myself for finding a loophole. Nuns didn't have to get married. The single life never looked so good.

When I told my mother she raised her hand as if to slap me, and when I recoiled, she paused. She shook me instead, shoved me onto my bed, and told me that only ugly girls became nuns, and a pretty girl like me would get married someday to a man that she loved so she could bear him children.

Even at six years old, I knew a lie when I heard one.

Or so I thought.

I stare at Gray, the man I thought I actually… loved. I gave him my heart. I told him things I had never told anybody else. He paid attention to me, and it felt so damn good I gave him one of my most precious possessions: my virginity. I felt empowered when I did because I knew that my father couldn't use me anymore.

But I knew the cost. I knew my family would, at best, punish and disown me. At worst… I tried not to think of it, but I knew none of the outcomes would work in my favor.

I'm not a rule breaker, I never have been. It took all of the strength and courage I had to go behind my family's back, and for what? Now this guy, who claims that he's part of the Rossi family ring, claims something happened involving Marialena.

Did Gray try to hurt my cousin?

I've been used. Manipulated. And after all I've been through… He must've used me to get at her somehow, to get at the Rossis—

"Oh my God, how fast are you going?"

No response. He only focuses on the road and pushes the accelerator harder. The car almost vibrates and my stomach plummets.

When the car accelerates, my musings come to a stuttering halt. This man sitting next to me, this Dario guy, is driving faster than I've ever driven in my life, and it is terrifying. He's terrifying.

I've never met him before, but it's no surprise he's a new inductee to The Family. I knew Leo betrayed them, and their bylaws state they have to induct a new member within a year of losing one. I know the laws so well I could recite them. The Rossi family's rules are nearly identical to the Montavios'.

I glance at Dario. An Italian name, yes, and he has classically Italian features, but I've never seen him before.

I… would know.

I watched as my cousins and brothers grew into adulthood, no longer gangly and arrogant teens with too much pocket money and too many adult responsibilities.

I watched them, all of them, my brothers and cousins, as their scant beards grew fuller and their jaws hardened, and their eyes grew calloused and steely under the weight of what they did. What was expected of them. We all were united by heavy-handed, authoritarian patriarchs and a too-short childhood. Some of us bear those scars better than others.

And Dario, his well-muscled body moving with fluid grace even when apparently running for our lives, his shoulders impossibly wide and powerful, muscled arms likely bearing the Rossi family's signature rose among other infamous tats… fits the mold. Ruggedly handsome with classically masculine features, his coal-black eyes are framed by a square face. The stubborn set of his chin tells me he does not back down easily. A fight with Dario's a fight to the death. With his athletic physique and general air of authority, I'd pick him out as Rossi mob in a lineup even though I've never seen him before.

"Put your head back. If I say duck, you fucking duck," he says in a low voice that expects immediate obedience and God help the person that questions him. I don't like how that makes me feel, so I look away from him.

Duck? He wants me to duck? From… gunshots?

Jesus.

I don't even know who we're running from.

I want to ask him where we're going, who's after us, and what exactly he thinks I did.

But I'm… still wallowing in the knowledge that Gray used me. Deep in my gut there's one thing I know: the professions of love were fake. Gray used me because of who I am. He knows I gave up everything in my life for nothing, and he doesn't care. He tried to blame me back in the restaurant.

The look on Dario's face when he did… but no, I won't think of that now.

"Motherfucker," Dario says under his breath.

Gray laughs mirthlessly behind us, and I hate him for it. Hate him. He tried to frame me, used me, and likely set me up.

I hope Dario gets another chance to hit him. He'd be a lot more thorough about it than I would. I liked Gray because he was nothing like the men I grew up with—softer, gentler, without the crass edge of violence about him.

"You thought you could get away from them," Gray says.

Them. Them?

Dario glares, the heat of his gaze making me cower against the back of my seat, and he isn't even looking at me. I don't know how Gray doesn't disintegrate in the power of that glare.

"The fuck are you hiding?"

"They're gonna take you. They're gonna torture you. They'll find out what they need, and then they'll get rid of you. That's how they work, and you know it." He looks desperate, his eyes wide, while his lips turn upward in a sick smile. He's out of his mind.

"You talk in riddles, asshole," Dario growls. "Real men use big boy words." He talks to him as if dressing down a child. Despite the danger we're in, despite my hurt and anger and fear, I'm tempted to smile. He's taken the upper hand with Gray in a matter of seconds, and it feels like poetic justice.

Dario curses under his breath.

My belly drops when Dario hits the accelerator even harder. He's obviously not someone who's easily ruffled, so his rising anger concerns me. Someone's coming for us, and fast, and we don't have the benefit of a solid guard at our backs this time.

The traffic hasn't died down on the highway, so he's jetting from one side road to the next, not an easy feat on the narrow, often one-way streets of downtown Boston. I don't know where we're going or why, but I can only surmise that we're in a shit ton of trouble.

This is someone Gray knows. Fears, even.

"You might as well tell us, Gray," I say quietly, trying another tactic. "If someone comes after us, we're all gonna die."

"I know," Gray says, and suddenly he isn't smiling anymore. His eyes are wide and frantic as they dart around the interior of the car. Suddenly, he grabs for the door handle with his cuffed wrists. I scream. I can't help it. We must be driving eighty miles an hour, and if he pushed himself out of this car, he'd splatter on the pavement like a watermelon dropped from a skyscraper.

"As if I'd leave the fuckin' door unlocked," Dario says, shaking his head. He's put the child safety locks on. "You stupid son of a bitch. You that scared of being taken hostage?"

"You have no idea," Gray says, his voice thin and afraid. "You have no idea what they're capable of."

"Who?" I flinch at the sound of Dario's voice, so harsh and raw it's like a slap on bare skin.

A gunshot rings out. The car spins haphazardly. Dario curses but doesn't lose his grip on the steering wheel or his near perfect control. Glancing in the rearview mirror, he scowls. His voice is a low command without a trace of fear.

"Take the gun out of the glove compartment."

Gun. Take the gun out.

So those are words you'd never hear come out of my brothers' mouths.

Uh, okay…

He narrows his eyes, his face tight. "Tell me Sergio or someone taught you how to shoot."

I shake my head. I feel so… useless. I wasn't even allowed to touch a gun. I can barely hit someone with a damn water pistol at a pool party. "I… I don't shoot."

"Of course not," he mutters. "Always had someone to defend your back, didn't you? Fuck it."

Shame colors my cheeks at the derision in his voice and the knowledge that he's right. Jerk.

"Take the wheel and give me the gun."

What? I feel like we're on a movie set in a high-speed chase, but the only problem is, I have no stunt doubles, and… this might not end with us magically escaping death. I've been in danger before, but nothing like this, where I fear for my life from my very own family.

My hands shake on the wheel, but I have one job to do, and goddamn it if I'm not going to do it as well as I can. I keep my hands on the wheel and my foot on the accelerator as we trade places. Dario grips the gun, turns, and points out his window at two cars coming at us. Gunshots puncture the air around us. A corner of the window next to Gray shatters. Bullets hit and sink into the metal. I jump with every impact.

"Give me the gun," Gray says. "I have a better angle."

"Like hell I'll give you a gun," Dario growls at him.

"Don't give it to him," I second. "Plus, he can't even shoot with his wrists cuffed."

"Shut the fuck up, you bitch," Gray snaps at me.

Fuming hatred boils inside me. The traitor. The goddamn traitor.

I jump at the sound of Dario hitting Gray. "I don't know who the fuck you are," Dario says, his concentration on the cars behind us as I try to keep our car from swerving. "But she's a Montavio, related to my family. You watch yourself."

Not gonna lie, it's hella satisfying. I may not have grown up with this guy, he might be a new inductee, but Dario's got Rossi in his blood.

Gray growls, as more gunshots pepper the back of the car. I can hear them ricocheting off the bumper, the sound unnerving and terrifying all at once, but even I know we should be Swiss cheese by now.

"What is this car, like, bulletproof or something?" We should be so hard to target, nearly invincible.

"Of course. It's an armored vehicle," Dario responds. "Reinforced and souped up."

Ah. Naturally. My cousin Mario and his friend Santo likely had fun with that job. Leave it to them to build a car sleek with luxury but as safe as a military-grade vehicle.

"So we just have to get away?"

"It's not invincible," Dario says. "There are certain spots impossible to fortify, and if we—"

As if on cue, the crack in the window next to Gray splinters, hit a second time in the same place. Again, and again, gunshots embed in the glass. Someone's found a loophole in the armor and it's working.

"Duck," Dario growls to Gray. "You're the one they want."

"I want them to fucking kill me," Gray says in a strangled voice. "I'd be better off than if they take me."

I hear the sincerity in his voice. I cringe at the thought of death before capture.

Dario curses.

Our tires scrape the side of the curb. Shit, that's my job. I quickly veer us back on course. The wheel shakes under my grip.

There's a side street up ahead with orange detour signs all around.

"Detour. There won't be any cars," I tell Dario.

"Do it. I hit their tire and one of 'em's off course."

"How many still following?"

"Two more."

Fuck.

I yank the wheel right, hard. Gray's head smacks against the glass as another shot fires. I focus on the road. It's late, so there's no construction workers, but up ahead are orange cones surrounding a torn-up road. I hold my breath but keep my cool, yank the wheel left to go around one hole, then right again to avoid another hole in the road. Someone screams in a nearby doorway, and on the corner a small group of teens smoking weed hoot and holler like they're cheering us on. Dumbasses.

At first, I don't see our tail, but when I hit the end of the road, I hear a screech of tires and see a flash of headlights.

Here they are.

Dario whips out his phone and makes a call as he pulls the trigger again once, twice, three times. One of the cars behind us spins out and slams into an unyielding bus stop pole, the sound of rending metal like nails on a chalkboard.

"Orlando, we've got a tail."

"Hot?"

"Fucking hot."

Shots ring out again. My cousin Orlando curses loud enough for me to hear him.

"Not sure we can get away from them, brother. Don't know their endgame. I've got two down and another still active. Want you to know where we are in case…" His voice trails off.

Cold fear grips my chest. He's calling Orlando to let him know we're gonna be killed. He wants surveillance and a heads-up for his brothers and mine when they go to identify our corpses in the morgue. My throat's tight, my eyes blurry with tears I refuse to shed.

My hands tremble on the wheel but I keep on course.

Orlando tries to assure us. "I'll get a drone on you. Sending backup. Your phone's set up to send an SOS with three pushes of the volume button. You get taken or one of you gets shot, one of you hit that button. Vivia, there's a tiny transponder in the glove compartment. They won't realize you have it if they take your phone. It works the same as a cell."

My hands shake as I realize they're not only making plans for our death, they're also making plans for our capture. Neither are planning on us getting out of here alive. One hand on the wheel, I lean over, open the glove compartment, and wrap my fingers around the tiny electronic advice I imagine is what Orlando is talking about, tossing up a silent prayer of gratitude for all those years I did my makeup while driving. My mama always said it was dangerous and would get me killed, but multi-tasking while driving is a damn good skill to have.

"Got it," Dario says, before he shoots again. Of course Mario took my phone before Dario took me away, so that's useless.

He hangs up the phone as another shot shatters the window. I scream when I see Gray in the rearview mirror, blood pouring from an open wound in his temple. He slouches to the side.

"Got his fuckin' wish," Dario mutters.

Oh God. He's next. We're next.

Oh God.

I stifle a whimper and keep going.

"Running out of road," I say in a shaking voice to Dario. My whole body's shaking and I can't seem to stop it.

When he speaks, his voice doesn't tremble. He talks to me like he's ordering his coffee. How?

"Keep the wheel straight. Stay on course. You're doing great, just like that. I'm gonna shoot them out but I need you to keep us steady."

Warmth floods my chest. There it is again, a completely unfamiliar and unexpected sensation that makes me want to do exactly what he told me to. I don't understand it, but I do what he says, nodding my head even though it makes no damn difference.

Seconds ago, we were enemies and I was his captive. Now, we're two people running for our lives. I remind myself that I'm his captive and I should hate him. Anything he says to calm me down is only because it's his job to deliver me to my brothers and cousins alive.

"Can you turn at the end of the road?" he asks.

"Too hard to see, it's all dark. I think I can— oh, God!" A bevy of detour and "Road Closed Ahead" signs, each in stark black letters against an orange background, are the only warning I get before there is no road. There's nothing but a thin wall of broken rubble and discarded cinder blocks before the road drops off to nothing, like we're on the edge of a cliff. It's probably no more than a foot or two of torn-up concrete, but there's no way I can drive over it.

I slam the brakes so hard the tires screech.

"Nowhere to go. It drops off."

Without missing a beat, Dario tells me to park the car. He's got the door open. I follow him, and when I get out, he grabs my hand.

"Duck and follow my lead," he hisses, yanking me down. Stifling a scream, I do what he says as gunshots rain all around us. I whimper but quickly scurry beside him. He runs to a vacant backyard behind a picket fence and slams the gate behind us. It's a small yard with a swing set and a little garden. Bile rises in my throat when I realize we've brought danger to a house with children.

"There are—there are children here—"

"No car in the driveway, they're away."

No one's home. Maybe he chose this house on purpose so there would be no civilian casualties.

"Will take them a minute before they see us. We can—"

Wood splinters as a car plows straight through the wooden fence and heads straight toward us. I scream. Dario pulls the trigger and shoots the driver in the forehead. The car careens past us and crashes into the back fence.

Three men jump out of the car.

There's nowhere to go. There's nowhere to hide. A sick feeling roils in my belly.

"Hands up," a cold, oily voice says in our direction. I blink in surprise and stifle a whimper. Three men wearing ski masks and all black stalk toward us, unhurried, as if they know we're cornered and there's nothing we can do about this. "Who the fuck are you? You ain't Mullet."

Gray Mullet. Ha, as if Gray would've fought them off like this.

Dario is not going to surrender. He shoves me behind a metal bulkhead as he pulls the trigger. I fall to the ground as they shoot back at him. One falls, the second, the third. I watch in shock, crouched behind the bulkhead as bodies fall to the ground like clay pigeons in a shooting game. It's inhuman. I've seen one shoot-out in my life and heard plenty of stories. No one can shoot this many without getting shot himself.

I will kill Sergio for not teaching me to shoot, and as soon as I get free again— and I will get free—I'm gonna learn how to defend myself.

They're dead. They're all dead.

We're… free?

"Stay right there." Dario doesn't look at me but scans our surroundings. I'd be a fool not to listen to him.

I lay as still as a corpse. I hear him traipsing across the yard as he looks for a way out. Sirens wail behind us. Of course. We don't have much time.

The cops will come, identify the car and probably Gray's body…

"This way."

I stand and follow Dario, which isn't hard to do since he grabs my hand almost painfully and yanks me to a gate. "Bulkhead's locked and they'll expect us to go there."

"Who?" I whisper.

"I counted twelve after us. I killed nine. There's three more."

My palm feels sweaty in his. I don't know what's gonna happen next or how I'm going to get out of this, but I know my only chance of surviving is following the lead of the guy that just hosed down nine guys single-handedly.

"You're a good shot," I whisper.

"Served ten years in the military," he says, without a touch of pride in his voice. Matter-of-fact. "Comes in handy in my present line of business, too."

Something whizzes past me and almost hits my ear. There's a sizzling sound and a blare of orange flame against the dark sky.

"Watch it!"

Dario shoves me down to the ground and covers me with his body. Smoke permeates the air around us so badly I'm choking.

Wood splinters. Gunshots ring. Dario heaves himself off me so he can shoot again, but blood pours from a wound on his head. He blinks, trying to clear his vision, then pulls the trigger. No one falls.

"There they are." An unfamiliar voice. Dario won't get off of me as if he can protect me by smothering me beneath his massive frame. I still have to breathe to stay alive, and we're surrounded. One gunshot and he's dead.

Apparently, they don't want us dead.

It takes three men to disarm Dario and haul him off of me, and it takes them a long time since he fights like mad. But in the end, even a huge former military Rossi man can't singlehandedly take down three heavily armed combatants without a weapon.

Someone reaches for me. Dario curses. A prick of something painful presses against my neck. My vision blurs. I'm aware of Dario screaming and kicking. Dimly, I'm aware that he's incapacitated one and the second and third are injured.

We could still escape, I think to myself, as my eyelids grow too heavy.

We…

Could…

I succumb to the darkness.

CHAPTER THREE

Dario

I WAKE UP IN A COLD, dark room. My eyes spring open, my body on instant alert. Once a soldier, always a soldier they say. I never really fully sleep.

There's a sliver of light in the far corner of the room. I've obviously been drugged so my depth perception's off, but it looks like the thin line you'd see at the bottom of a doorway.

I try to remember what happened.

We were cornered. I'd watched as they held my arms back, pricked her neck with a needle to drug her, then probably did the same to me. I don't remember that, but I feel my body covered in bruises. I didn't go down without a fight.

Doesn't matter. Here I fucking am.

I do a quick mental inventory. Broken ribs. Bruises, lacerations. Gunshot wounds are superficial. Hard to see out of one eye. They hit my temple with a bullet, but it was a graze and didn't penetrate. Stings like a motherfucker but if they knew how to fucking shoot—or were shooting to kill—I'd have been a lot worse off.

I keep my breathing slow and regulated in case they're monitoring me.

I still don't know who the fuck they are.

I've been here before. Not this exact location, but I've been taken hostage before, and I know the most important thing to do is stay calm and observant then fight like hell when given the chance.

And I will get a fucking chance. The blood thrums in my veins knowing how I'll fight when I can.

Most prisoners are overwhelmed and even paralyzed with fear, and the few that aren't rarely have the training necessary to fight.

I do.

I feel a warmth at my back and hear slow breathing. I look over my shoulder. Vivia's passed out against my back. We're strapped to each other. Doesn't make sense at first why they'd do that unless they were short on restraints and wanted to make sure neither of us tried to escape with the other.

Clearly, they don't know the Rossi family code.

I don't dare wake her up or move.

I plow through the slog in my brain to put facts together.

Fact one. Vivia and Gray were considered suspects by the Rossis for the attempt to assassinate Marialena.

Fact two. Vivia says she didn't know about it, but I can't trust what she says. Gloria was the one that pointed the finger, and I trust Gloria more than I trust Vivia.

Fact three. Vivia isn't innocent. She's hiding something. She's clamped her mouth and refused to answer, was tracked down by Gloria and Mario, and there's no way she was supposed to be without her guard in an underground sex club. Her brothers would lock her up in a chastity belt and move her into a convent first.

Fact four. Gray tried to pin it on her, which means there's a pretty good chance that he was the one responsible and he tried to get out of it by throwing her under the bus.

Is she innocent? Fucking doubt it.

I narrow my eyes in the darkness. What kind of a douchebag tries to get someone else to take the blame? A fucking pussy, that's who. I wish he wasn't dead so I could kill him all over again, the asshole.

Who was really behind it all, though? Whoever's responsible for us being brought here, for attacking us on the streets of Boston, and for drugging us. Someone pulled out all the stops, knowing that Gray could've spilled all. At least that much I can guess.

Why are Vivia and I still alive?

They had their chance to kill us and didn't. That leaves only one plausible explanation: we're useful to them for another purpose.

I sift through what I know to make sure I'm not missing anything. We weren't sure who tried to hurt Marialena at first, but Mario and Gloria did some investigative work. Romeo was livid and nearly lost his shit when someone tried to hurt his baby sister, but the rest of us kept our heads on straight and found out what we could. As far as I know, the Montavios knew shit, but I'd guess that's changed by now.

There's no way she acted with their knowledge. I've worked alongside the Montavios long enough to know they're as loyal as the Rossis, and they'd fucking die before they'd betray any one of us.

Vivia's in a lot of goddamn trouble.

Right now what's more important is finding out if Vivia is alright, and then the next is figuring out a plan to get out of here. I was tasked with bringing her home to The Castle safely and goddamn it, that's exactly what I'm gonna do if it kills me. I have one job to do. I won't fuck up.

I shift a little to see if I can rouse her silently. I whisper a hoarse, "Vivia." My vocal cords don't want to work.

I call her name again, and she moans a little. Jesus, I wish we weren't attached to each other. I need to see how badly she's injured, and if she's okay. Cracked ribs and some scrapes won't hold me down.

But before I can turn around and try to unfasten these bonds, the door opens. A masked man comes inside wearing nothing but black. My eyes aren't accustomed to the bright light, and I blink a few times to adjust to the sudden change. I can't tell if this is the guy from earlier.

The door clangs shut behind him.

"The guard's awake and alive, she still seems asleep."

Guard?

Ah. They think I'm her bodyguard. Makes sense. How would they know the Rossis were involved?

I can feel her tensing against me, too much in control for a person who's supposedly asleep. I gently move my hands that are behind me until I find the warmth of her skin. I give her hand a little squeeze. She squeezes back. I'm struck with how small her hand is in mine, but how strong her grip is.

I don't care who she is or what she did. I'm sworn to protect my family, and the Montavio family is part of that.

"Good. Looks like she's awake, too, aren't you, princess?"

"Fuck off," she mutters, her words slurred. I grit my teeth. I'm the one that can piss off the people that took us, not her, because I'm the one they'll beat up. It's a fine line. If they touch her, I'll have to kill them and that'll make things really complicated.

He only chuckles, though, and marches over to us. "And who do we have here," he says. "Vivia Montavio's trained bodyguard put up quite a fight, didn't he? Impressed, man." He shakes his head. "Never seen a guard ready to throw down like you. Should hire you for our outfit."

Outfit. Not a single person, then.

Noted.

This guy's smaller than I am, but he moves with the grace of an assassin. I don't move.

I tense, bracing myself for a blow but it doesn't come. He kneels in front of me and says in my ear, "How many you kill, brother? Nine? Ten? We'll take that outta you."

There it is, the threat before they beat the shit out of me. Been here before. I won't cave, and I won't die, and neither will she.

If he thinks I'm her bodyguard and doesn't yet know he's captured a Rossi, that could play into my favor. I rack my brain trying to think of how I can hide it or if I should even try—one glance at the rose on my forearm and he'll know exactly who I am.

"And you." He lets me go and reaches for Vivia. I tense, trying to assess the damage I can do when my hands are bound. If he hurts her—

"You've got a lot to answer for, don't you?"

She spits in his face. Motherfucker, didn't Sergio teach her anything about hostage situations? God. Seems like Sergio didn't teach her anything.

He grabs a fistful of her hair. I lean back, swivel my leg hard and knock him off balance. He falls in front of me which makes it easy to jam my foot in his neck to hold him in place. I won't be able to restrain him for long with my hands bound and he's got the advantage, but the element of surprise is working in my favor for now.

"Apologize, Vivia." I can toss him a bone.

"For what?" she snaps.

Of all the fucking times to give me shit—

"Better for you if you don't provoke them."

"Oh, like sweeping his legs and pinning him by the throat isn't provoking at all."

I grit my teeth and shove my back against hers.

"Fine. I'm sorry. Shouldn't have done that," she says. He shoves me off of him and gets to his feet, reaches for his gun, cocks it and aims at her. If I don't intervene and get the attention focused back on me, he's gonna hurt her.

"You gonna blow my brains out like a pussy? With me tied up?" I shake my head. "Untie my bonds and let's fight it out, brother. Make me earn that fucking bullet."

The door opens further, letting in more light.

"Why'd you keep him alive?" I can't see much but a dark shadow against yellowed light behind him. "Should've shot him already."

I don't recognize their voices. I don't detect any accents. They're working together for a larger group.

"I wasn't instructed to kill him, too. Mullet was useless to us, but the bodyguard might prove useful and the Montavio girl is the best bargaining chip we have."

Someone yells, and his voice sounds distant, like he's yelling down a hall. I wonder where we are. Seems like the basement of a warehouse or something. I barely refrain from rolling my eyes. Original.

The voice becomes louder. "Ace, the boss wants to talk to you."

Ace. Noted.

The guy pointing the gun at me kicks me on his way out, and without missing a beat, I trip him. He goes sprawling, falls hard but braces himself on his arm, and swings his gun back at me, cocking it.

"Ace! He ain't in a patient mood."

He curses under his breath. "Gonna kick your ass, you son of a bitch," he snarls before he gets to his feet and hurries to the door.

"Look forward to it!" I yell after him.

The door shuts hard behind him, plunging us back into darkness.

We sit in silence for only seconds before Vivia starts to talk. "So you think it's—"

"Shh." I shove her back with mine.

"So you get to—"

"Shut up," I hiss. "I'm trying to hear anything that could tell me where we are."

She's quiet, but I can feel her fuming with her back against mine. I don't give a shit, I'm not happy about this situation either.

I keep my voice low. "What do you hear? Whisper."

She's silent for another moment. "Water, but it seems distant." We're both silent as we hear the unmistakable sound of a plane flying overhead. I hear her breathing along with mine as we continue to listen, when in the distance I hear one short blast of a horn. It's a ship's signal.

"The wharf," she whispers.

"Bingo."

Jesus, it kills me knowing we're right in the North End. The Rossi family owns so much property here, there's likely a few of them nearby. Backup and a rescue team within five minutes from here. One of our own could be ordering a cappuccino within earshot of us.

"Wharf could be a problem," I whisper to her. "Means we could be taken on a plane or boat easily."

"Yeah."

I wonder if we're bugged.

"What do you remember?" I ask her.

"We were chased into someone's backyard. They cornered us. Destroyed the fence. Killed Gray, drugged me. I saw them hit you before I passed out, and that's all I remember."

So she has no idea if we're being bugged either.

"You okay?" I ask her. Voices echo in the hallway outside the door. I'm piecing things together about who this is and why they want us, why they killed Gray but didn't kill us.

"Other than being drugged, watching my boyfriend get killed, and being taken hostage first by you and then whoever the hell they are? Just peachy. You?"

Boyfriend... the asshole she was with was her boyfriend. Good to know. There's more to this story than it seemed at first.

"Cut the bullshit. We're both hostages here for who knows what or how long, and there's no telling if we're a better use to them dead or alive, though it seems alive, and it might be the only reason we're still breathing."

"Yeah."

"Tell me your injuries."

"You gonna doctor me up?" she asks, her voice dripping with sarcasm.

The little brat. "Tell me your fucking injuries."

She sighs. "Hit my head. My lips feel swollen, but that might be from the meds."

"Yeah." Okay, so, so far nothing sounds like it will prevent her from running if we have to.

"My wrists hurt where I'm tied, and my—oh! Oh, shit," she says, her voice dropping. "I just remembered."

"Yeah?"

"They—do you think we're being bugged?"

"No idea. If they have cameras in here, they won't see anything because it's so dark. And it's a small room, so the chances they took the time to set anything up are pretty slim."

"How do you know it's a small room?"

"Took him four steps to get to us from the doorway and saw the corners when the door opened. Plus, the air in here's getting stale now that we're both awake, but it's probably still a good idea to talk discreetly so they don't pick up shit."

"Right," she whispers. "Do you remember what Orlando said to get before they got us?"

My mind feels like thick sludge, and it makes me want to punch a wall. I hate someone fucking with my mind more than anything. I'd rather die a painful, drawn-out death than lose my mind to illness or disease. I close my eyes, remembering… I called Orlando, that much I know.

I push, trying to open up my mind and replay the conversation, when suddenly it comes rushing back with such vivid clarity. I sit up straighter.

"Your phone's set up to send an SOS with three pushes of the volume button… there's a tiny transponder in the glove compartment. It works the same as a cell."

My voice is husky and low in the darkness. "I remember. Where is it?"

"I shoved it in my bra."

If they're tapping us, we have to move fast.

"Fuck. We're tied together and I'm guessing you can't reach it."

"No, I'd have to be a circus performer to reach my bra with my chin."

"A sight I'd pay good money to see."

"Jesus."

"Just sayin'."

I'm thinking.

"What kind of a bond is this?" she asks.

"Feels like rope. They weren't prepared to take us."

"Right. Okay. Okay, alright," she says, her voice getting excited, as if she's just had a good thought. "If we work together, we might unfasten these bonds if they're just ropes."

"You were drugged when they tied you up, and I don't remember when they tied me up, but if I was tensing in any way when they did, or fighting, if I relax in the restraints, they'll likely be looser."

She nods. "Okay, alright. That's a good plan."

"They did a shit job here. My legs are free, you?"

"Yeah, same."

"So all we've got is our hands tied together and something holding us together. Remember that.

Your untied legs are your best weapon. Actually, any freedom of movement you have at all is."

I can feel her straining as she looks over her shoulder. "There's only one tie that's binding us together."

"Right. Good. Okay, so you can't move your hands in front of you if you've got them behind your back, and I can't either. But if we unfasten the short rope tying us together—"

"We can undo each other's wrists," she finishes.

"Exactly."

"Okay, so I'm gonna go slack. You go slack, too, and let's see if that loosens the bonds at all."

"Right."

My heart beats faster as her body gentles against mine, going limp. I relax as much as I can, my body loose and slack. The ropes around my wrists feel looser.

"I get more slack that way," she says, so low I can barely hear her. "Definitely. I'm gonna try to see if there's any difference in the two bonds. See if I can't distinguish them."

I thread my fingers over rough rope, touching my wrists first. Hard, thick rope binds my wrists together, and I can't get much more than my thumb across one. But I can feel her hands up against mine, and it's easier to feel the rope along her wrist. As I wriggle, finding the rope, I feel something around my waist.

"Wait," I whisper. She freezes. "Got another one around my waist. Looser. You?"

She sighs a second later. "Yeah. Me, too."

"It's alright, we might be able to use that one to our advantage." I can already see the asshole who came in here wriggling and kicking for his life as I use the rope around our bellies to strangle the life out of him. It would be a much better weapon than the thick rope around our wrists. Suppler, easier to hide.

"Oooh," she whispers. "It's coming loose, the one tying us together. I don't think they did a good job tying them."

Likely criminals, not Boy Scouts, and tying ropes isn't in their bag of tricks. Probably thought they'd get Gray and Vivia but didn't count on taking a two-hundred-fifty-pound guy like me with them.

"Okay, good."

"The longer length is at your side, can you feel it?"

It takes long minutes, we curse up a blue streak, and when we're finished, she's panting and sweat pours down my face in rivulets, but the rope tying us together falls to the floor. We can tell it is the same as they used around our waists, so once that's gone, all that remains is the tie around our wrists.

"Come here."

I swivel, still held back a bit by the rope, but not enough that I can't strain against them to reach her. "Let me get the transponder out."

"Can you please just take the ropes off my wrists first? I don't relish the thought of you coming anywhere near my breasts."

I can't help myself. I grin in the darkness.

"Afraid I'll turn you on, baby?"

She curses like a sailor.

"Shh, now. Words like that shouldn't come out of the mouth of a pretty girl like you." I shake my head. "Could take a long time to get our wrists unfastened, and we want to send that signal as soon as possible."

When she doesn't respond, I hope she sees the logic in this. She wants out of here, too.

"Fine." She wriggles so that her front is facing my hands. "There. I'm going to lean down so that you can reach for the transponder."

"Good. Lay down flat so I can reach you."

"Obviously."

I grunt at her, but she only falls to her belly and pushes her chest up against my hands. I swipe along her cleavage, feeling for the hard, cold transponder, and keep my touch as chaste as I can. She's a

Montavio sister after all, and it's a shitty idea to do anything that might piss her brothers off.

Still, I don't miss the feel of her silky skin against my fingers or the way her breathing hitches when I touch her.

This is a woman unaccustomed to being touched by a man who knows how to.

I wish I didn't know that.

I'm tempted to push, to make this more than just an exploration down her breasts looking for a damn object. So she knows that I'm controlling this, I'm the one in charge.

But just because I have asshole thoughts doesn't mean I have to act on them.

Not all the time anyway.

This woman's still not only my prisoner but my ward. Our status and roles demand that I protect her at all costs, even if the tables have turned a little bit. For now.

When we escape, however...

Finally, I feel the transponder. I slide it between my thumb and forefinger, and don't waste any time. Orlando said it would be set up so three taps will signal our location, just like our cell phones. It's a high-tech little number with a thumbprint ID, so not only will they know where we are, they'll know I was the one to activate the signal. I slide my thumb to unlock it, then quickly hit the button on the side three times. I watch as it silently goes from red to a flash of green, then pull away from her.

Voices are getting louder in the hallway. I don't want them to know yet that we've unfastened our bond. I sit up quickly.

"Sit up. Make sure they can't see the lead of the rope." She scrambles as fast as she can with her wrists still bound. But she loses her balance and falls, landing hard on her shoulder.

"L," she whispers. I reach for her, and with my hands behind my back, help her sit up clumsily as the doorknob turns. I feel for the rope and tuck it behind myself just in time as the door swings open.

"Food." Someone marches in with a tray. The smell isn't all that appetizing, something savory but overly processed, like a warmed-up MRE. Nonna would have a fit. I'm half ashamed my mouth waters, but it's been hours since I've eaten.

"How are we supposed to eat with our wrists bound?" Vivia asks.

The guy only chuckles. "You think I didn't think of that?" He fists her by the hair, and she stifles a gasp. My body tenses, but I can't do anything about it right now.

He touches her as if it's his right. I'll remember that, too.

He takes a knife from his belt and undoes her rope, then the one holding us together. I hold the end tight, so he doesn't feel the slack and thinks we're still bound. Then he opens a closet door and shoves her and the tray inside. "Eat. You have one minute." He slams the door behind her. Out of the corner of my eye, I can see the tattered end of the rope we unfastened. I grab the end and quickly tuck it into my palm. It's thin and supple and will do the job I need well.

"Vivia," I yell to the closet.

He kicks me. "Shut up."

"Best weapon," I yell back at her, earning me a fist punch from the asshole. I hope she remembers. Untied hands are going to come in handy if she's smart about it.

I hope she's got some of the Montavio fight in her. We'll need it.

CHAPTER FOUR

Vivia

I'M SHOVED in a closet with a counter ticking on how long I have to shove this food in my mouth. I wouldn't eat food they gave me if I were starving to death on a remote island. Who knows what kind of drugs or whatever they put in it.

I try to will my body to stop shaking, but I'm not having much luck. I hate closets. Hate them. When I was little, my mother would lock me in a closet as punishment, sometimes for hours. I'd cry until I vomited and since then have always hated small, enclosed spaces. I will myself not to remember that, not to let the fear of the past sweep me under. I can't. I won't.

My hands are free, the transponder's safely back in my bra, and I have twenty seconds before that door opens again. I quickly assess the closet. Nothing. Not a hanger or shoe in sight. I look down at the tray. A bottle of water, a plastic plate with gray-colored meat on it, next to a sad mound of... potatoes? Gravy? Congealed pasta? Blech.

So the food and tray are my only weapons. There was a knife, but he has it now. The same one he used to cut my ties.

"Ten seconds," he shouts, his voice louder. He's outside this door. He's expecting me to shovel down this sad excuse for a meal in record time.

I'll use the food and tray to take him off balance, then either take the knife off him or off the floor, wherever he's put it. I never used a knife on anyone in my life.

I'm not sure what I'd even do with it except blindly stab at him. I wish he'd fed Dario first. Something tells me he would know exactly what to do with a knife. Probably wouldn't even need it.

"I'm ready. This food's bullshit," I say through the closet door, baiting him.

"Don't bite the hand that feeds you, princess."

The door swings open. I stand with the tray in my hand.

"You didn't eat a damn thing," he mutters.

"Oh, I ate all of it," I say, and when he looks up at me in confusion, I make my move. I toss the water I've hidden tightly in my grip into his eyes. He curses and blinks, flinching as his hands come to his face. I don't see his knife. Where's his damn knife? He gasps and takes an involuntary step backward. I shove the tray at his neck, and when he doubles over, I kick him between the legs. He sinks to the floor. My whole body quakes, expecting immediate and violent retaliation when I hear Dario.

"Push him over to me," Dario says in a hoarse whisper, probably not wanting to make any more noise than necessary.

I gather up my strength and shove him toward Dario. Dario moves just as the guy gets back up.

Seconds ago, he looked restrained and captive. Now, he springs into action. Dario gets to his feet and swivels his leg out, kicking the guy so hard he snaps bone. The guy falls to his knees but not before he slashes at Dario with his knife, which conveniently reappears when he needs it. He probably hid it somehow.

Dario expertly dodges the knife slash and bites, gripping the man's hand with his teeth. It's too brutal, too animalistic. I can't watch. Blood drips to the floor and the man gives an inhuman scream.

The guy pivots beneath Dario and claws at anything he can find. His fingers latch onto one of Dario's sleeves, and he yanks, trying to get away. The fabric tears. Dario pulls away, but it's too late. Dario's rose tattoo's obvious, and our captor doesn't miss it.

He freezes, suddenly terrified.

"Rossi," he mutters. "No fucking way. I didn't know —I didn't mean—"

Dario quickly uses the knife to cut his rope. We have to move because it's seconds before someone will come and find out what's going on. I reach for the tray, lift it, and smack it on the guy's head with all my might. It shatters like glass and falls to the floor around him. It's enough time for Dario to undo his bonds, grab the rope, and in seconds, he's got the guy pinned beneath him, the rope around his neck.

"Lock the door and get the knife, Vivia," Dario says, his voice as calm as if he were ordering pizza for a Friday night special. I can't look at his blood-smeared mouth without wanting to vomit.

The man's legs are twitching, and his face is purple. He's…strangling him. He releases him only long enough to grab the guy by the hair. "You touched her hair. You bullied her. You acted as if she were yours." He lifts the man's shoulders and whacks his head on the unyielding floor. I flinch. "That's for touching her."

Calmly, unmercifully, as if he has only one job in the world now and he's dedicated to seeing it through to the bitter end, he lays him back on the ground and wraps the rope back around his neck.

I stare, watching, horrified and fascinated. Dario barks at me to wake me out of my stupor. "Vivia. I said lock the door and get the fucking knife. Now."

I look around me wildly and finally see the glint of a blade a few yards away. I grab it, then run to go lock the door when two more large, masked guys come in. Dario abandons the guy, who's either passed out or dead, and launches himself toward me.

"Get behind me," he growls. "Now." His arm circles my waist, and he hauls me behind him as the other two quickly assess the situation and charge.

The first guy swings and Dario ducks as the second one comes in and reaches for me. I kick him between the legs but miss. He comes up swinging and connects his fist to my jaw. My head snaps back, stars blinding my vision from the pain and impact of it all.

"Come after me, motherfucker," Dario fumes. "You leave her the hell alone."

He knocks one guy on his ass as he puts himself directly between me and the guy about to attack me. I fall to the floor and cover my face in instinctual self-protection and flinch at the sound of flesh hitting flesh. Dario sinks a vicious punch in the first guy's jaw, swivels and kicks the second in the face so hard I hear a sickening crunch. He fights as if he were made for this, as if his body knows exactly when and how to bend, strike, and block, every move instinctual like a predator's hunt.

Blood pours from his nose. Someone tears Dario's shirt. Screams wail around us like the gnashing of teeth.

I hear a car approaching outside. Just one. No sirens. Could be damn near anything right now. Nothing would surprise me.

"Fuck! Fuck!"

One of the guys attacking Dario backs away, his hands up in a sign of surrender. "Jesus, man. Stop!"

Both men stop defending themselves against Dario. Dario blinks, as shocked as I am.

"He's fucking Rossi!" One guy points with trembling hands at the now-visible rose on Dario's arm. "Run! Get out of here!"

They scramble out of the room and Dario looks like he's going to run after them, when he turns to me. "Someone's coming," I whisper. "I heard a car outside."

"That'll be Orlando. He got our signal and wasn't far. We have to go, now." His voice still commands, but he's gentled the tone. "Are you hurt?"

Of course I am. My eyes are blurred, lacerations and welts cover my body. But my bones feel intact, still, and I think I'm okay this time.

"I'm—I think I'm okay," I whisper.

He grabs my elbow and drags me to my feet. "You do exactly as I say while we get out of this place. Exactly."

I can only nod my head.

All around us, they're oblivious to our escape, as all run for their lives. There's something about knowing they've mistakenly crossed into Rossi battle territory that's put the fear of God in them.

I stumble out of the hold we were in with Dario. At first it seems like it's some sort of landing within a warehouse by the wharf.

I blink in the bright overhead lighting. We're not only on a wharf, we're on a ship, and the men that were kidnapping us are leaving as fast as they can. One dives into the water, two more jump into a car park at the end of the pier as my cousin Orlando, huge and bigger than life, marches on the pier leading toward us bearing the largest gun I've ever seen. Right here in broad daylight as if defying someone to snap an Instagram shot or call the police.

He sees them trying to take off and lifts the gun. Tires squeal as they peel out of the lot to escape with their lives.

I cover my mouth with my hands. Dario grabs my arm and pulls me with him toward Orlando.

"No matter what happens, get to Orlando," he says.

No matter what happens? What does he think will happen?

Orlando shoots as the car peels away. He shoots at the water until air bubbles rise, until the water's coated red and no one surfaces again. Nausea grips my stomach.

When Orlando reaches me, he takes me by one arm and Dario takes me by the other. There's no warm greeting, no reassurance that I'm okay. He doesn't even look like he knows me.

They drag me off the pier and shove me into a nearby waiting car. I'm breathing heavily, panting. I don't feel as if I've been rescued. It's not like I get to go home free and clear now, though I guess I'm relieved I'm alive. Dario was taking me to The Castle.

Have others shown up to rescue us? It was a quick signal and it wasn't long between sending it and Orlando showing up, but a rescue from the Rossis should mean more than just one comes. I look around for more guards, another brother, anyone else but Orlando, but he's the only one here.

It's the first sign to me that something's off with this rescue.

And then... then I realize. This isn't a rescue at all.

I look around a second time, half expecting to see our captors coming for us, but no one comes. They're all fleeing as if the wharf's on fire. I glance from side to side in the bright light of day, trying to get an idea of where on the wharf we are.

Cold dread fills my belly when I realize the predicament I'm in. Orlando and Dario aren't going to take it easy on me. They'll have questions and want answers.

I have to get out of here.

I reach for the handle on the door, but it's locked from the inside. I look frantically around for another way out when the shadows of two large figures loom outside the window. The driver's side door opens, and Orlando slides into the driver's seat. They're having a hushed conversation that stops the minute they know I'm in earshot.

Dario opens the door next to me and sits beside me.

"Hey, Orlando." I greet my cousin, hoping for some kind assurance. He glances in the rearview mirror at me and gives me a stern, curt nod. Lovely.

He's bigger than I remember, taller and more heavily muscled, his chin lined with a dark beard and those eyes of his as uncompromising as ever. I haven't seen him since we were invited to The Castle for his father's funeral services years ago.

"Vivia." There's no warmth in his greeting, not even the slightest hint of familiarity as Dario's large hands grab mine in his. I go to pull away, but he holds fast as Orlando reaches in his glove compartment and something metal clinks. He tosses cuffs over his shoulder and some kind of soft fabric.

No.

Dario snaps the cuffs on, tightens them, then in one swift motion, tugs me down so my head's on his knee. My struggle's laughable in his strong grip as he slides fabric over my eyes and ties it behind my head, then follows with a gag. I scream and swear but every sound I make's muted.

Fuck.

The car moves quickly and nearly silently as Dario keeps my head on his leg, keeping me out of the sight of anyone who might look in here. They talk in low, concerned voices.

"Called one guy Ace, was the only name I heard."

I mumble against my gag that I heard a Shark, but they wouldn't know that since I'm gagged, when Dario's hand claps down on my ass. "Lay still and stop fighting." I'm so stunned I don't move at first.

"Vivia." Orlando's voice rises, directed at me. "You've been taken into custody for attempted murder against my sister. Sergio's been notified and he's on his way to our family home, where all members of both the Rossi and Montavio inner circles have been called." The car slows down. Traffic? "You're in Dario's custody until further notice. Do not fight him. He's been given free rein by

Romeo to use whatever means of restraint or force are necessary to both hold and question you."

A chill slides down my spine. They think I'm a traitor.

Once, when I was ten years old, my father discovered a traitor among them. My father made no pretense of hiding the man they found from anyone, even his children. We all heard his screams when he was ordered to be beaten. I heard the pleas for death when they burned the tattoos marking him Montavio from his skin with a blowtorch, his flesh sizzling like roasted meat. I heard my father's cold voice order him killed as an act of mercy when he'd almost died by the torture alone.

Betraying the mob is one of the most serious crimes one could commit. Internal betrayal is the worst of all.

I feel cold and numb. I don't realize I'm crying until the blindfold's wet against my skin.

I didn't try to hurt Marialena. But if I tell him the truth, my brothers will know I snuck behind their backs. They'll know I'm "damaged goods," that I broke the rules. And once they find that out… what will become of me? Other women have been exiled and disowned for what I've done. My father's no longer here, but I'm not sure Sergio will be any more merciful.

Orlando keeps talking.

"Until we sort things out… until we know who was after you and why, you and Dario have gotten into a car accident. And you didn't survive."

What?

I stop breathing. He's going to tell my family that I'm dead? I know now why he gagged me. I wouldn't accept any of this without a fight.

"This will give us a chance to do several things. First, Dario will question you, and if you value your life, you'll answer him as honestly as possible. Remember what I said. Dario has free rein. He will not answer for anything he does that hurts you in an effort to bring justice and seek truth. Do you understand me? Nod if you understand me."

No, no, no. I start to shake.

But I nod my head. Dario's hand is on the side of my head to keep me in position.

Pathetically, I imagine that he's comforting me.

He isn't. He's going to hurt me.

"As Dario questions you, we'll deal with Sergio. When Sergio found out you were complicit in the attempt on Marialena's life, he wanted to come for you himself."

I shake my head, but I can't defend myself.

"He would've killed you himself if you weren't already dead. His exact words were, 'she's dead to us.'"

My stomach clenches as if I'm going to be sick. I shrink inside myself and wish I could lift my hands to my ears to block all of this out.

"While you're in hiding with Dario, whoever kidnapped you will think you're dead. We'll do what we can to make it seem that way."

My family will mourn my loss and think I'm gone. I can't imagine what my mother will go through under this plan.

"Whoever took you now knows you were with a Rossi. They'll expect that you'll be brought to us. We'll have to secure The Castle and prepare for an attack. They also may look for you at your family home. You aren't safe anywhere but in hiding."

Safe in hiding with my captor who's going to interrogate me.

Sounds lovely.

I close my eyes and wish I could sleep, that I could block all this out forever. That I could wake up and this whole nightmare was only a dream I could blink away.

CHAPTER FIVE

Dario

I WONDER at first if she's fallen asleep. Even though she's our prisoner, and it's my job to get answers out of her, I saw the way she reacted with real fear, the way her blindfold dampened with tears. She's distraught.

I won't give her comfort, though. No. Until I know the truth, I have to remind myself she either attempted to take the life of one of the people I've been sworn to protect, or she was complicit in the murder attempt. She isn't innocent.

"Brother." Orlando looks at me in the rearview mirror. I knew when he came for us that we wouldn't be going to The Castle. I knew I'd be taking her into custody, so I was the one that recommended we pretend we were killed to throw any potential attackers off track. Word will spread, quickly, and the people who kidnapped us today will drop their search if they know that not only was she killed, she was killed at the side of a Rossi.

"Can you have Mario and Gloria send me everything they have on her?"

"Of course. I haven't talked to them yet. So far, it's just been you and me, and I'm going to keep this circle as small as possible. But I can ask them to send me what they had that caused the search yesterday."

I nod. "We going to where I think we're going?"

He grins. "S'mores?"

I nod. If Vivia's anything like the Rossi girls, she's gonna lose her shit when she sees where we're going. La Cabina, a rustic cabin off the Rhode Island coastline, is nestled in the woods. Bordered on one side by the ocean and on the other side by nothing but trees, La Cabina has no running water or neighbors for three solid miles. I've been there once, for a bachelor party. I personally like the little retreat, but something tells me Vivia won't share the sentiment.

Orlando hasn't spoken to the rest of our brothers, not yet. We're better off just working together for now. The fewer people who know our whereabouts, the better, at least until we figure out who came after us, because that one tie will for sure lead us to whoever called the hit on Marialena.

I'd like to think Vivia's innocent, but in my line of work, you're guilty until proven innocent, and the evidence against her isn't looking good.

It takes about an hour for us to get there, and the whole time Orlando tells me what he knows.

"Contacted one of our associates on the coast already, and you should have everything you need," Orlando says as he cruises to a stop at a red light. "There's everything from food to clothes to cash if you need to buy something. Burner phones and chargers."

"Marshmallow sticks?"

"Yeah, man. You want a fuckin' marshmallow stick you find it in the woods. And there's no way I'd give that girl something that could work as a potential weapon."

I can't help but smile at that.

"There's some fishing gear, though you'll have to be careful."

"Got it."

"As far as Sergio and the rest, you let me handle them. Sit her up, bro, will you?"

I sit her up. We're away from the miles of traffic now, and alone on the stretch of road that will take us to La Cabina.

"Vivia," Orlando says, as he looks in the rearview mirror, though she can't see him with her blindfold.

She nods silently. Her only choice, really.

"You're not in a good place. I told you Sergio wanted retribution himself. He said if you were complicit in the attack on Marialena, you were dead to the Montavios."

She flinches as if struck but otherwise doesn't react.

"You're not gonna like being here alone with Dario. You won't like what has to happen to get to the bottom of this. And it pains me to see it come to this, cousin, but you know our rules."

She clenches her jaw and turns her head away but doesn't respond. I don't know how old Vivia is, but she's spent at least a couple of decades deeply immersed in the rules of mob life. She knows how close she is to a very, very serious consequence… if not several.

And I'm not gonna lie. I'm good at this. I'm not easily swayed by feminine wiles or pleas. I'll get answers, and she'll be out of the line of Sergio's fire for now, while my brothers will have a chance to investigate.

Alone in the woods with a beautiful woman who's my captive and my charge? Yeah, I've had a lot worse assignments than this one. Probably most.

You wouldn't find La Cabina on any GPS. You wouldn't find it on a map, even. La Cabina is nestled deep in the woods that surround the Narragansett Bay in Rhode Island, and it's the only rustic cabin for miles. About ten miles down the road, there's a small, private campground run by a husband and wife who've been friends with the Rossi family for so long, they're practically family themselves. We're guaranteed privacy and isolation here.

It's a coolish, early summer day. We spent the night imprisoned and left bright and early this morning, barely before the sun rose. Now the morning is heating up, not a cloud in the sky to inhibit the warmth of the sun. It still gets cool in the mornings of June in New England, but midday warms and occasionally we even have a heat wave. Today's slightly overcast and a bit chilly.

I smile to myself. Good. We could get cozy by the fire.

To get to La Cabina, you take a left on a dirt road that looks like the entrance to someone's driveway, follow it until you see a bright red hand-painted sign for the beach, then take a second turn down an unlit gravel driveway for about a mile until it looks like you'll drive straight off a cliff into the ocean below. The entrance to La Cabina is hidden behind a blanket of pine trees. There's no running water though there's a nearby pump, a clean but otherwise rustic outhouse, and outside the small cabin there's a well-used fire pit and grill. There's no electricity, but Orlando's furnished me with small portable chargers so I can call out if need be. He'll notify me when it's time to come home.

Orlando parks the car. I see a shadow quickly skirt behind us and vanish into the trees, but it's far too small to be human. A raccoon, maybe. Small woodland creatures inhabit these woods, since they're so rarely disturbed.

"Saw some turkeys roaming nearby," Orlando says, and even blindfolded and gagged, the disgust on Vivia's face is evident.

"He's joking," I tell her, as I grab her cuffed wrists between my fingers. "I'm sure we've got mac and cheese and Top Ramen for days. No one eats wild turkeys anymore."

"And fish. Don't forget fish," Orlando says.

I nod. "I'll make Nonna proud."

But when I look at the pale, wan face of the girl I've taken hostage I don't joke anymore. I might be a ruthless asshole, but I'm not inhuman. She's lost a lot in the last few days. Her circumstances both then and now are no laughing matter.

"Thanks for everything, brother," I tell Orlando, shaking his hand. He's brought me up to speed and promised to text later with more details and updates as they come.

"Of course," he says, scowling as he looks at her. "I'm sorry this has come down to you."

"No, I get it," I say in a soft voice. "It'll be a lot easier for someone like me who isn't related to her to do what I have to."

He scrubs a hand through his dark, short hair. "Exactly. Still, I owe you."

He owes me shit. I playfully punch his shoulder. "Owe me? You were the one that gave me life after The Big House, man. Consider us even."

He fist-bumps me, gets in the car and leaves. I watch until his taillights are little more than a flash of red firefly lights against a night sky.

Vivia hasn't moved. She obviously hasn't spoken. She knows we're alone in the middle of nowhere, and that I have carte blanche to interrogate her any way I see fit. She's probably terrified.

Good.

I lay my hand on Vivia's elbow. Again, my fingers touch the softest skin I've ever felt. I remember what she looked like wearing the red hair, how it felt when I finally took off that layer of lies and revealed what she truly looked like. I wonder what she'll look like when I unveil another layer of lies.

Her shoulder-length, warm brown hair caresses her cheeks. They're damp from her tears, and little strands of hair cling to them. Without thinking, I clear the strands from her face and brush them behind her ear. She lets me do this without flinching or showing that she's even aware that I touched her.

That'll change.

I'm not sad about that.

"I'm taking you inside. Lean on me and follow my lead."

She does exactly what I say. Our rustic getaway's surrounded by trees, so the ground is bumpy, a sea of tree roots and fallen, rust-colored pine needles. It would be easy to slip or fall without keeping a close watch on her footing. I guide her to the door. The key dangles from the lock.

"Stand here while I open the door." I turn it, and the door swings open. I step over the threshold, lead her in behind me, and walk straight to a small circular table in the middle of the room. "I'm going to sit down, and you'll sit with me so I can remove your bonds. For now. We'll eat, freshen up, and get some rest. We have all the time we need, so we don't have to rush."

She nods.

I'm confident I'll get what I need from her within twenty-four hours. I have no idea how long we'll have to hide her. Both of us, really.

The interior of the rustic cabin's nothing short of charming. A round, circular wooden table on roughly hewn legs sits in front of a wood-burning stove, three chairs on each side. A checkered tablecloth and oil burning lamp complete the look.

Beside the wood-burning stove are a few wooden shelves filled with non-perishables, and a large cooler likely filled with perishable items that will last a few days.

Behind us there's a fireplace, a small loveseat, several rockers, and a large metal basket filled with split logs. Matches sit beside the wood.

A small table houses sunblock, insect repellant, a well-stocked first-aid kit, and something that looks like a hand-powered radio. Haven't seen one of those in a long, long time.

A doorway opens to the only bedroom in the cabin. The door's ajar. There's a queen-sized bed covered with a quilt, a pile of folded blankets, and wooden end tables on either side of the bed, each with a few books on top.

I take this all in in seconds, and since it isn't my first time here, I only look for anything that's changed. The only difference is that this visit, I have supplies already laid out for us.

I pull out one of the chairs by the table, fold myself into the seat, then draw Vivia onto my knee. I'd have to be blind and heartless not to respond to the soft, gentle weight of the beautiful woman in my lap.

Alone in the woods with full control over a stunning woman? No one can hear us for miles? Twist my arm.

We're going to become very, very intimate over the next few days whether she likes it or not. And that starts now.

She doesn't protest when I sit her on my knee, nor when I reach for her gag and unfasten it. She opens and closes her mouth, then releases a labored sigh before I unfasten the blindfold. I watch as she blinks, unaccustomed to the bright natural light filtering in through a window.

I spin her around to face me and hold her chin between my fingers. "I'll only take the restraints off your wrists under one condition."

She nods, probably not trusting herself to speak.

"You'll do exactly what I say. You heard your cousin, and you're a smart girl. You know what these stakes are, don't you?"

She nods.

"Then tell me. What will happen if you disobey me?"

"I'm sure you'll punish me," she says, disgust coating her voice.

"I will. And what will happen if you try to get away?"

"You'll catch me and punish me again." The way she grits her teeth suggests she's schooling her features so she doesn't roll her eyes. Smart girl knowing that wouldn't go over very well.

"Precisely. Would you like a few minutes of freedom?"

She grits her teeth. "I'd like a lot more than a few minutes of freedom but yes, of course, I would like at least that."

"You're a long, long way off from earning full freedom, Vivia. You're being accused of some of the most serious offenses our families have ever known. The fact that you're even here with me is a mercy."

Her lips thin. I doubt she'd phrase it quite that way.

"For now, you can answer some questions for me. I'm an excellent judge of character. So it's in your best interest to answer as truthfully as possible. If you do, I'll completely unfasten your bonds and let you use the bathroom."

I watch as her back goes ramrod straight. She narrows her eyes at me. "I'd be grateful for that." She gives me a sidelong glance. "You like me sitting in your lap." She squirms on my lap, holding my gaze. I don't know if she's uncomfortable or trying to get a rise out of me.

"Of course. You're beautiful. I might have a job to do, but I'm not dead."

Something shifts in her eyes. It isn't the first time I've noticed a response to a compliment. I keep note of this because I can use it to my full advantage.

"We're going to start with some very simple questions. Straightforward answers. Don't sugarcoat anything. Understood?"

She swallows hard. I can't help but notice how thin and vulnerable the skin at her neck is.

"Yes, of course."

I have a few ways I could interrogate her. Brute force is one, but with a woman like her that likely isn't going to go over too well. If she's been raised in the mob, she's probably more accustomed to brute force than anything else.

I'll try another method.

"What was your childhood like?"

No reaction at first, then she clears her throat. She likes to think before she speaks, then. Formulates her words. "You probably know more about the Rossi family than any other family, I'd guess. Our childhood in some ways was very similar. We had similar expectations. My father, like theirs, was heavy-handed and authoritarian. He thought nothing of harsh, vicious punishment at the slightest sign of what he'd call disobedience. His favorite expression was 'Mazze e panelle fanno i figli belli.'"

Ah. I'm familiar with his favorite saying. Literally translated, it means "sticks and bread make beautiful children." In other words, hard discipline and good food are the recipe for a good childhood. Most of us grew up with a variation on the principle. My grandma used to say walk softly and carry a heavy wooden spoon. Good times.

She continues with a sigh. "But fortunately for me, I wasn't around him much. My biggest jobs were to look pretty and… keep my legs closed." She can't hide the note of bitterness in her tone or the way her voice wobbles. She knows as a woman of the mob, her parents likely only valued her virginity with an eye toward potential marriage to someone of high rank above literally anything else she could offer them.

I nod my head. "I understand. And your mother?"

She shrugs. "Still alive, as you probably know. She's a good enough mother, I suppose, but cowered under my father and made the rest of us toe the line. She sent me to boarding school when I was little, and I never fully got over that rejection."

I listen to everything that she says, but I try to read between the lines. Her home was nearly loveless, the only affection she likely ever received was when she did something her parents approved of. Knowing what few expectations they had for her, I would venture to guess that wasn't very often. I can use this to my advantage. I'll have to.

While brute force is only one way that I could interrogate her, I could use the carrot instead of the stick as well. Personally, I prefer using both methods, but we'll get there.

While I listen to her answers, I gently slide my hand to the small of her back. It's a gentle, possessive move that should reassure her, and while she's talking, she might not even be aware that I'm doing it, except for realizing that it's comfortable for her.

"Tell me about your brothers."

She bristles. I watch as an unreadable expression spreads into a thin-lipped smile. There's a touch of sadness there. "I got along with my brothers when we were younger. We were on the same side, really. But once my dad was gone, and Sergio took the lead, he was almost as bad as my father."

I don't know much about Sergio, but I'm not surprised. He takes his job very seriously.

"Do you trust them?"

She looks away and doesn't answer at first. Finally, she shrugs. "Trust them to save me if I were in danger? Yes. Trust them to take care of me if I needed something like a roof over my head or money in the bank? Yes, of course. That's part of their job. Trust them to know who I am and to take care of my best interests?" She shakes her head with a laugh. "Not on your life. "

I catalog all this information in my mind. I'll process through it later and compare what she tells me to what I find out from Gloria and Mario.

I have a few more questions to soften her up, to get her used to talking to me. If I can ask her about her past and get her to open up to me about it, I'll go in for the more important questions and likely get better answers.

"How old were you when you went to boarding school?"

"Six."

Six. So young. Barely first grade. I remember how at that age the whole world started when I woke up and ended when I went to sleep. There was no past, no future. Everything in the six-year-old mind seems to be focused on the present. What they're going to eat for breakfast, how they're going to entertain themselves for the day. How to stay out of trouble, how to make friends, how to do well in school. Does a stray puppy on the street have a home, and how high can they swing without falling off and breaking a leg? How much does it hurt to break a leg anyway?

She has an odd expression on her face, her eyes level under drawn brows, her lips set in a frown. She doesn't like talking about her family or her past.

Time to make this a little more heated. Press a little further, even.

"Tell me, Vivia. Were you a good girl?"

Her brittle smile falters a little bit. "According to whom? The pastor at the local church? My mother? Or you?"

I don't hesitate.

"Me."

She doesn't answer this question at first but takes a deep breath and gives me an almost demure smile. "Up until recently, I was a good girl by everyone's standards."

I can't deny the fact that I want to protect this woman. It's a flaw I need to be aware of, one I can't ignore. An instinct I'll have to stifle and choke. Even as I tell myself that I have a job to do, even as I tell myself that it is crucial I find out information that could lead us to the threat against my family, I see a wounded person. I see someone in such desperate need of approval it's choking her. I see someone who knows there's no turning back from what she's done, and anything she's ever known is gone to her.

Vivia knows that her family won't take her back. She doesn't quite know the extent of the damage that's happened yet, but Sergio says she's dead to them, a punishment worse than death for a woman like her.

She doesn't know that the Montavia family will no longer see her as one of theirs. She doesn't know that the protection, and every provision that was hers, is gone now. All she has is me, and this one last chance to save her life.

CHAPTER SIX

Vivia

HE ASKS me more about my upbringing, my brothers, my schooling. He asks me if I've ever dated anyone, what I like to listen to for music, do I like to read? The questions seem almost pointless, but I make it a point to answer each one honestly. I don't know why I wouldn't.

Why did he ask me if I was a good girl? It was the only question that hit a nerve for me.

I can't help the way my body reacts at the slightest hint of approval from him, and it unnerves me. It's an erotic touch, a sensual kiss, a come-hither smile, and a crooked finger. I don't understand why, and I feel as if a part of me is broken to even crave this from a man like him. Or from any man, for that matter.

My stomach growls, and he nods. "We need to eat and then get some rest. Do you need to use the bathroom?"

Of course I do. I've had to pee for like an hour.

Cringing, I ask hesitantly, "… I don't think I saw a bathroom around here?"

He gives me a smirk. "There's an outhouse, toilet paper, and soap. That's about it."

I cringe and think I'm grateful this hasn't happened when I'm on my period because gross.

I hold my chin up high. I can do this. I can do this. "Yeah, I could definitely use an outhouse."

"I'll go with you."

"Oh, no. I don't think so. That's just…"

His hand claps against my ass. "Yes, I will." I flinch at the unyielding sound of his voice.

I feel my cheeks heat with mortification. It's not so much that it hurt, but I'm humiliated. I look sharply at him to see what his game plan is. What was that?

"From now on, we have rules, Vivia. No back talk. I'm the one in charge here, and the sooner you accept that the better. There's no privacy. There's no you and me, there's the two of us joined at the hip indefinitely. There's no way you're going anywhere alone, and you will not have a chance to escape until we've gotten to the very bottom of this. I'll give you the tiniest bit of privacy to use the facilities, but that's all you're getting." He stares at me, so angry it makes my heart beat a little faster.

"Do you understand me?" he says, with that ultra-fixation that's making me squirm. It was nice when he was focused on asking questions, but now that he's correcting me, I feel as if I'm withering under the laser stare. Yes, yes, fine.

"Fine," I breathe. "I guess I'm a prisoner and all that." I turn my head away from him so I don't have to look at him. Something tightens in my throat when I realize that this is part of what my family is. This is what they do.

"Off we go," he says with a grip on my arm as he marches me outside.

Okay, so the outhouse is one of the most disgusting concepts ever. It's a literal tiny shack in the middle of the woods with a hole where I'm supposed to—no, wait, we're both supposed to do our business?

Gross. I don't even use public restrooms if it can be helped.

Something tells me things are going to get a lot grosser before they get better, if they ever do.

How do the Survivor people do it? No one ever talks about peeing or... worse... in the woods and having to use like leaves to wipe your ass. What about shaving your legs? There's no way he's giving me a razor. I shudder. I shave every day and feel like little trees are growing from my stubble if I go longer than twenty-four hours without shaving.

And then I realize with a cold sort of fear… this is part of my punishment.

I've been stripped of all the comfort that I was raised with, every luxury my family could afford. I have no one to drive me anywhere, no house cleaner to make my bed, no personal chef to give me my platter of food or make me a side salad. No mother to give me an allowance, or older brother to bail me out if I get in trouble. No luxury car to drive me to the city to meet my friends, and I am definitely not getting a manicure anytime soon.

Why do people like situations like this? I shiver and open the door to the gross outhouse. I scream. Dario's two paces behind me so when I scream, he's right there.

"What is it?" I don't realize at first that he has a gun drawn.

I point a shaking finger to a disgusting spider with the longest legs I've ever seen.

"It's—it's—it's a spider." I manage to stammer. He laughs, actually laughs at me, the asshole.

"Arachnophobia's a real thing," I mutter.

He reaches down and picks up the spider by a leg. My heart's racing so fast I feel like I'm gonna pass out. I turn away, woozy, trying to calm my racing nerves and he has the audacity to look amused.

"This isn't even a spider, it's a daddy longlegs. Looks like a spider, kinda, but just an insect with really long legs. It's completely harmless." I want to tell him to skip the science lesson, but I can't talk.

He throws it back into the woods, then sobers, his voice hardening. "Now get in there before I bring you in there myself."

Even in the dark, kind of smelly outhouse, I take a minute to appreciate the fact that I'm alone for the first time.

This is my… luxury. I need to think about how I can get away. This story doesn't end well in my current predicament. He'll interrogate me, probably violate me somewhere, and report back to my family. My family will probably turn on me, or at their most merciful marry me off to someone I've never met. There is no freedom at the end of any of these roads.

I need to find a way to get out of here. It has to be the pinnacle of my focus: my escape. If I'm already dead to them, the only risk with me escaping is that I'll be found out and killed.

What do I have to lose?

Is living a life orchestrated by someone else any different than dying anyway?

But Dario won't be easy to fool. The only time I'll probably be able to escape is when he's sleeping. He barely even lets me pee alone. But knowing him, he'll probably cuff me to the bed and then hold me while we sleep. That isn't gonna work.

I can find a weapon, or at least observe a way to escape when we're out of the cabin, maybe if we take a casual stroll in the woods. I can't outrun him, that much I know for a fact, because he's definitely athletic and taller than I am, and if I tried that I think that I would really end up regretting it. He would capture me, and punish me, and neither one of those things sound like a good option.

I circle back to the weapon idea.

"You're taking a long time for someone who just wants to pee," he says right outside the door. I roll my eyes.

"You're a guy. Girls don't just point… and… spray… then shake it off. Ew."

He makes a low sound that could either be a growl or a laugh.

Weapons… weapons. That is a viable option and maybe my only one. Of course, he's the one with the gun and I'm just me, with no knowledge of weapons at all. Dammit, I wish I had more experience.

But at least I know what I have to do now. I have to keep an eye out for an escape. I don't really care where I go or what I'll do after I get there. I don't care if I have to find some menial job and take a different identity and become broke to do it. I've had a life of wealth, and it is very seriously over-rated. Nothing comes free.

So my best bet right now is to play a long game. To "obey" him. Eye roll.

Do every single little thing he asks and bide my time until I have the freedom to escape. This isn't like my captivity back on the wharf when I was tied with a rope. This affords a lot more freedom, and I only have one person to escape from.

It's doable.

I make up my mind. I'm probably dead to my family by now. They don't care about me anymore, and Vivia Montavio is no longer who I am.

I'll take on a new identity, I'll find my way.

I finish my business and leave the smelly outhouse. He stops the door with his palm, and steps in my space. "Stay right there." Any trace of gentleness I thought I imagined before is gone, and now he's nothing but bossy and implacable. Whatever.

With his back to me, he unzips his pants. Door still open.

"Oh my God, you're not just —"

"I am just taking a piss with nothing but air between the two of us. Get over yourself," he says. "I don't trust you enough. Stay right there."

Guys are so disgusting. I turn and look away, and remember my purpose. I quickly scan the woods for anything I could use as a weapon. There's a thick, fallen branch that could work as a club, but I grimace at the thought of actually bringing that down and hurting him. Sharp sticks yes, but God I can't… impale a guy. Jesus, I don't have the constitution for shit like this.

Maybe I don't need to hurt him. Maybe I can just… sneak away.

He takes me by the arm and leads me back to the house.

"I don't suppose there's any instant hand sanitizer around here."

He sniffs. "Poor little spoiled, sheltered Montavio sister," he says without a trace of sympathy. Is he mocking me? Whatever. Any woman would be grossed out by this. Spoiled my ass.

When we're back inside, he sits me down in a chair and cuffs my arms behind my back. The hardback wooden chair is stiff against my back. Once I'm secured, he goes over to the supplies and retrieves a large jar of peanut butter and another of strawberry jam, along with a loaf of white bread. My stomach growls.

I've never been a peanut butter and jelly sort of girl, but anything sounds good right about now.

He makes three, presumably two for him and one for me, takes two blue speckled camp mugs from a rustic shelf, and I watch him go outside to pump water. My heart pumps a little faster when he does, but he's only paces away. I can't run. I'm not even prepared, and I'm starving. My lips and mouth are so dry, and I haven't really thought about it until now, but I'm seriously dehydrated.

When he comes back in, he's all business. He stands by the table, his large frame unencumbered by the loose, dirty clothing he wears. I must look a sight myself. It would be good to change into something clean.

He's something to look at, I'll give him that. His profile speaks of power and an ageless strength. Square jar tinged with stubble, framing a handsome, square face. A girl can at least admire him.

I wait for him to unfasten my cuffs so I can eat. I suppose I'm pretty naïve since he has no such plans. He pulls a chair directly across from me and straddles it, lifts the sandwich in his large, rough hands, and takes a huge bite.

Did he wash those hands? I saw no washing. I imagine he washed them in the water outside and stifle the wave of nausea.

"Open up, buttercup." I stifle a sound of disgust, open my mouth, and actually let him feed me little bites of sandwich. My cheeks flame with embarrassment. You don't realize how much you value your own autonomy until you're reduced to feeling like a child. Someone providing for your food, watching your every move, hand-feeding you. It's demoralizing, which is probably exactly why he does it.

"So," I say to him. "Do I get to ask questions? Or is that only your job?"

The peanut butter sticks to the top of my mouth, making it hard to speak. I move my lips and try to swallow. Wordlessly, he lifts the cup and brings it to my lips.

I have to intentionally mute the part of me that likes this. The way his hand cradles the back of my head. The way he gently tips water into my mouth while I swallow, not so much that I choke, but enough that I get a nice full sip. When I give him a little shake of my head to tell him I'm done, he rests the cup on the table. He's so careful it's almost gentle.

I don't think I'm the only one affected, either. He reaches over and brushes a droplet of water from my lips, his face pensive.

"Need more?" he asks, his voice a little husky. He looks straight into my eyes. We're sitting only a few feet away from each other.

I swallow hard, and when I speak my own voice is affected. "I'm all set, thank you."

It takes me by surprise how emotionally I react to his feeding me. I've gone from feeling humiliated to feeling... something decidedly very different.

There's a crumb on my lip. I capture it with the tip of my tongue, and he watches every move. I like the way his Adam's apple bobs when he swallows hard, trying to mask emotion. He's sitting so close to me, he could kiss me if he wanted to. But we both know that's not allowed.

"Go ahead," he says. He's waiting on another hard edge. Pulling himself back. "Ask me. I won't promise I'll answer everything."

I dive right in, feeling stronger after some food and water. "I grew up within the Montavio family. We were always with the Rossis. And you were not around then. When did you join their family?"

He takes a large bite of a sandwich. No, scratch that. He eats half the sandwich in one gargantuan gulp, swallows, then swigs down some water before he answers. "I served time with Orlando," he says in his raspy voice. "I got involved with the wrong crowd. Unlike some people I know, I grew up poor."

Ouch. Jerk.

"Hit the streets to survive. My grandma raised me, and she never knew how I got my money. She wasn't dumb, so I'm sure she suspected, but she decided it was in both of our best interests if she didn't ask questions, so she didn't. I started with small theft, when one of the local guys took me under his wing. Showed me how to work for money, and for a long time, I was clean. Enlisted, because I looked up to the military and found it was a way out. But it didn't last. When I was on leave, I came home to find my grandmother sick and in need of more medical care than I could afford. So... I didn't re-enlist and went back to what I knew would bring me money. People respected me. I graduated to being the best car thief in the entire neighborhood. I got away with it for a long time. I'm fast, I'm not stupid. And it paid really fucking well."

Well, that was more than I expected.

He takes a sip of water and sees me watching him. "More water?"

I nod just because I want to see if he uses his cup or mine. He doesn't put his cup down but places his to my lips. I take a long, refreshing sip and try not to think about the Rossi family tradition about two people drinking from the same cup. I wonder if he knows it.

"Spent some time in juvie when I was sixteen but didn't serve real time until I met Orlando."

"And that was after you'd served in the military."

"Yes."

"So this was... when Orlando was arrested for manslaughter," I say, putting the pieces together. All of us know when one is arrested. My brothers and cousins do many things that skirt the law, and they mostly get away with it, but every once in a while, someone gets caught, tangled in a net, and dragged to jail like a fish on a line. We all knew when

Orlando was arrested because it was shortly following my uncle Narcisso's death.

"I served two years." He doesn't give me any more details, but I know that's all it takes serving that much time. Hell, serving any time. The guy serving time, or a guy at war, both suffer. "When Orlando got out, he told me to find him. So I did. It didn't take long to prove myself to the Rossis, and they inducted me in because they were short a man." He looks at me seriously, all traces of humor gone. "And they are the best family I have ever had. I take my loyalty to them very, very seriously."

"I know," I say. "Believe it or not, I take loyalty seriously too."

"I'll choose not." His voice is cold again, detached. I tell myself it doesn't matter. He's no friend of mine.

I go back to the questions.

"What's your job in the Rossi family?"

He gives me a slow smile. "I do what no one else wants to do. And I do whatever they tell me to. "

I swallow because I feel suddenly nervous. Without speaking, he lifts the water to my lips again. I drink.

I don't want to think about things that he would do. He does the dirty work. The leg breaking, threatening, and so, so much more. If Romeo says jump, he'll ask how high.

Time to change the subject before I let myself imagine him pulling someone's fingernails off or conducting an interrogation with a drill.

I've seen both and you don't forget that shit.

"Why did your grandmother raise you?"

"Because my mother was in no position to raise a child. She was a child herself."

I don't ask him why he uses the past tense when talking about his mother. She's either dead, or so far in his past she no longer matters. Both options pain me. Sometimes I hate how I feel.

I can already see him in my mind as a young boy too tall for his body, who hadn't grown into himself yet, maybe bullied at school because he lived with a poor grandma in the poor part of town and had to wear faded clothing and old sneakers. Maybe he learned to fight then. Maybe he got the attention of his classmates when he started to earn more money. Maybe they feared him when they found out how he did it.

But I don't ask about those details. I don't know if I want to ask anything else that would make him seem more human to me. It's important that I keep a very close distinction between who he is and who I am and where this is going.

He tells me about school, about his grandmother, and all the while feeds me small bites of my sandwich until it's gone. He lifts the cup to my lips again, and this time I look straight into his eyes as I swallow. It's the only control I have in this entire situation. He holds my gaze, and I wish I could read his mind.

"We had a long night," he says. "It's a lot of work living in a rustic cabin. You look exhausted." I wonder if he has to point out how tired I look to justify his own need for rest. Men like him don't rest easily. They work, and work, and work some more. They wake up at a moment's notice and put their own lives on the line as a matter of routine.

There I go with the damn compassion again. Why couldn't I have inherited some of my mother's ruthless genes?

"We're gonna take a nap."

We. We, together, because there's one damn bed in this place. Involuntarily I look at the only bed in the only bedroom.

"So did they leave, like, any toiletries? Toothbrush perhaps? Cleansing wipes? Exfoliating body wash?" I looked down at my dirty, ragged nails. "No chance there's a nail file somewhere."

"You won't need much more than soap and water."

I try to hide my disgust. "At least I don't have to boil lye to make my own soap or some shit like that," I say with a shudder.

He makes a low growling sound. "We don't have to get that rustic. But remember what I said about those words coming out of a pretty mouth like yours." His voice hardens and takes on a lecturing tone. "I don't want to hear you swear again, am I understood?"

What will he do if I swear again?

I don't know why my body reacts the way it does. The control he has over his voice… the subtle implied threat… the knowledge that he could so easily overpower me it would be laughable, feels strangely erotic.

I decide to try something. Without a trace of humor or sarcasm I nod my head obediently, giving him the submission that he supposedly wants. "Yes, sir."

"Don't do that, Vivia." His voice is husky, barely civil. I struck a chord in him.

There's a certain desperation in his tone. I'm genuinely curious, though. What about my reply affected him?

"Do what?" My voice is a whisper. We're inches away from each other. He shakes his head at me.

"Tempt me. Play with fire just to see how hot it burns."

His voice drops to a lower register, dark and dangerous and terrifying. "They'd scorch the tattoo from my flesh before they murdered me. And you…"

I don't reply because I've lost the ability to speak. There's nothing pretentious or fake about what he just said. And then I realize... he's every bit as captive as I am.

"Let's get some rest," he says, his raspy voice taking on the stern register he likes to revert to. But he's not fooling me. I heard every word he said.

He brushes the crumbs off the table into the palm of his hand, walks to the door and scatters them outside. I assume for birds or something, like some kind of altruist. He leaves the two water cups on the table.

We walk together to the bedroom. I don't ask him about the bed. I don't talk to him at all. It's the middle of the day, probably lunchtime, and I'm suddenly exhausted. He's right. We've had a long night and I do want to rest.

I haven't taken a nap since I was a child. Somehow, I feel justified.

I don't think that I can actually sleep lying next to him, though. Not when I have as many questions going through my head as I do. I don't think I'll rest at all. But I'm wrong. He turns down the blanket, lifts me up since getting onto the bed with cuffed wrists is impossible, and lies me down on the mattress. Without a word, he unfastens my cuffs and arranges me on the bed so my hands are in front of me and then his hands are the shackles around my wrists. We lay so close together there isn't an inch of space between us.

"Don't move," he whispers in my ear, his mouth so close to me the hair on my neck flutters. "Close your eyes and rest. If you try anything funny, I'll punish you."

"Yeah," I say on a yawn.

"I wouldn't be so blasé about it if I were you. I'll pull you over my knee and spank your ass. You'll wish you hadn't, Vivia."

Again, his raspy threat makes curiosity and something else, something darker and erotic, flare across my chest.

Fine, whatever, I'm tired.

I only nod my head and close my eyes.

I tell myself I don't like the way his body feels pressed up to mine. I tell myself I don't like the warmth, the feeling of protection, or the way his hard length pressed up against my ass tells me he sees me, and he likes what he sees.

I tell myself we're captives here in the middle of nowhere.

I tell myself my only chance is to do what he says and survive while I plan.

And then I'll escape.

CHAPTER SEVEN

Dario

I HAVEN'T TOLD her that much about myself, but the little I revealed seems like it may have been a mistake. I have to keep our rules in mind, and it's not going to help at all if I'm letting myself grow soft in any way.

But I am a good judge of character. And something tells me she might not be as guilty as we thought.

Yes, she's spoiled. I'll fix that while we're here in the woods. Nature itself will be a good teacher, and I'll make up the difference. I won't let her act like a spoiled brat.

But the women in the Rossi and Montavio families are held to high expectations. Their lives are not their own, and it seems the only trade-off in exchange for everything they're expected to do is leading a comfortable life. None of them want for anything, whether it's clothes or shoes or a spring break trip to Maui. I'm told Marialena's first car was a luxury BMW worth over a million.

She was attached to the car, until she got into a fender bender about a month ago, at which point she went crying to Mama who soothed her by buying her a new one. Romeo allowed it because he knows as well as I that material possessions and luxury are pretty much the only freedom she has. And I would hazard a guess that Vivia has experienced much of the same. She's never had to get her hands dirty or even so much as drop bread in a toaster for breakfast.

I think of everything Orlando told me. Vivia may have suspected but doesn't know for sure yet that her family no longer recognizes her as one of their own. I'm expecting any minute to get proof from Gloria and Mario about her guilt, or at least a lead on what she might know that would be helpful. But for now, I do my best to rest. It's a tricky feat when you're using your own body as human handcuffs. It's even harder when the person you're restraining is stunningly beautiful and the soft breath she releases when she sleeps is the most fetching whistling snore you could imagine.

I close my eyes and slacken my grip only a little. I'll know the second she wakes, or if she tries to move. I fall into a deep and dreamless sleep.

An hour later, she's thrashing in my arms, crying out. I'm instantly awake. Something's wrong.

I sit up. Vivia's crying. I look around the room to see if there's anything I missed. Did someone break in? Did she see another "spider?" But there's nothing in here except the two of us and the fading sun outside the window.

"Are you okay?" I'm immediately awake, one of the many benefits of being a former soldier. "What happened?"

I pull her over to me so she's lying flat on her back and I can see her face. It's contorted in pain, and her eyes are flooded with tears. "It's nothing," she lies. "I had a bad dream." That much at least is probably true.

"Tell me about it." What someone dreams about can often be very telling.

"I don't want to." She shakes her head. But I wasn't asking.

I retrieve a strand of her hair and give it a sharp tug. "I said tell me what it was about, and that wasn't a suggestion."

She blows out a disgusted breath. "Ugh, fine. I don't know if it means anything at all, so I don't know why you care. I dreamt I was at The Castle. I'm certain it was there. My brothers were there, all of them, but Sergio was in the front. He said that I was dead to them. My mother walked in, too, and it got worse. She said everything was over, that they might as well bury me in the graveyard with my dead aunt and grandparents."

She shudders and closes her eyes. "And the next thing I knew we were at that graveyard, and my body was in a box being lowered into the ground. I could see out of the casket, it was me in there, still alive. I watched my mother throw dirt on my casket and knew they were going to bury me."

She sighs and pinches the bridge of her nose. "See? Stupid. It doesn't even make any sense."

"I don't know," I tell her. "That makes perfect sense to me."

She looks at me as I continue. "It's also true." I don't like to sugarcoat things. I call things as I see them. "Your family thinks you tried to kill your cousin. You are dead to them. Your only chance is here in the woods with me as your only opportunity. Orlando brought us here because he thinks that you'll be able to give answers you otherwise wouldn't because if we were at The Castle Sergio or one of your other brothers would intervene. They will want to see you dead, Vivia." I'm not telling her anything she doesn't already know.

"Orlando is telling them all that we died, not just so that the Montavios don't look for you but because we want the people who kidnapped us to think that we died. If they think we're still alive, they could come after us again," I say, turning around to look at her and holding her face in my hands. "It's the safest option until we know who they are and we can defend ourselves."

I knew from the beginning that brute force wouldn't be the way to get answers from Vivia. The only way to get the truth is by building some kind of trust between us. "Do you know who took us?"

She shakes her head. "No." There's a firm confidence in her voice that tells me she doesn't know anything.

"Did you try to murder your cousin?" Again, she shakes her head. "No, I would never. I love my cousins. Even though some of them drive me crazy, we're family, and that's all I have. You should know that. We don't have friends, or romantic relationships. Literally all we have is each other. Why would I ever try to hurt my cousin?"

I shake my head. "People do stupid things when they're in love."

She sighs shakily. "I only thought I was in love with Gray. I was with him because he paid attention to me, and my brothers didn't like him. I've lived a very, very sheltered life, Dario."

She tries to turn her face away, but I won't allow it.

She shakes her head. "I had a feeling from the beginning that he was using me. I'm not sure what his plan was, but he would… say things. Ask questions. He definitely liked having things like the privilege of sitting at high-end restaurants and enjoying the status of it all. So whoever worked with him definitely promised him all of those things. Prestige, honor, money."

"I see."

I have to go in for the truth. "Did you sleep with him?"

She doesn't look away but only nods her head. "Yes," she whispers. "I wish I hadn't, but I did."

It was a fatal error. It would've been at least understandable if she loved the guy.

"Is there a chance you're pregnant?" She looks outraged.

"I… no," she says. "The last time I slept with him was two weeks ago. It's impossible."

"I suspected as much."

She doesn't ask me why I wanted to know. I'd have to take that into consideration when I question her. A part of me doesn't want to go hardcore on her, doesn't want to really hurt her. After what I've seen and what we've been through in such a short time, I'm not sure she has much more information than she's letting on.

"All right," I say to her. "I'll have other questions for you as well."

She thinks that over. She doesn't seem to like the idea of answering my questions. I don't care if she likes it or not, the sooner I eliminate her as a suspect the better. And I'm not going to let her soft voice and her pretty face sway me from my loyalty to The Family.

I push out of the bed and stand beside her, when I hear a beep on my phone. I reach for the cuffs on the bedside table and snap them on her wrists before I pick up my phone and read the messages.

Message from Orlando.

Romeo knows you're there. He's the only one. Everyone, including Sergio and the rest of the Montavio family, believes that you were killed en route home. We believe that will help them go into hiding, and prevent them from looking for you. Sergio has shown no reaction, but Romeo believes it is for the best because Sergio would probably kill Vivia unless you can prove that she's innocent. I'm not sure that's possible, brother. And I think you'll share the same opinion when you see what I'm going to send you from Gloria.

A chilling detachment suffuses me.

Dead. We're dead. We faked Gloria's death after she went dark and began to work for us, and that was the strangest, most emotional funeral I've ever gone to. Not many people get to watch their own funeral.

I wonder if my grandma has figured anything out, or if anything has been announced. She's an elderly senior citizen comfortably residing in an assisted living facility, thanks to Romeo. I don't know if she has any access to news or would even process this information if she did because she's got dementia. For once in my life, I am thankful that she's most likely blissfully ignorant. Romeo will know not to tell her I'm dead, to somehow shield her from the pain of that.

Files begin to show on my phone. Audio messages, PDF files, pictures. I glance at the bed where Vivia lays on her back. I don't know if there's guilt or fear in her expression, or both. She knows I'm going to delve into this. She knows I'm going to have a lot of questions for her. And I'm sure she suspects that the real interrogation will not be pretty.

I walk out of the bedroom because I don't want her to see my expression when I go over the files from Gloria. It's a good move. I feel my brows snap together, my pulse racing as my blood pressure rises. Vivia might say that she is innocent, but I can absolutely see why Gloria says otherwise.

Her phone sent texts to Gray. Identifying locations of Marialena, the weak spot at The Castle. Explanations as to when and how they travel, how many bodyguards she'll have on her at any time. And for some reason the pictures I see of her and Gray intimately connected, in bed, making out at a club, make my blood boil more than anything.

Twenty-five thousand dollars hit her bank account an hour after she sent those text messages.

How much did she trust that asshole? How much did she tell him?

How much is she lying to me?

Another update text from Orlando.

NOW THAT YOU *have this information, do with it what you will. Find out everything, brother. We have a lot riding on it.*

I respond with a text of my own.

ME: *You can trust me. I've already begun to question her, but I'll need to ask more. Do you have any way to identify who she sent the texts to? Have you been able to trace the payments into her account?*

ORLANDO: *Gloria says they're from an unnamed source, but they originated in Canada. It looks like there's a strong connection between Canada and here. You said you heard one of them call the other one Ace?*

ME: *Yes*

ORLANDO: *We can't find anyone with any local moniker. Doesn't mean there isn't one, but Gloria is starting to believe that this is not an established group. It's more likely one that wants to become an established group.*

. . .

I NOD as I start to put the pieces together. Why would they go after Marialena? If Vivia is innocent, why would they use her in particular? But one thing I need an answer to before I can answer anything else: is Vivia guilty?

I take a deep breath and text Orlando. *I'll get information this afternoon and evening. I'll update you as soon as I have anything new.*

Orlando: *Thank you. I trust you. Do you need anything where you are? I know it's rustic.*

I chuckle to myself.

Me: *We have better provisions here than I had when I was overseas. It's a little bit of a retreat honestly. Vivia is not as pleased, but that's probably a good thing.*

I can almost hear him laughing on the other end.

I put the phone down and go through the rest of the files from Gloria. As I do, it's starting to look more and more like Vivia has something to hide. I'll strip her down and ask everything I need to. I'll get answers if it kills me.

Based on the footage here, she's already lied to me. I'm a fool for taking anything she says at face value.

I stalk back in the room. Her eyes snap up to me, guarded. She's hiding something, and I don't know if it's because she knows I spoke with Orlando, I have more intel on the situation, or because she knows that I'm going to get the truth out of her, but the innocent expression on her face is gone and now instead she wears a cold, hard mask. Montavio stock through and through.

I snap my fingers. My voice is cold. I need answers, and I want them now. I point to the floor in front of me. "Get over here."

"A little hard to get out of bed with handcuffs around my wrists," she says, a sarcastic twinge in her voice.

I stare at her. "I'm sure you're capable."

I anchor my hands on my hips. I don't know why I allowed myself to flirt with the idea that she was anything more than my captive. I don't know why I allowed myself to soften around her. She's either a very good actress, or I'm a sucker. Maybe both.

I watch her struggle to get out of bed, and she finally sits up. She's got herself off the bed and stands on the floor in front of me. I think over my options about how I can interrogate her. Straight questions are going to get an answer. I need her vulnerable. I need her afraid.

"I got some information from my team, and it's not looking good for you, Vivia."

I look at her, waiting to hear what she'll think and to see how she'll respond.

When someone's lying or planning to, the micro expressions on their face often show two things at the same time: what the liar wants to show and what the liar wants to conceal. You have to watch carefully because micro expressions don't last longer than half a second.

The quick half-smile and widened eyes show me exactly what I need to know.

Ah. The spoiled Montavio princess is not as innocent as she looks. I cluck my tongue and shake my head from side to side. She's responded well to the little bits of praise I've spoon-fed her. I wonder how she'll respond to disapproval, rather than raw aggression.

Maybe I'll try both.

I step over to her. It's such a small room, two steps and I'm there. She doesn't flinch or back up but holds her ground, even when I reach for her. I thread my fingers along her scalp and watch as her eyes flutter closed.

She likes that. She won't like what I'm doing next.

I weave my fingers close to her skin, grip, and yank. She gasps and her eyes fly open. I take her by her hair to the door and march her into the main living room.

"Dario, what are you doing?" she asks, her voice wobbling.

"I told you. I got information that implicates you. I need truth from you. You've lied to me already, and I don't want to give you another chance for more lies."

"What did I lie to you about?"

Oh, she's a good fucking actress.

I don't answer her. We'll get there.

I stand her in front of me and uncuff her. "If you try anything, I will tie you to the bed and take my belt to your ass until you scream for mercy." I stare at her, letting those words sink in. "Am. I. Clear? "

Her chin wobbles, but her lips are set in a thin line. I wait for her to say something in response, but she doesn't. I yank her hair harder.

"I asked you a question."

"I thought it was rhetorical," she says with a haughty air.

She swallows hard and meets my gaze unflinchingly. She even goes so far as to shake her head so that her hair falls across her shoulders in a gesture of anger and defiance. Every line, angle, and curve of her body speaks defiance. We'll see if it still speaks that when I strip her.

I can almost hear her thoughts. She's used to brutality. She's used to violence. She'll just grin and bear it and get through.

We'll see about that. Something tells me her father and brothers have never questioned her naked.

She's my little captive.

With her wrists unfastened they hang by her sides. "Clothes off." I sit only inches from her and watch. She blinks at me and doesn't make a move to obey. I almost imagine she shakes her head, barely perceptibly. She wants to defy me but fears the consequences.

I grab her waist and yank her in front of me. I tug at her flimsy clothes, letting them fall to the floor like torn paper. Being stripped seems to unleash something within her.

I pick up her clothes and toss them into the fireplace. She won't need them again.

"You've already earned a punishment for your disobedience, haven't you?"

"I—"

Before she can respond I grab her waist and yank her over my lap. She knows my plan and quickly tries to stop me. She recoils and squirms and pushes. "Let me up! No! Let me go!"

I'm ready, though. In seconds, I pin her legs with mine and throw my arm across her lower back to hold her in place. I find perverse pleasure in the challenge. I'll enjoy taking this out of her by force better than any other way.

So fucking sue me for being a sadist.

I slam my palm against her perfect ass. Glad that she's looking at the floor because I'm unable to mask my face that shows I like what I see. She's slender but curvy in the right places, two little dimples in the small of her back I want to kiss and lick in reverence. Her ass is full and heart-shaped, now bearing the pink imprint of my palm, and I want to worship that, too. She has long, slender legs and her dainty feet kick every time my palm slams against her naked skin. Before I yanked her over my lap, I noted perfect, round breasts with pretty little blush nipples I can't wait to lick and suck.

Here in the woods, we're alone. We might as well be on another planet.

She stoically doesn't respond at first, but I can feel her struggling. I wonder if she can feel how aroused this makes me.

I don't fucking care. I hope she does.

"What was that for?" she grates out.

"Because you lied to me. You said you haven't had sex with Gray in two weeks. Dated video footage I got this afternoon says otherwise."

She slumps over my knee, guilt-ridden if ever I've seen it. I give her six more hard slaps. I'm not sure why she lied, but I am sure she won't do it again.

"Anything else you wanna confess to?" It would be convenient while she's over my knee.

"I used birth control. I'm definitely not pregnant." She says it like it's a dirty word.

"Then why did you lie to me about something so stupid?" She doesn't answer but only shakes her head from side to side, her hair falling about her face and kissing the floor. I don't like that she doesn't answer when I ask her a question. I give her another hard slap where her ass meets her thighs.

"Because I'm trying to deny that I had anything to do with an asshole," she says, her voice tense. "I hate that I let him take advantage of me. And I hate even more that you saw us having sex."

I rest my palm on her heated skin while I speak to her. "What do you think Sergio would do with that footage?"

She knows exactly what he'd do, and so do I.

Vivia makes a sound like a strangled sob. "You know exactly what he'd do," she says angrily, but she can't hide the emotion in her voice. "I'm flawed now. I'm useful to no one. They can't use me to marry off, they can't use me as property. I'm worthless to them." Her voice catches at the end, and as she says this, I wonder if this isn't part of her reasoning. Maybe she wants them to know that she can no longer be used as a pawn.

I have other questions to ask her that are more important than this. That was only to satisfy my curiosity.

"Texts were sent to an unknown person disclosing Marialena's whereabouts, how many bodyguards she had with her, and where she would be found.

The weak links in Castle security. They were sent from your phone. Answer me honestly, or this punishment gets a lot worse."

One might think that a barehanded spanking on bare skin doesn't hurt that much, but they would be wrong. When I strike her just the right way little fingerprint-shaped marks rise on her skin. Welts. She screams in agony. She has sensitive, tender skin, and her body reacts instantly to the pain.

"I didn't know any messages like that were sent from my phone," she says.

I give her another slight slap. "And how do I know that to be true?"

"I never saw them. So maybe you could check to see if the texts were deleted after being sent? Because it wasn't me."

I rest my hand on her ass again, to remind her that punishment is only a breath away, and she better answer as truthfully as she possibly can.

"After your phone disclosed information to the rivals, twenty-five thousand dollars hit your bank account. Are you telling me that you didn't notice that?"

She doesn't respond again; she knows what that means. Anger surges in my chest as I secure her over my lap and give her six hard, relentless smacks with my palm. She flinches with each one and still doesn't respond. I shake my head, willing and able to punish her more. I shift her on my lap so my fingers reach her breasts, cup one and finger her nipple.

She gives a quick, sharp intake of breath. "What are you doing?"

Will she tell me no? Will she tell me to stop it? Is she going to try to tell me that she doesn't want this?

But… she's responded really well to my praise. She has a natural submissive streak a mile wide, whether she wants to admit it or not.

So while I finger her nipples, I watch her reaction. I watch the way her cheeks flush pink, how she involuntarily parts her thighs. I dip my fingers between her legs and feel the evidence of her arousal. A dark, powerful sense of possession washes over me.

No one will ever touch this woman again. No one else will question her.

I will get the truth out of her one way or another, but every shudder of pleasure in her body belongs to me. I long to taste her, to devour her, to feel every spasm of ecstasy that crashes through her body when I make her sing for me.

"I'm questioning you."

She doesn't respond, but her breathing hitches and gets quicker when I stroke between her legs. Gentle, tender. Then my fingers close around her nipples and tweak, hard. She screams and arches her back.

"I asked you a question. I can tie you up and whip it out of you. I could use other forms of torture to get my answers and you know that no one else will hear you. No one's coming to rescue you." I could restrict her breathing, threaten to hurt her. But she's a delicate woman, and I can't allow myself to do anything that would cause permanent damage. A good spanking or whipping she'll recover from quickly.

Which is good, because something tells me I'm going to have to rely on that method a little more often.

CHAPTER EIGHT

Vivia

I'M LYING over his lap feeling helpless and furious and so aroused I could scream. It isn't fair how quickly he strips me not only of my clothes but of my pride, my dignity. I have nothing to hide behind with every slap of his palm and stroke of his finger. Nothing.

"Now answer the question."

Part of me doesn't want to answer the question because I'm embarrassed. Another part of me truly doesn't have the answers, and further, I don't want to tell him the full truth. I know I betrayed my family, even if ignorance was my biggest sin.

I can't hide behind silence anymore. He will do everything in his power to make me tell him everything.

"Yes. Yes, fine. I saw the deposit. At first, I wasn't sure where it came from. I get an allowance from my brother, but it's… less than that." Not much less, but he doesn't need to know that. "I didn't think much of it because I have a credit card and all my expenses are met."

He can't hide the note of derision in his tone. "So twenty-five grand wasn't a blip on your radar for you then, was it, little princess?"

I grit my teeth, fully aware of the fact that he can and will punish me when I talk back, but I don't care right now. "I hate it when you call me that."

That earns me three more searing smacks of his palm.

"No, it didn't bother me. I wasn't sure where it came from, and I didn't care. "

I didn't care because I was planning my escape. And I figured wherever that money came from, I would use it to get the hell out of Dodge. That plan went to shit, and I'm not telling him because it'll get back to my brother. And if I ever escape this, I'd be in indefinite lockdown for the rest of my life.

"So you didn't know that was a payoff for information directly related to Marialena?"

I tell him honestly, "No."

"You didn't know that the information was sent from your phone with the information they retrieved?"

I squirm over his lap, scared of what can happen next, when he asks me something I can't answer.

"No."

He strokes his palm over my sore ass, and I try to steel myself so I don't feel, I don't respond.

It doesn't work.

"Did anything at all tip you off that the guy you were with was using you at any point?"

"Of course," I tell him. "But I didn't think much of that either, because every man I've ever been with was using me for one reason or another."

Truth. I gave him the truth.

Finally.

"Did you know that the man you were with was on another's payroll? Did you know he was working for someone?"

I don't know how to answer that either without implicating myself. I think about what to say, but apparently, I'm too slow, because the next thing I know he's spanking me again, hard, and this time he really means business.

He's lecturing me like he's in charge of me, and it makes me want to punch him. "When I ask you a question, I expect an answer. No answer is disobedience. Hesitation is disobedience. You have five seconds to answer before your ass feels my belt."

I freeze. At the threat of him taking his belt to me, I don't know how to respond. I realize in a panic I don't even remember the question.

He shifts, still holding me against him, and I feel him reach for his waist.

"No! Dario! Ask again!"

But he doesn't listen. With one rapid tug, he holds his belt in his hand and slides it along my ass.

It's at once scary and erotic.

"I said," he says in a curt, stern tone, "did you know that Gray was working for someone else?" I feel the cold leather on my body, and I'm frozen. I don't know how to answer the question. And I know my time is up. I tense, ready for the strike, but nothing can prepare me for the way it feels.

I expect it to burn, I expect excruciating pain like he's taking a whip to me, but he's doing something different. He slides the leather over my skin, until every cell feels as if it's primed. I open my mouth to speak, but nothing comes out and I'm not sure what I'd say if I could. My hands reach wildly in front of me until I feel his pants. I anchor my fingers in his clothes because I feel like I'm going to fly away if I don't. I stop breathing when he lifts his arm. But when the belt finally lands with a swish and a whap, the bite of leather is nothing but a sensual caress.

He does it again, and again, and again. I feel if he continues, I'm going to climax right over his lap. My cheeks flush at the thought. I'll never be able to look at him again. The whole situation is vaguely disturbing, my emotions perplexing and unpredictable. Anxiety knots inside me because I'm out of control and he's taken full command.

I don't trust him, but I have no other choice.

If only I could be sure of my own reactions, but even those betray me. It's impossible to calm my erratic pulse, my mind an unruly jumble of fear and hope.

"Dario," I finally manage to breathe, though I don't know why I'm calling his name or what I'm asking.

His hands find my breasts again. I hear a little moan that rushes over my skin like the rumbling of thunder. I don't realize at first it's coming from me.

"You're a good girl, aren't you, baby? I believe you, Vivia." As he speaks, he traces his rough fingers over the softest, fullest part of my breasts, weighing and worshipping them as if I'm as delicate as fragile glass. The juxtaposition of the hard punishment just moments before and the tender way he touches me now makes a flicker of disquiet hum along my nerves.

Suffice it to say, I have never been touched like this before. Whereas Gray's sexual advances were bold and fearless, there was an unpracticed, selfish flavor to them that put me on guard. He wanted to take. Dario, however… my God, the way he touches me it's like his life's purpose is to pleasure me, and he knows exactly how to do it.

The interlacing sensations of fear and arousal make me pant. I'm dizzy and lightheaded, still helplessly prone over his sturdy, unyielding lap. Far back in my mind, I'm aware that this is intentional. In no way has he let me off the hook. He hasn't softened even an inch. This is all part of his plan to master and manipulate me.

And goddamn, is it working.

I'd promise undying devotion, I'd give him anything he wants, hell I'd give him my firstborn child if he only touches me again. I need him to satisfy the yawning need, the almost feral pressure between my legs that's driving me mad. I would fall down and worship his cock if it brought me relief. The wait is interminable.

As I moan and make a complete fool of myself, mumbling incoherently and begging for him to touch me, he alternates lashes of his belt with sensual touches across my naked ass, between my pulsing legs. The pressure builds, and builds, until I can't breathe.

Somewhere in my state of half-consciousness, he loops the belt gently around my neck. I should be afraid that he's going to strangle me, or at least threaten to. He definitely could. It wouldn't be outside the realm of possibility.

But no. It's only another one of the tricks up his sleeve.

He tightens it so that my pulse races, a delicate play between fear and sensuality as he touches my nipples and fondles my breasts with such languid, skilled strokes, it's as if he holds a magic wand.

"Did you know," he whispers, punctuating every word with a salacious swipe of his fingers, "that Gray was on someone else's payroll? That was the question, Vivia." His fingers freeze right above the place I want him to touch. "That was the question I asked you."

I whimper and squirm, but I can't reach his fingers on my own.

"Of course," I tell him. "Of course I did. I assumed he worked for my brother at one point, and I knew he wasn't poor. He never told me what he did, and I didn't ask questions."

"Why not?"

That's an easy one. I answer in one breath.

"Because when you grow up the way I did, you realize that sometimes it's better not to know."

He rewards me with another brush of his fingers, driving my need up even more. I wantonly writhe against his hand, unable to stop myself from wanting more, harder, faster.

"Answer this next question honestly," he says, a latent threat in his tone. He pauses all movement, his voice tight and commanding. "Did you give your virginity to Gray?"

Slowly, wordlessly, he removes the belt and fists it. I clench in anticipation.

I throw up a shield to my mind so fast my body tenses. What does that have to do with anything? No, God, no, anything but that. I hate that he's asking me.

I don't want to tell him the answer to this. Again, knowing full well that I'm going to be punished, I clamp my mouth shut and close my eyes. He shifts me on his lap, my only warning to prepare for more punishment.

The belt falls so hard I lose my breath. I feel as if I'm being split in two. I scream until I lose my voice, garble words in a hoarse cry as he lashes me with barely a pause between strikes. I lose count of the strokes. I'm submerged in pain. I want it to stop, and I don't know how to make him.

I'm crying freely now, tears falling onto the wooden floor. The tiny wooden cabinet absorbs my screams as if it were meant to. This is why I am here. No one will hear me scream or come to my aid. If Dario decided this was my last day on Earth and it was his duty to take my life, no one's coming to my rescue here.

He finally stops. He's panting from the effort, no longer whipping me, but poised as if he's ready to strike again.

Why? Why does he care?

Why this time of all times is my punishment so much worse than it was before? Why does questioning my virginity make him so harsh? I would've expected fury from Sergio, or Mama. Or any of my brothers, to be honest.

Why does Dario care?

"You know I did," I say, my voice choked with tears. "You know I gave it to him. So why do you need me to tell you? What's it to you?" My voice sounds small and accusatory, and I don't care.

"You know why," he says, his voice so harsh it feels physically painful to hear. "What happens to you next is fully contingent on how honest you are."

Maybe he's also experimenting with the best way to get the truth from me. Sensual caresses, and the need to climax? Or harsh punishment?

I'm fully aware of his hard length pressed into my belly, and it suffuses me with a sense of power. I like that he's affected by me.

He feels what I do, every inch of my body pressed against his. This is more than his job.

Dario wants me. And is there any such thing on this earth as a woman who doesn't want to be wanted?

I admit the truth, even though it's embarrassing. "I didn't like that my virginity wasn't mine to handle or control," I tell him truthfully. At this point I don't know why I would hold anything back from him. Every time I have, he's only punished me and known that I had something to tell him.

My reward comes as he spreads my legs with his strong, capable fingers, teasing and possessing every inch of me until I'm on the very cusp of climax again.

"Vivia," he says, "tell me everything now. I want to hear it. Don't make me extract it in pieces."

And then his voice dips to a lower register, molten and seductive. "You took your punishment like a very good girl, and I'm so very proud of you. Do you know how proud of you I am?"

I tell myself not to fall for it. I tell myself he doesn't mean it. I tell myself that this is only part of the whole game.

But it doesn't matter. Nothing I tell myself makes my body respond any differently.

I melt into him. My pulse raises. My breasts feel fuller and tingly, and I want to feel anything, literally anything, against my nipples and the underside of my breasts. The pressure between my legs is unbearable.

I can handle the spanking. I can handle his anger. But the way he praises me unravels me. I fall to pieces like a deck of cards. And he knows this, fuck it.

I wish I had better control of my emotions. But I can't control my reaction any more than I can control my heart beating or my eyes blinking. It's instinctual, inexplicable. In my entire life, no one has ever spoken to me the way he does, and even though a very small part of me feels that this is just part of the game, and he doesn't actually mean a word of it, I don't care. It feels so good, I'll take even this parody of affection.

Harsh direction, cruel words, brutal punishment... They are my bread and butter. They were my daily diet. I don't like being punished, but long ago I learned how to steel myself against it. This, however? This... praise? Gentleness? Whatever it's called... It's so foreign to me I'm completely taken off guard.

"Open your legs, beautiful," he says to me, and even that feels so good it makes me want to cry. Mama told me that I'm beautiful, yes. My nannies did too, as did my extended family. But there's something about the way he calls me beautiful, as if it's a term of endearment, that it sinks into my skin and warms me from the inside out.

I do exactly what he says. I lie prone over his lap as if I'm part of him. My naked skin is on fire and my heart beats so fast I feel dizzy. I close my eyes as if that will help me withstand the torrent of emotion, but it doesn't do much good. No. I don't stand a chance against this.

Flames lick at my body, warming me to the point of pain. I half expect he'll make me come like this, right over his lap, and I won't stop him. But no. That would be too simple. He releases me on his lap, reaches down, then lifts me and cradles me to his chest.

Aw, Christ, I love how that feels though.

"I've never seen anyone more beautiful in my life," he says. "When they told me what my job was, I thought I was the luckiest man alive." He's playing me, he has to be, but why does it seem like he's sincere? "I'll take a gorgeous woman like you into custody anytime." He shakes his head from side to side. "And I didn't even know the half of it. Tip your head back, lovely. Just relax, let your head fall back."

When I do as he says, he makes a low, male groan of approval. Oh, he likes it when I obey him. Dario has a strong sadistic streak, that much is clear. Lucky for him I'm a pretty damn good match.

"What a good girl. Look at you, you're doing so good."

His praise makes my heart beat faster, and I feel as if I'm wrapped in a silken cocoon of utter bliss. I feel blissfully happy, and my heart sings as I bask in his praise. I silence the inner censor that tells me not to trust him, that this is only an act, that this is a—

Oh, hell.

My mind becomes a blissful chasm of nothingness when he bends his mouth to me and kisses the valley between my breasts. He continues to praise me, his words igniting a need in me so ferocious I can't control it. Every word is an adulation, every sentiment pays homage and I forgive his sins with the benevolence of a saint. "Look at that perfect body," he moans. His lips are fire against my skin, and every time his eyes meet mine, as his tongue circles my nipple, he kisses the swell of my breast, the slight pain of teeth against the hardened buds, my heart turns over in response.

He looks at me as if he wants to remember me, like he's painting a portrait in his mind he'll hang where he can worship it every day. His mouth softens when his gaze slides down my body to my curves. "Damn, woman," he growls. "You're fucking amazing. Say my name, Vivia. I love it when you say my name." His gaze bores into mine in expectation, and my heart jolts. A tingling warmth spreads to every part of me until my nerves are fire.

"Dario," I whisper.

"Good girl," he approves. His voice takes on a harder edge, as if he knows he has to do a job but wants this over with. "Have you told me everything?"

"Everything I know," I tell him with utter sincerity. "I met Gray on vacation. He seduced and used me. I was naïve and stupid and I slept with him, but I used him right back because I wanted control over my life." My voice trembles. "I would never hurt my family, Dario. Never. I love Marialena, and hate that Gray tried to hurt her." I swallow, my voice shaky with emotion. "And I'll do everything I can to help you find who did try to hurt her."

He stares into my eyes, reading me, then after a long moment, nods. "I believe you," he says. He doesn't apologize for interrogating me or bringing me here, and I know why. He was following orders. He's bound by oaths to obey Romeo and the others in authority over him.

He may not apologize, but he's going to make this better.

"You like it when I praise you, don't you?" he asks curiously, as he adjusts me so he can reach between my legs. My hips jerk upward involuntarily. I need him to touch me. I'm craving his touch so badly I want to cry.

"Yes," I whisper. It's true. Butterflies erupt in my stomach when he says anything to praise me. His words of adulation and approval make me warm from the tip of my head to my toes. I'd give him anything in that moment. The truth. My pride.

My heart.

It might prove to be my fatal flaw, but I'll die happy.

I don't care if he means it. I don't care if he doesn't. I'm so starved for his affection and praise it's almost alarming to me. I've never had anything like this before and I'm not sure I'll ever have anything like it again. The precariousness of my situation is scary when I think about it, but I don't want to think about it.

I want him to touch my breasts again. I want him to make me climax. I want to feel him inside me, stretching me so full he takes my breath away. I want to see him in the throes of ecstasy when he empties himself inside me.

I want it all.

I know he's going to kiss me right before he does. Hope and fear hold me captive. And when he finally does… when his lips meet mine… I finally taste him.

You wouldn't know by looking at a hardened criminal and veteran like Dario that he is capable of such tenderness. His lips are scorching, the touch of his hand on the back of my head so fierce I lose my breath. Our tongues tangle before I lick his lips. He tastes like fire and need and warmth, and I want to taste more of him.

He stands suddenly, taking me bodily in his arms without breaking the kiss. His teeth graze my lips, and when I moan, he devours my mouth as if he's starving. His grip on my body tightens, his arm around my back and at the fold of my legs, but all I feel is his mouth, his tongue, his teeth, and the low moan of approval he gives when my tongue licks his.

I don't know how we make it to the bedroom, but the pillow is under my head and the bed sags with his weight on me. His fingers are tangled in my hair sending frissons of arousal through every nerve like sparks of fire. I'm vaguely aware of a deep, lingering pain where he spanked me, the heaviness of my breasts, the liquid fire between my legs as he moves his fingers from my hair and captures my wrists. I want to touch him, to hold him, to anchor myself to him, but I'm pinned to the bed under his weight and grip. The loss of control and reminder of his strength only feeds my growing need.

With his mouth still on mine, both my wrists pinned above my head with one hand, he lowers his other hand between my legs and parts them. I shiver in expectation, so eager I can't breathe. The first feel of his hand between my legs makes me spasm. The second and I lose my ability to speak. The third, and my body erupts in flames. My hips jerk and ecstasy claims me. I'm grateful no one can hear my scream because I couldn't stop myself if I wanted to. I ride his fingers and lick his tongue, the only thanks I can give for the bliss he's giving me. My body explodes in a sudden torrent of fire, and when I finally breathe again, I gasp deep, soul-quenching breaths of air. I shatter into a million little shards as ecstasy claims me.

I gasp as I slide down from my pinnacle, the sweet agony like nothing I've ever felt before. He releases my wrists so he can hold me, and to my surprise my cheeks are wet.

"I—holy—mother of—what was that?"

"Beautiful girl," he says with a chuckle, as I bask in the warmth of my post-orgasmic climax. "You climaxed. Your reward for telling me the truth. Don't tell me you've never climaxed before?"

"I—that—"

Apparently talking in complete sentences is out of the question.

I close my eyes and drop my arm across my forehead, incapable of movement for long moments. He slides off of me and rests beside me. I can feel his warmth radiating like fire. "That was a... climax... the same way the little... stream... behind my... house... is the Hudson River."

I close my eyes.

I love the sound of his laugh. "Lie still, Vivia," he commands. He could tell me to walk a tightrope over the Grand Canyon and I'd nod and say "yes, sir." So I lie as still as I can which is pretty easy because I'm confident I'm actually paralyzed. "I want to drink you in with my eyes, lovely."

I close my eyes and let him do just that, still numbed from ecstasy.

I'm not sure what's happened. I'm not sure what will happen next. But sometimes, living in the present is the very best choice one can make.

CHAPTER NINE

Dario

VIVIA MONTAVIO HAS A PRAISE KINK, why yes, she does. I've never seen anyone so eager for approval. I've never seen anyone respond like her to the slightest accolade. She longs for affirmation so desperately, I have an almost unfair advantage.

My instincts were right. Hard interrogation and harsher punishment will not be the most effective means with her. While others would scoff at the way I've mostly handled her, the most practical methods of interrogation are the ones suited for a captive's needs. Or, more accurately, the methods best suited to take advantage of their weaknesses.

And I've found hers.

I'd feel like an asshole if I didn't make another discovery: interrogating her further is fruitless. She doesn't know fucking *anything.*

I lie in bed next to her, and she half-dozes beside me as I update Orlando.

ME: *I've fully interrogated her. She knows almost nothing.*

Orlando: *Dammit. I mean, I'm relieved though. Would hate to think she was really behind any of this.*

Me: *Everything Gloria found leads to her, but it wasn't actually her who betrayed us, it was her boyfriend who's now dead. Biggest question is, who would try to hurt Marialena using Vivia?*

NO ANSWER AT FIRST. Vivia blinks and rolls over slowly, like she's drugged.

ORLANDO: *It's a good question. It would be someone who'd do anything in their power to prevent the Montavio and Rossi families from uniting in any way. We're stronger if we unify, and that makes us nearly invincible.*

NEARLY. A merging of two mob families is tricky business. In-house fighting is what typically does them in.

I nod to myself.

ME: *I think that's right. The question then is, who would be trying to prevent that from happening?*

Orlando: *That's exactly the question. Gloria's working around the clock with Mario to see what she can find. I'll update with more information. But listen, brother.*

I WAIT FOR THE RESPONSE. I watch the little dots on the phone indicate he's typing, then stopping, typing, then stopping. Finally, a message pops up.

ORLANDO: *She's safer with you for now. If she were to come here it... would not be good. Sergio believes she was behind this. And we know she slept with Gray. So even if she had nothing to do with what happened to Marialena, that alone means she's fucked.*

I WINCE. I know it.

ME: *Yeah. So we stay here for now.*

Orlando: *You have to. It's better for you and for her while we get to the bottom of this.*

Me: *Sergio will be pissed when he finds out we lied to him*

Orlando: *I'll take my chances. Lie low, brother. Call me if you need anything.*

Me: *I will*

VIVIA ROLLS over again and opens her eyes, looking up at me. She blinks as if she's surprised I'm there at first, then looks around her. She grows still when she remembers where she is.

I sit up and stretch. "I'm starving. You?"

She nods quietly.

"It's getting to be about dinnertime. And since there's no electricity here, we'll have to light the oil lamp and build a fire, too." I look down at her. "Even though it would be my preference to have you walking around here without any clothes on, we have to go outside and you'll get eaten alive. It's better for you to wear something."

She gives me a frown that borders on petulance. "You threw my clothes into the fireplace, remember?"

I lean closer to her, a silent reminder she'd better watch her tone. "Oh, I remember. Dance club clothes won't serve you here, lovely. You'll need something a bit more practical."

I push out of bed, keeping her in my peripheral vision, and reach for the duffel bag Orlando's had brought here. I take out a pair of jeans and a long-sleeved top way too small for me and toss them at her. "Here. Put them on."

She eyes the clothes suspiciously, then sits with her arms crossed on her chest. "Go on. You can give me some privacy to dress."

I shake my head at her. "Now why would I do a thing like that? I've already seen all of you. What benefit is there to pretending otherwise?"

I watch as her back goes rigid, and slowly shake my head, heading back toward her. "Maybe," I say slowly, fully aware of how resistant she is and how necessary it is that I teach her to obey me, "I didn't make myself fully clear earlier."

I watch as her face turns ashen, and I can't help but think to myself how pretty she is. She wipes her hands on the bedspread as if her hands are clammy. Almost as if she doesn't realize she's doing it, she presses her elbows into her sides, as if trying to make her body as small as possible, to avoid attention or to somehow make herself disappear.

None of it bothers me. I have a job to do, and I'm not going to let her sway me.

I sit on the edge of the bed and give her a contemplative look. "Any freedom you had before you came to this cabin is gone. Anything that was yours, well and truly yours, before you came here? Gone.

Life as you knew it? Gone. All that we have left is this one opportunity."

She shakes her head and scans the small interior of the cabin. "I don't understand… "

"We're in the cabin surviving. I am your captor. You're my charge. If your brothers knew you were here, they'd kill you. Without a second thought. If the people who tried to kidnap us knew you were here, they wouldn't be as merciful. They'd probably take advantage of you, rape you, take turns using you, send pictures of you to your family, and *then* they would kill you. Maybe they would kill me first and make you watch. Maybe they would make me watch as they abuse you. Before they killed me, too."

I grind my teeth together because I can't help the way those images affect me. My body tenses, adrenaline coursing through my veins as if the picture I painted is about to happen. I don't like that idea. And in a short time, I imagine what it would be like to beat those men. To break their bones. To make them bleed. I draw in a slow, steady breath to calm my fury.

She flinches and recoils, obviously noting my anger and attributing it to her own actions. I don't bother clarifying. I want her afraid of me. I want her to obey.

"I spanked you earlier. I have literally zero qualms about doing it again. In fact, since we're being honest here, I fucking hope you give me a reason.

Over, and over, and over again." The image of her splayed out over my lap, crying for mercy while she scissors her legs and braces herself for every slap of my palm against her naked skin, makes me so hard it's painful. I lean closer to her.

"So go ahead, beautiful. Make your choice. Disobey me and give me shit, and give me a reason to punish you. Or obey me, and we'll get through this night together. Have some food. Make some preparations for the days ahead. It won't be as amusing to me, but we have time."

She rubs her arms together as if she's cold and shivers a little. When she speaks, her voice is a little shaky and husky. "Fine. I'll dress in front of you. Would that make you happy?"

Her words sound as if she wants to defy me. As if she wants to hold herself aloof… but her tone is barely audible. She's afraid.

I gave her a smile, and almost actually feel it this time. "Elated."

She flinches when I reach my hand to hold hers. I slow my touch, not surprised she doesn't welcome it. I flick a wisp of her hair behind her ear and drag my thumb down her cheek until I cup her jaw. Vivia Montavio will be putty in my hands in a matter of days.

I bend my head closer to her and contemplate kissing her. I can already taste the sweetness of her mouth, the seductive warmth of her lips. Our breaths mingle. I remember how she responds to praise.

"Be a good girl for me," I whisper. "Can you do that?"

Her gaze is frozen on my lips. She doesn't breathe. The sound of her swallowing is audible, as she quietly nods her head.

"I can do that," she whispers back. I cup the back of her head. I move closer to her. Her eyelids flutter like the beating of butterfly wings before she closes her eyes.

I kiss her forehead.

When I pull away from her, she looks stunned. Her lips are slightly parted. I want to kiss them.

We'll get there. I want her questioning what I'll do next.

When I glance at the window, it's getting dark outside. We'll have to play later.

"Maybe you need a little help."

I lift the top and snap it open. She's so on edge she flinches.

"Arms up." I half expect her to defy me, and I'm curious what her response will be to being dressed as if she were a child. But she does nothing but obey. Her slender arms reach heavenward, then she holds my gaze as I slide the top over her head and guide her hands through the arm holes.

"No bra?"

"I thought you girls hated those things."

"They're torture devices. But I'm hardly a hippie, and I was raised right. A woman needs to protect her assets."

"Unfortunately, it appears the department store wares were a little short. You'll have to make do."

I smooth the fabric over her skin, and let my palm linger on her breasts, a reminder that going braless might not be as bad as she thinks. Her cheeks flush pink when her nipples harden against the fabric.

If she reacts to my touch, she schools it well.

"Lay back."

She obeys. I lift one leg after the other, slide them into her jeans, then pull them over her little butt. She hisses.

"You're smiling because that spanking you gave me earlier still hurts?"

"Of course. You're adorable."

"And you're a *sadist*."

"Thank you."

Her mouth parts. "That wasn't a compliment."

"Where I'm from, it most certainly is. It means I did my job well, and we're off to a really fucking good start. Let's go." I gesture for her to follow me. "I'm not going to cuff you right now. We're running out of daylight, and we have work to do. I need two sets of hands. And you don't need me to tell you what will happen if you try anything funny."

She rolls her eyes. "Nope. Hey!"

Her eye roll just earned her a good hard smack to the ass. "Roll your eyes at me again, and I'll take you straight across my knee. Consider yourself warned."

She opens her mouth as if to protest, and then thinks better of it. She only sighs and walks beside me.

I take her hand in mine.

"Do you see that lamp over there?"

She nods.

"Bring it here."

I release her hand with reluctance, but I need to make sure she's going to obey me. This is a simple request, though. She brings me the lamp and hands it to me.

"Where did that come from? Little House on the Prairie?"

"Oil lamps are incredibly useful tools. You'll see."

"They look very flammable, too," she says apprehensively.

"We'll be cooking with open flame, heating ourselves by a fire, and any energy source in this cabin is from propane or kerosene."

"So in other words, this entire site is explosive?"

"Exactly."

I show her how to light the lamp, but it's self-explanatory. Flick a match, strike the wick, and off you go. We place it in the center of the round table in the kitchen area and go outside together for firewood.

Dusk has fallen over the quiet campsite. I don't miss the way she sighs. Yeah, I feel the same. All around us, tall pines rise out of the earth and kiss the sky.

The blue of dusk creates art through the dappled leaves; flickering shadows dance with light. We gather up kindling and broken bits of wood. She doesn't make a protest through any of this, and we work in near silence. The only sound is the wind rustling the branches, the crunch of leaves under our feet, the caw of birds, the nearby hum of moths and butterflies, and the scattering sound of animals rooting around in the underbrush. I expect her to react in fear, but she only stands closer to me.

"Who owns this place? The Rossis?"

"Yeah. You've never been here then."

She laughs. "Yeah. You could say that. You have to understand the Montavio and Rossi women would rather die than live in a place like this. Anything five miles away from the nearest shopping plaza is rustic. Three bars of a cell phone signal instead of five is practically roughing it. I heard vague references to cabins, and camping, and I knew my brothers came here from time to time, but I always assumed that it was like a Boy Scout adventure thing. None of us asked questions because we didn't care."

We have two sisters in the Rossi family, Rosa and Marialena, and now that many of the brothers have married, there are more women in the Rossi family than the Montavia family. Only one of Vivia's brothers is married, which gives her one sister-in-law.

"You didn't have any sisters growing up," I say to her. "Did you?"

"No. Did you?"

I shake my head and reach for the split logs lined up outside the cabin. We'll need to start a fire soon. I make preparations for a fire and keep an eye on her the whole time. "I was an only child. And I think I was enough for my grandmother to handle." I can't help but smirk to myself thinking about all the antics I got into. My poor grandmother was gray way too young. If I could go back in time, I'd kick my own ass for being a little punk.

She reaches for the logs, to help me. I don't think so. I shake my head at her.

"No. You focus on the small twigs and kindling; I'll take the heavier things."

She gives me a curious look. "I'm fully capable of helping you with this."

"Didn't say you weren't, but do you really think it's wise to test me right now?" I reach for one of the slim, supple branches from the pile of kindling and flick it against her ass.

"No." She turns away from me, but I don't miss her cheeks flushing pink. "Kindling it is."

She continues to gather the small branches, and I continue to stack logs. "I'm glad I had no sisters," she says. "I wouldn't wish for anyone to be treated the way I was growing up."

I'm no fool. I'm well aware of the fact that she wasn't treated well, and she doesn't like the restrictions she's had, or will continue to have. It's no secret that the expectations for Montavio and Rossi women are practically medieval and fly in the face of modern feminism so starkly, it's almost shocking.

Still, I see my chance. I want to needle her a little. I want to see how she'll react, see if I can learn a bit more about her.

"Oh, stop it. You act as if you're enslaved, and not as if you haven't lived in the lap of luxury your entire life. You've had everything you wanted handed to you. Tell me the truth. Did you have a nanny?"

"Of course," she says, unable to hide her terse tone. I'm getting under her skin.

"Didn't you go away to school?" The pile of wood is more than we need tonight, but I want to keep her working and talking so we continue.

"Yes." She won't look at me.

"Did you ever have to make your own bed, cook your own meal, or mop a floor?"

"No, but I…"

"If you were to ask your father or your mother or your brother for money, what would they say?"

"They would give it to me, but that's not the —"

"Did you have bodyguards?"

She clenches her jaw. "Of course."

I don't miss the way she starts flinging the wood at the pile, or the way her breathing becomes noisier as her nostrils flare. She picks up kindling and whips it at the pile with a sweeping gesture, and when she looks at me her chin is high in the air, defying me to paint her childhood as idyllic.

But still, she doesn't speak, only curls her lip while she reaches for more kindling.

"Did you vacation in Italy?"

"You know I did." Her eyes snap at me. How far do I need to go to make her break?

It's a dick move, intentionally baiting her. But we're here for a reason.

"What were your vacations like? I spent my school vacations raking leaves in the fall, shoveling driveways in the winter, eating Top Ramen for lunch while my grandmother worked two jobs. So tell me, Vivia. What were *your* summers like?"

"Oh, let's see," she says with a sarcastic twinge in her voice. "Yes, they were beach vacations, I traveled to Europe, I ate good food, and I wore designer clothing. But maybe you'd like to hear about the time when I was sixteen and the cabana boy accidentally touched my hand when he gave me a towel by the beach. Then later that same day, I had to watch my father beat him before he cut off his hand. Should I go on?"

"Oh, poor baby, raised by a protective daddy. Wonder what that's like."

"Or maybe," she says with a sickly-sweet tone, "you'd like to hear about the time we took a Mediterranean cruise, only we had to cut it short because my father had a mistress whose husband died, and it was this big *mystery* about how he died, and my mother had to pretend she didn't know that her husband had called for the execution of his mistress's husband simply because he wanted a blow job on the Mediterranean." She shrugs. "But maybe that didn't really matter, because I was drowning myself in my virgin mimosas, because I was never allowed to drink anything but wine and that was only over in Italy, and those luxury fabrics against my skin made me immune to evil, my mother's tears, or the fact that everyone we encountered cowered in fear at the sound of our names."

"Ah. Scary." She only purses her lips and doesn't respond to me.

So I found out a couple of things. Her dad was unfaithful—shocker. It's almost a given in these circles.

She has no sisters, was the only Montavio sister, so lucky her, likely received the weight of responsibility afforded a mafia woman. She has no respect for her mother, nothing short of hatred for her father, and probably feels the same way about her brothers. That's one thing that's different about the Rossi girls and their brothers. While they were all joined by a commonality in childhood, and the Rossi brothers are protective of their sisters, it appears the Montavio brothers cared more about what their father thought than their sister. But I also wonder how much time they actually spent together if she spent a good portion of her childhood in boarding school. Do they even know each other?

All the Montavio brothers—Sergio, Timeo, and Ricco—have been faithful to us. I know them to be hard-working and loyal, but neither of those things matter to her. They took after their father's tradition of treating her with disrespect and control. She might never forgive that. This is all important information for me to know going forward.

Vivia doesn't appear to be shallow, but she's been terribly sheltered from the basics of day-to-day life.

She makes a little squeaky sound as she slaps at her arms. Mosquitoes fly around us.

"Go inside. Sit at the table where I can see you, and keep your hands folded in front of you."

The screen door slams behind her, and she does exactly what I say—none too soon because the fluttering of wings warns me there are bats nearby, and something tells me Vivia would lose her shit. Not that I don't like the idea of her running into my arms for protection…

Stay focused.

We spend the next ten minutes in silence. She sits obediently at the table with her hands folded in front of her, and I build a fire inside the fireplace. There's a definite satisfaction in watching the flames leap to life, in the earthy smell of burning wood, the smoke. I sit on my haunches and watch the flames lick around the kindling like eager fireflies, igniting the dried pieces of wood as I build a furnace. Within minutes, I've stacked the firewood to maximize the length of time it will burn. It's a small fire, one that will warm us and help us cook our food, but will burn quicker than one might think, especially seasoned, dry wood like this. I'll either have to feed the fire all night long, or make the most of it while it's lit.

"Where did you learn to do that?" she asks curiously. Her hands are still folded in front of her, but she's been watching me the entire time. "There's definitely like a method to your madness. You don't just toss one in there and light it. I watched. You took the lighter, smaller things first to get the fire going, then you stacked it all."

"I grew up on the streets. We did this for fun." I don't tell her that my best friend was arrested for arson when I was ten years old, and that crime followed him for the rest of his life. "We were expert at building fires, and it served me well when I was in the military."

"Why do you do it like that?"

"If you light damp wood, or light too big a log at first, the flame will smolder out. It's a rookie mistake, not building a small fire first. If you build a fire just right, and stack dense, long-burning wood, it will burn for hours. If you don't, it will either burn out quickly, or smolder into nothing."

As I talk, I wonder about stoking *her* flames. A part of me can't help but wonder if I'm kindling a fire with her or if the flames will smolder and collapse into smoke.

I shouldn't let this bother me. I don't know why I care.

She sits at the table thoughtfully, then changes the subject.

"Is there anything I can do to help with dinner?"

"Do you know how to cook?"

She shakes her head, her eyes bright. "No. Not at all. But it doesn't mean I can't… like, husk corn or… peel a potato or something."

"We'll keep it simple tonight. There's some fresh food, a bagged salad, a package of hot dogs. We'll eat up the perishables first, because I don't know how long we'll be here, and it makes sense to do that."

"Do we have, like… plates or something?"

"We might, but I don't want you getting out of that seat, and I want your hands where I can see them at all times."

She has the nerve to look hurt. She almost winces. "What do you think I'm going to do? Stab you with a potato peeler? You're twice my size, and I told you I barely know how to cook. You know I know absolutely nothing about self-defense? You were in the military. You're a Rossi man. You're the one that has the advantage here."

I stand and fold my arms over my chest. "I'm well aware. I want *you* well aware that you're still my prisoner."

She nods and purses her lips. "Yes, *sir*."

CHAPTER TEN

Vivia

HE LIKES it when I submit to him.

And if I'm honest with myself... really, truly honest and not lying just to make myself feel better about things... I like when I do, too.

I may not know much about relationships, but I've seen enough that failed that this counts for something.

I don't care how much money you have, most every woman I've ever known would choose fidelity over material possessions. Not all, but most.

I don't care how attractive you are, or how high-ranking or powerful, most women I've ever known would choose attention over *things*. I watched my mother's spirit wither and die under my father's neglect.

Don't get me wrong. She is no innocent. My mother is a selfish bitch.

It doesn't mean she's not human, though. It doesn't mean she's incapable of being hurt. I know I definitely am. I saw what it did to my mother knowing my father chose a mistress over her. Did she blame herself? I don't know. It takes a certain kind of man to cheat on a woman, regardless of how he's treated.

So when Dario tried to make it look like I lived in some sort of picture-perfect childhood because I had money and material possessions, I know he's bullshitting. He's smarter than that.

And there's one thing I know for sure about him: he might be mean, he might value loyalty to the Rossi brotherhood, he might pretend he's not affected by being alone with me, but I know better. I watch how his nostrils flare when I obey him. I watch his Adam's apple bob when I call him sir. He says I have a submissive streak, and I don't deny it. But he likes having control over me in more ways than one. And I won't let him forget that.

I didn't look for a means of escape when I went out with him. It's more important that I know what his weaknesses are. He's obviously stronger than I am. He obviously has more people on his side. But every person walking this Earth has a weakness if not several, and I'll use that to my advantage.

I watched how he lit that fire, and I took note.

If he thought I was in danger, or if both of us were, he would do everything in his power to prevent that from happening, that much I know.

I tuck all these things away in my mind.

I watch him prepare salad, hot dogs, then toss a bag of chips on the table. My stomach rolls with hunger. I could probably list a hundred things I'd rather eat than a hot dog, but there's something about the way it sizzles over the open flame that makes my mouth water. I'm starving.

He turned the hot dogs over the open flame until they're blistered and sizzling. There's a package of rolls but no condiments. We're not here for fancy meals, I know.

He puts paper plates down, opens the bag of chips, and puts two hot dogs in buns on my plate. The salad is a bagged affair, pre-washed lettuce with prepared dressing which he forks onto my plate without a word. Next, he takes a few chips. I wonder if he'll allow me to feed myself this time. A small part of me hopes he won't.

What's wrong with me? Why do I like the control he exercises over me? It should unnerve me, or make me feel belittled, but I can't deny the erotic vibe every time he touches me. The way he fed me earlier was nothing short of foreplay.

"Am I allowed to feed myself?" I ask, unable to hide the seductive tone of my voice. I want him to spoon-feed me. I want to ask him permission.

He takes his place next to me, piling food on his plate before he answers.

"You've been a good girl. You have permission to feed yourself."

Good girl. Those words feel like light and warmth and all things good and wholesome.

They say starvation is an excellent seasoning agent. They're not wrong. A simple fare of hot dogs and chips and salad taste like I'm dining in a five-star restaurant. I eat quickly, eager to stop the gnawing pain in my belly.

"Careful, Vivia. There's only one thing I want you to choke on and it's not a fucking hot dog."

Ah, very classy. Still, my cheeks flush. I wish I had better control over my reactions, but before Gray I'd never been touched by a man, and something about the way Dario touches me makes me crave more. Even his lewd comments don't shock me the way they really should.

We eat in silence, both of us clearing our plates. I sigh contentedly now that my stomach is no longer aching with hunger. He pushes away from the table himself, walks over to the fire and crouches before it. I watch as he takes a long metal skewer thing and pokes the flames. He's so intent on it, I give myself a minute to look about the room. Where did he put the matches?

I don't see them at first, but finally note the little brown package.

They are right there in his pocket. Dammit. I need those. I'll get them.

I sit as quiet as a church mouse watching him, not giving him one chance to catch me doing anything I shouldn't. Not giving him any excuse for going all commanding on me again.

When he stands the matches fall out of his pocket onto the floor. The sound is almost noiseless, eaten up by the crackling of the stoked fire. I stare at the matches, memorizing where they are. He walks toward me.

"Clear the dishes. Put them in the sink. It's a lot of work washing dishes in the wilderness, so we'll pile them up until we need to wash them."

I do what he says without a word, taking the dishes and stacking them in a little sink. I wonder what the whole production is to wash dishes if there's no hot water. I guess we'll have to… boil water or something? It doesn't really matter that doing anything will take ten times as long as it would if we were in a modern place, because what else will we do with our time anyway?

He's sitting in a rocker by the fire when I'm done.

"It's hard to imagine people do this for fun," I say to him honestly. "What's the appeal?"

He shrugs. "Some people like being away from modern conveniences. They find them distracting. Some people find it cathartic being in the woods, with the earthy smells and stars overhead. There are lots of reasons people like to unplug."

"I get it, but at the same time, is it really worth having to wipe your ass with leaves? To wonder if a bear is going to come into your cabin? To have to boil water to wash your dishes? I mean, can't you just, like, go sit out in your backyard and leave your cell phone inside?"

The corner of his lips quirks up. "You could. But that would probably get you punished, wouldn't it?"

I look away, unwilling to face the truth. Yes, some people could disconnect and go sit in their backyards, but if I did it, I'd be fucked. Maybe there is a certain advantage to being alone in the woods.

"Tell me about your brothers," he says, leaning back in his chair with a cup of water. He takes a sip every now and then as I tell him everything I know. The eldest, Nicolo, died a few years ago, right around the time Orlando was imprisoned and Dario met him.

Ricco is the only one married with a child, and he's close to my Aunt Tosca. Timeo's done well for himself with investments, the most book-learned among my brothers. Sergio is a fair but hard-ass Don.

I shrug. "I don't really know them that well, we've never lived together for a long period of time."

He strokes his chin thoughtfully. "It feels as if that was intentional. Like your father didn't want your brothers to get close to you."

"Yeah. I wondered why he did that. I wondered if it was a 'divide and conquer' kinda thing. I noticed it was... different with the Rossis."

"Very much so. The brothers and sisters are all very close, and if it came to a choice between his father or his sisters, Romeo has and would choose his sisters, every time. But that isn't the case with your brothers. Keeping you separated from your brothers, your father insured their allegiance to him."

Though he's contemplative, there's a certain heat to his words, a possession to his touch that unnerves me when he touches me.

I can't let myself think of him as anything more than my warden. But it's hard for me to think that way when I witnessed the way he's touched me, his responses to me, the way he commands. I'm not immune, no matter how hard I try.

When he commands my body responds like a tuning fork, vibrating and humming. And there's a small part of me, which I can't deny, that wants to feel so much more.

I yawn, exhausted, but don't want to go to bed yet. This day has felt like a week in and of itself. He feels the same it seems, as he sits in the rocking chair in front of the flames.

I look around at the limited seating arrangements near us. There's a love seat, but there's no way in hell I'm gonna sit there because if he decides he's going to join me we'll have to get all cozy. Nope. There's a little stool, but that wouldn't be comfortable for very long without back support, and it's so far away from the fire I wouldn't feel the warmth.

I feel his eyes on me. Cautiously, I look toward him, my heartbeat racing. Dario looks at me with a predatory gaze that makes the little hairs on my arms stand up. He looks at me as if he wants to devour me... It would be a lie to say I don't like that.

"Come here, Vivia." When he says *come here* like that...

He pats his knee. He wants me to sit on his... lap? I don't know about that. I'm thin and fit, but that rocking chair looks like it's straining under his weight never mind with two of us sitting on it. Still, he gave me a command, and I'm expected to obey. I walk to him, shuffling my feet.

But he doesn't drag me onto his lap. He gestures to a footstool in front of the rocker. Interesting.

"Sit here, please." He parts his knees and puts the footstool between his legs. He wants me to sit by his feet?

Why the hell does that appeal to me?

I shouldn't want to. I should feel insulted or demeaned, but instead, I feel… I'm not sure how to describe it. Small in a good way, not belittled but more like I'm… taking one step closer to intimacy with him.

Weird.

I swallow my rising nerves, and nod. I already feel half naked wearing these clothes with no underwear, but the way his eyes take me in, I feel even less clothed than before. I'm vividly aware of what little separates us from each other.

I slide myself onto the footstool, and he quickly adjust his legs. To my surprise, this is very comfortable. I lean against him. His strong, sturdy legs provide good back support. The flickering flames generate a radiating warmth, so I'm not cold anymore. And while I sit at his feet, he starts doing something I'm not prepared for. He threads his fingers through my hair, combing the strands almost methodically. I fight against the urge to close my eyes and relish in this feeling. It's soothing, and luxurious, and I'm tired.

I put the weight of my head against his knee while he continues to play with my hair.

"Beautiful. Your hair is beautiful," he says, threading his fingers through it. I feel a lift and tug, curious what he's doing until it dawns on me.

"Are you... braiding my hair?" I ask, incredulous.

"I am. It'll be hard to wash it here, but this way it won't tangled as much."

"How do you know that?" How does a man like him know anything about hair care? But I don't really care how he knows it, I'm just talking nervously, because him braiding my hair feels so intimate, I feel uneasy. I shiver.

"Cold?"

"A little." He spreads a blanket over my legs.

He continues quietly braiding my hair and doesn't answer my question.

"I don't suppose you have a hair tie?"

"No." I clear my throat. "Why are you doing this?" I ask.

I try to keep my tone casual, curious, and not guarded, but I fail.

"Doing what?" he asks.

"You know."

"I don't like insinuating or assuming anything," he says. "I want you to be very specific with me. I've kidnapped you, instructed you to sit between my legs, and now I'm braiding your hair. What is it that I'm doing that you want information about?"

"Okay, so... braiding my hair and having me sit here."

"I told you. I'm braiding your hair because it will keep it less tangled. You're sitting by my feet because I want you to be within arm's reach of me. Also, I like you here. And if you were sitting beside me, you might forget your place."

My place.

My place.

Hmm.

That should make me angry. I should want to slap his face. But now, my body has to go and betray me again with an accelerated heartbeat and curiosity.

"Okay, so earlier today, you practically beat me. And now you're treating me with tenderness. What changed?"

I can feel the tension in his legs from where I sit. He doesn't like what I just said, but he's holding himself together. "That, lovely, was hardly a beating. Believe me when I tell you, you would know the difference." The chill in his voice sets my nerves on edge. I know then that I would.

"I spanked you. And I can say with confidence that wasn't the last time that will happen. But I can also say that if you behave yourself, most of the time you'll enjoy it." Well of all the arrogant things…

He continues, so I clamp my mouth shut because it's definitely the best thing to do right now.

"But I understand your question. Do you wanna know why I'm not interrogating you right now? I'll tell you why." He sobers, and there's a sincerity in his tone that I don't miss. He is telling me the truth.

"I've thought it over. I don't believe you're guilty. I'm rarely wrong. And if I am right, that means that our roles have changed significantly."

Really.

"How so?"

He leans forward, his hands on my shoulders. It feels so good I want to close my eyes and sigh.

But I don't. I have to stay alert. Without a word, he brushes the braid over my shoulder so he has access to my bare neck before he presses a kiss to my naked skin. I imagine my flesh sizzles. My God, his command over my body.

"YOU ARE A BEAUTIFUL WOMAN, Vivia. Your family has disowned you. My job with you right now is to keep you safe and protected until the time comes where we can prove your innocence. If you were in good standing with your family, what would be the rules your brothers would have for me?"

I START BLINKING RAPIDLY, chewing my lips. I force my hands onto my lap to study the fire. My breath comes in short, rapid gasps. "You wouldn't be allowed to touch me. If they thought that you did, they would hurt you." Vivid memories of bloodstained sand fill my mind. It wouldn't be the first time. I swallow. "He… They would…" I'm having a hard time forming a complete sentence because of the nerves that shatter my body.

I KNOW exactly what he's insinuating. We're alone. My brothers have disowned me and think I'm dead. Anything he does now is off the record. We both know that only he could hear the words, and he probably will. I don't know what that will mean…

HE PLAYS with the braid on my shoulder. "My job is to bring you to them safely. My job is to find the people who tried to kill us, and more importantly, Marialena. But there isn't much I can do about that here in the woods, so I'll leave that part to Orlando. Tell me this. If I were to bring you to your brothers and we were to prove your innocence, how would that change things?"

"I WILL BE REINSTATED as a Montavio sister."

"AND WHEN THEY find out you gave your virginity to the man that betrayed your family?"

. . .

I BREAK out in a cold sweat. I can't speak. I grip my knees so that my knuckles turn white. "I don't know what they would do," I say in a trembling voice. The truth is, I don't know exactly what they would do. But it wouldn't end well for me.

"SO YOUR ONLY chance at survival is easy. Your only chance is here with me."

I'M NOT MENTALLY sure of what to do. I swallow hard, fruitlessly trying to calm my frayed nerves. I feel a little dizzy to have a choice before me. Or more accurately at the lack of choices before me. I want to flee and hide to escape this dreadful feeling in the pit of my stomach, but before I can do anything else, he brushes his fingers over my temple in soothing circles. My eyes flutter closed. Wordlessly, he bends and kisses the bare skin at my neck.

AND I KNOW exactly what he's doing. Excitement, and fear, and lust flood me.

I know what he's going to do, but I don't know how I am going to react. I've never been here before, and I can't forget who he is, or who I am. But there is one thing I know for a fact. If he shows up in front of my brothers, proves my innocence, and then proves that I belong to him, it will be a radically different situation than if he brings me before them guilty and no longer a virgin.

DARIO HAS the choice to own me. And if he does, it will change the course of both of our lives forever.

I TRY to mentally sort through the options, try to think what will happen. I try to anticipate what could happen next, but I can't. Because the next thing I know, his mouth is on my neck, his tongue is drawing circles on the sensitive skin there, and the moan he draws out of me makes me wet between my thighs.

I DON'T KNOW what his plan is, but right now I don't care. All I want is for him to touch me again. For him to claim me, to lose myself in this moment and forget who I am. I need this. Maybe he does, too.

HIS VOICE MOVES over my body like foreplay, the ring of command making my nipples stand hard at attention and a growing need throb between my legs.

. . .

"YOU'RE SUCH A PRETTY GIRL," he whispers in a silky voice. "That's a girl. Close your eyes now. I love the way you look when you're at rest."

WHEN HE BEGINS to praise me, my body sings as if he's playing me like an instrument. "You're such a beautiful girl. Lie still so I can keep drinking you in with my eyes. I hated having to take you as my prisoner." He stops talking. His voice sounds amused. I keep my eyes closed obediently, as he smooths over the apple of my cheek. "No, that's a lie. I loved being in close proximity to you. What I didn't like was that you were with another man."

HIS VOICE HAS CHANGED, no longer soothing but now more corrective. "I should punish you for that. Shouldn't I?"

MY HEART BEGINS TO RACE. I know this is foreplay, that he's trying to turn me on, but I couldn't stop myself now for all the money in the world.

MY EYES FLUTTER open and I look at him. The mystery in his gaze begins to heat me. There's a sharp, almost sassy nature, a dark insolence, he brings out in me. He doesn't play by anyone's rules but his. And I'm drawn to the compelling nature of his. I can't help it. There's something in those depths that says "you're safe with me. There's nothing I wouldn't do for you." And scarier still, "there's nothing I wouldn't do to you."

THERE'S a little heat in his eyes that makes my already swimming body silently beg for more. I want him to do all kinds of wicked things to me, and that look in his eyes promises exactly that. His gaze falls to my neck, and his eyes rove over me as he lazily appraises me. I can't imagine I look that good, but he looks as if he's taking in a masterpiece.

MY HEART RACES when he reaches down and holds me, his arms coming around my back and shoulders to cradle me against his legs. I try to throttle the dizzying arousal that races through my veins, my limbs, my nerves, but I can't. He radiates something that draws me to him in a way that's out of my control.

IT'S EVERYTHING ABOUT HIM. The smoldering flame in his eyes, the possessive sound of his voice, the way he touches me.

"THAT'S MY GIRL," he says. If he touches me right now, one stroke of his fingers between my legs would make me soar into nothingness. I'm completely helpless when he begins to praise me, and I couldn't stop my growing need with all the reserves in the world. "That's my girl," he says while he drags his thumb down my collarbone and circles the tender skin right above my breast. "Damn, woman." I expect him to finish the sentence, but it seems like that's all he has to say. "Say my name," he commands.

I SWALLOW and look up at him. He's asked me this before. He loves when I say his name. I wonder why.

BUTTERFLIES ERUPT in my stomach at the eager look in his eyes. "Dario," I whisper.

"THAT'S IT LOVELY. I love it when you call my name. You're such a good girl."

GOOD GIRL, good girl, the words are like fire in my veins, igniting my desire so strongly I can't stop myself. "Come to bed with me, love. And I'll make you forget everything."

My eyes flutter closed when he reaches down and lifts me into his arms, carrying me to the bedroom.

He slides me unceremoniously to the floor.

"Clothes off."

His voice is a command, it does just as many wonderful things to me as his praise does I quickly move to obey.

"Beautiful girl. Such a good, obedient girl for me. I bet if I were to reach my fingers between your legs, you'd be sopping wet for me, wouldn't you?"

I NOD SILENTLY.

"THEN SHOW ME, lovely. Show me what I do to you." His voice lowers. "Show me what's mine."

I'VE NEVER FELT SO proud of myself before, never felt so confident in my body. But as I strip my clothes and he drinks me in, I feel as if I'm the most stunning woman this world has ever seen.

The humble, plain clothing falls to the floor like discarded baggage. I shiver.

"COLD?" he asks. I shake my head. No, not cold. It isn't as warm here away from the fire, but it's insulated, and the earlier fire did warm this room, too. It isn't cold that makes me shiver.

"Ah," he says with a lewd, lopsided grin. "You shiver for another reason."

I swallow and nod.

"Put your hands behind your head."

I obediently lace my fingers behind my head and watch him. I hardly breathe. He's still fully dressed, and I'm stark naked, a contrast that isn't lost on me.

"I've never seen anything more beautiful in my life," he whispers. "Never."

"Dario," I whisper, disbelieving. His eyes come to mine alight with curiosity. "How can that be true? You've… you've been with women before."

He nods. "None have ever looked at me the way you do," he whispers, stepping closer. When he draws nearer to me, my pulse begins to quicken again. "None have ever melted into a puddle when I praised them. And I love that about you."

Love that about you.

"I don't understand," I whisper, because I truly don't. What's changed with him? I shake my head, bewildered. But soon, my thoughts and questions are silenced when he reaches the bed. He lowers his mouth to mine, covers my mouth with his, and the world ceases to exist.

CHAPTER ELEVEN

*D*ARIO

I LOVE everything about this moment. The tender way she holds onto my shoulders as if to secure herself to me. The soft flutter of her lips against mine. The way she moans when I lick her lips. The tentative feel of her tongue when it brushes mine. I capture the back of her head with my palm and hold her to me, a moan escaping my own lips before I can stop myself.

"Good girl. You're so beautiful. You please me so much, Vivia," I whisper, taking a moment to whisper in her ear before I kiss her again. She shivers and leans into me, eager for more.

I didn't completely verbalize my plans for her in the other room, because I don't know how she'll react, but we both know that bringing her to her brothers as she is, no longer a virgin, a suspected traitor, would mean her swift and sudden death. But I know she's innocent, and we have a chance at redemption that no words or actions would say louder than I can right now.

I know exactly what I need to do.

I need to claim her as my own.

I need to make her fully mine.

I need to own this woman, through and through.

And if I put my baby in her… if I bring her to our families claimed, owned, and carrying my child, there isn't a thing they can do against either of us.

I kiss her again. I don't want anything between us.

Her hands loosen around my neck when I deepen the kiss.

Long ago, when I was barely out of high school, one of my military brothers taught me how to seduce a woman. *Kiss her all over, every inch of her, and she'll be putty in your hands.* Kissing a woman on the lips is only the beginning.

I kiss her neck, her jaw, the fullest part of her cheek, and the delicately arched eyebrows over her eyes. I kiss each eye, first one then the other, then her hairline, and as I kiss her, I hold her close to me. She smiles and bites her lip when I tug the loosened braid draped over her neck, her eyelids fluttering open.

"Close your eyes, lovely."

When she quickly obeys, I praise her again. "That's a girl. Such a good, obedient girl, aren't you?"

She nods. Her lips part on a moan when I kiss the top of each breast and linger just before her hardened nipples.

"Touch yourself," I command, my voice a husky whisper. I'm so hard it's painful. I imagine her tight, hot cunt around my cock and moan into her ear.

"Touch myself?" she questions, apprehensive.

"Don't tell me you don't touch yourself."

Her cheeks flush pink and she shakes her head. "I… it's odd to me. I don't… really… think about it."

So fucking innocent. How is this woman a Montavio? She defies everything I've ever known about women.

"How can someone raised by Montavios act like she's been holed up in a convent?"

"Did you miss the part about boarding school?" she asks in a teasing but husky voice. "It was a Catholic boarding school."

"Ahh." Cute. "So I want you to do this," I tell her, reaching for her hand and draping her thin, tapering fingers between her legs. "Feel that pressure between your legs. Touch where it aches. Stroke yourself."

I love the way her cheeks burn, the way her eyes brighten and the slight parting of her lips when she does what I ask her to.

"Good girl." Goddamn, she pleases me. "Just like that."

She releases a little moan as she finds what feels good to her.

"Yeah, baby," I encourage her, pressing my own hard length against her body. Every stroke of her fingers between her legs stokes my own lust. "Keep going, baby. Work that pussy for me. I want you wet."

I want to take her, claim her, feel the tight walls of her pussy gripping my cock before I empty myself in her, but we aren't there yet. She's as turned on as I am, but I want her to trust me before we go that far.

"Oooh, *fu—*" she catches herself on a moan, her head lolling to the side. She fingers her clit while I suckle her nipple and flick the other with my fingers. I want her to feel the heightened pleasure that comes from pain, but I don't want to pull her out of this moment. I start with a gentle increase in pressure with my tongue on her nipple, then flick the second nipple.

"Dario," she says in a choked voice. "I'm going to... I think I'm going to..."

"No. Not yet. *Wait.*"

"I can't," she moans.

Yes, she can, and yes, she will. "If you come, I'll whip your ass black and blue," I threaten in her ear. "You come when I tell you to, or I will turn you over my knee and spank you until you scream for mercy."

She whimpers to herself and slows the friction of her fingers between her legs. Perfect.

"Ah, baby, yes. Just like that. Mmm."

I can tell the threat of a spanking turns her on, but she doesn't want to push things with me. I can tell she wants my praise more than literally anything else I could give her. She could make herself come, but the loss of my approval wouldn't make it worth it to her.

And I fucking *love* that about her.

"Good girl," I continue to praise. "Keep working that pussy for me baby."

I brace my body over hers, my hard length pressed up against her belly. I crave the friction of her body against mine and watch her as she works herself.

Her fluttering eyelashes. Her soft moans. The way her lips part and she makes the most painful look as she tries to wrestle back from the edge of climax.

"May I touch you?" She asks it in such a soft, pleading voice. So eager to please. So submissive. *Damn.*

I nod my head. I don't wanna lose control, but I want her to touch me too.

While she continues to work her pussy, she slides around to the waistband of my pants, her hand shaking as she reaches for me. I groan at her soft, gentle touch on my cock.

I bend my mouth to her ear, whispering praises and adulation until she's moaning with pleasure.

"Let yourself come, baby," I whisper in her ear. I take my cock from her grip and stroke myself while she works her pussy. "Atta girl. That's it, baby. Just like that."

I jerk my cock, on the edge of climax myself. I won't come now.

"Stop," I grate in her ear. "And stop touching yourself."

"Dario," she says on a half-sob. "Please, please don't make me stop now. Oh, God," she whimpers, her head lolling to the side.

"I told you what I want, Vivia." My mouth is at her ear as I tuck myself back into my shorts, my balls aching for release. "I told you. I'll own you. The only chance we both have is if I own you. Fully. Completely. Irrevocably."

I lower myself onto her body and kiss her breasts before I bring my mouth to one nipple, then the next. "I own your pleasure," I say, reaching for her pussy. She arches her back into my hands and shudders with the first spasm of ecstasy. "I own your body," I whisper against the fullness of her breast before I nip each bud in turn. She gasps and writhes as I stroke her again. "And I own every drop of pleasure you feel."

I roll over to her side, while I keep stroking between her legs and I bring my free hand to her neck and flex. "Do you understand me?"

I want her to feel the threat. I want her to feel how easily I could hurt her and choose not to. I want her to feel all of it. When she doesn't answer at first, I still my hand and cup her pussy.

"I asked you a question."

Nodding, she blinks. Her cheeks are wet with tears. "I do. I understand." She nods, then meets my gaze and gives me exactly what I need. "Yes, sir."

I feel the vibration of her throat against my hand as I flex again. "That's my girl," I whisper, circling her clit while she gasps. "Then come for me, baby. Ride my fingers. Take what's yours, Vivia. Come for me."

Her screams of pleasure fill the small cabin as she comes against my hand. I hold her neck, just on the edge of choking her, deliberate control as she climaxes so hard, she screams herself hoarse. She rides every wave of bliss on my hand until she slumps in the bed beside me.

Panting. Exhausted. She rolls over and tucks her full body against mine for comfort.

"Oh my God," she moans, her eyes fluttering closed. "Holy sh—holy smokes," she says adorably, censoring the profanity before she gets punished for a naughty word. Adorable.

"That's my girl." I lavish praise on her like icing on a cake, sweet and decadent. She eats it up, her slender arms circling my neck. I make myself wait, ignoring the raging hard-on as I hold her.

Soon, I'll take her. Soon, I'll claim her fully.

I can wait.

Something tells me she's worth it.

She falls asleep tucked in beside me while I hold her. I love the feel of her body pressed to mine, her breath on my skin, the trusting way she lays on me in slumber.

Little by little, I'll possess every inch of her.

When she's fully asleep, I close my eyes, my breath joining hers.

I dream of The Castle, meetings with my brothers, and long, empty hallways that lead to dead-ends. Vivia's crying in one of my dreams, but in the next she's eating breakfast at one of the long tables in The Great Hall with Marialena and Rosa. Sun pours through into the sun room while we walk the halls hand in hand. I don't know the details of my dream but I know our enemies are dead and Vivia's mine.

I'm exhausted from everything that's happened. When I wake in the middle of the night, she's rolled over on her side but still touching me. I sling my arm about her reassuringly, and as I drift back off to sleep, I rest in the knowledge that she's safe with me. And I'll do everything in my power to keep her there.

CHAPTER TWELVE

Vivia

WE FALL into a sort of rhythm over the next few days. And I have to admit... it's nice. *Really* nice.

He hasn't really gotten any more lax with me... he's still strict and bossy, but that's just in his nature. It's what I'm used to, having grown up the way I have around the Rossis and Montavios, but with him it's more that I just need to be in control. I know he's dedicated to my safety, and I'm not exactly sure why, like what's in it for him... but I'm not going to look a gift horse in the mouth either.

In the mornings, we make a simple breakfast. Oatmeal or fried eggs, and when we have a small sink full of dishes, we boil water with dish soap, wash them, then rinse with warm, clean water. We fall into traditional roles—I wash the dishes, help with food, and he does the dirty work like cutting wood and building fires.

Even though I've never done this sort of work before, and there's a bit of what I'd call a *learning curve*, I have to admit I sort of like it. There's something so simple about seeing dishes come clean under a stream of running water, washing them dry on a dish towel, eating simple meals by the campfire, and wiling the time away by gathering kindling.

I'm starting to actually almost understand why people like to *vacation* this way. Almost. I mean, I wouldn't choose it myself, but I kinda get it.

I definitely would not call this vacation. It's nothing like our trips to Bali, or Maui, or Turks and Caicos. Nothing at all. But it is a sort of retreat, away from the demands of my family and society. And there's something invigorating about the clean, brisk forest air, the soothing smell of burning fire, or even eating a meal cooked by your own hands.

He feels it, too, I know he does. Three days after we arrived, I sit in the cabin and watch him prepare to go fishing. It's a warm, sunny day, and he's bare from the waist up. I don't even bother to hide the way that I gawk over every inch of his masculine physique before he tugs on a tee. Bummer.

"It's a good time of day to get some fish," he says. I don't care about the perfect time of day to get fish, which direction they swim, or how he's going to get them, but I like listening to him talk to me about it. He's like an overgrown Tom Sawyer, barefoot and suntanned, with muscles in places I never knew could grow muscles.

There's a little ache inside me, though. And I don't know exactly what causes it. I don't like having emotions I'm unfamiliar with, so I push it aside while I watch him.

And far back, in the recesses of my mind... I know we can't stay here forever. I know there will come a time when we have to leave here, and the future's so uncertain it's got me on edge.

"...and yesterday morning, I noticed a whole school in the inlet that stayed longer than usual."

I nod, pretending I'm listening. I think this is cathartic for him, too. I've seen lesser men buckle underneath the demands of the job he has. Here, without the ever-present pressure from his Don and brothers, he can breathe a little more freely. Dario has one task, and that task is *me.*

He's got a small bucket of little minnows in water and a smaller plastic container of worms he's captured for bait. I've grown a little less squeamish in the past couple days and actually watch the little minnows dart around in the water like bolts of silver lightning.

"You're actually going to use little fish to get bigger ones?" I feel my lips turn down.

"Do you have any idea how many of those you'd have to eat for a real meal?" He shakes his head. "You'd be better off boiling roots than trying to make a meal of those little things."

"Still, it doesn't seem fair. What did they do to deserve to be fed to the bigger guy?"

"It's the circle of life," he says, a corner of his lips tipping upward. "And both of us know how that works."

We do. *Sigh*. Do we ever.

"You're adorable when you pout."

"I'm not pouting."

"You are, though. You don't like the idea of a squiggly fish on a hook." I think what I'm trying to do is not lose the contents of my belly.

He gives me another little half smile. I wonder what he thinks about me.

Things have… heated up.

Every single night, he's made me come—on his hands, on his mouth, and last night he went so far as to let himself climax on my belly. After, we bathed together by heating water, soaping up and washing each other off, then rinsing in the outside shower under silvery moonlight. He told me it would ward off vampires, but I think he's the one that's warding off anything that could threaten us.

But after all that... we haven't had sex. We've done everything but. And most of the time he spends on my pleasure and not his. I feel as if he's trying to build trust, or do something to make me less wary of him. But what he doesn't know is that building trust sexually is the least of my concerns. I'm so inexperienced, it's barely on my radar.

It's all the other ways he builds trust that mean so much more to me.

"Get your shoes on, baby."

I don't even think to question him at this point. He likes to command, and I like to obey. Him, anyway.

Part of me basks in his lavish praise, and I've begun to silence the inner voice that tells me this is wrong. Why should I question what I like? Why should I question who he is? He told me a few days ago he no longer thinks I'm guilty, and that means so much to me.

I don't know what the future holds for us, and I know that we have mountains to climb and valleys to cross before we have any type of peace, but I also know that something's growing between us.

I never suspected that I, Vivia Montavio, beneficiary to the Montavio throne and under the rule of my merciless, hard-hearted brothers and family, would ever consider falling for someone. I've never even entertained the thought of having any real feelings for another person. It seemed so outside the realm of possibility, it was as relatable and attainable as a Disney movie. I no sooner imagined myself falling in love than I imagined myself flying a jet solo over the Grand Canyon. Things like that don't happen to women like me.

Why would I change the course of things now?

"Hey, so, we don't happen to have any razors, do we?"

He doesn't respond at first, as if thinking over his response. Finally, when he answers, I know why.

"We do. I hid them, because I didn't want you to have access to anything that could be used as a weapon. But you've behaved yourself." His eyes come to mine as he says this, and I'm not sure if I imagine the lewd, lust-filled look, or if it's part of my imagination.

"Why don't you come with me, I'll fish, you can have a swim and shave down by the beach."

"The beach?" I haven't ventured far outside this cabin. I knew we were near the water but assumed it was far below a cliff or something.

"Of course," he says gruffly. "We're on the Narragansett Bay. It overlooks the ocean. And we have a private beach here all to ourselves. It's nothing fancy, it's really small, but you're allowed to go with me."

Every time he's gone fishing, I haven't joined him. He's cuffed me before he left, and I was perfectly fine staying behind so I didn't have to see him spearing a little fish on a hook.

"I can't shave with salt water, though, it'll sting like crazy."

"There's fresh water nearby."

Alrighty then.

I gather my supplies when he shows me where the razors are. For crying out loud, I had no idea we had these things. Lady's shaving cream, a disposable package of five-blade women's razors, several soft washcloths. My God I am *dying* for a good shave.

I tuck the things into my pockets, put my shoes on, and follow him with all his fishing gear down to the beach.

It's early morning, the sun barely peeking over the horizon, but it's already warm. Yesterday, it was so warm it felt like summer, and today is starting to look similar. Locusts sizzle in the background, warning us of a warm day ahead.

"Are you sure this is a good time of day to fish?"

"It's always best if you can come earlier in the day or late in the day, but there are no other fishermen for miles. No competition. And with the way the sunlight reflects on the water, this particular cove is shuttered in darkness, and the fish like to gather here."

I think it over. If he's fishing… that means he's going to bring smelly, scaly fish back to the cabin, and he'll have to… clean them and… things like that.

"This really is an excellent time for me to become a vegetarian."

He stares at me a full second before he bursts out laughing, his laughter full-hearted and resonant. When he breaks the laugh off his eyes smolder. It's rare that he laughs out loud like this, and a part of me feels very pleased.

I can't help myself, as a ripple of amusement makes me giggle. "What's so funny?"

"YOU TRY TO BE SO BRAVE," he says as we walk toward the steep bank that takes us to the ocean's edge. I've walked with him this way before, but we never went as far as the ocean.

It's beautiful here. The wind rustles through the leaves, and there's a slight hum of insects in the underbrush, but they don't bother me. It's like background noise in an isolated land, unadulterated or unpolluted with raucous sound or human interaction. Nature's symphony. The screech of a gull overhead, the fluttering of a flock of birds as they soar skyward, the distant tap of a woodpecker on a tree, and growing closer now, the swish of the waves coming onto the shore. It sounds as if it's a recording, something created to soothe. I could close my eyes and drift off to sleep with a lullaby around me.

"But then every once in a while, you're a spoiled little city girl."

"Hey!"

He gives me a look that's half teasing, half stern, and my heart thumps. "Do you disagree with me?" He's begging me to defy him. He loves it when I do, I know he does. I imagine him laying down his fishing gear, capturing my wrist, finding a tree stump and hauling me across his lap.

Fine, then. I can play along, too. I ignore the thundering of my heartbeat as I scoff at him.

"You are full of *shit*," I say, thereby breaking two rules. Not only am I defying him, I tossed in a naughty word. Oh, what's he gonna do now?

DARIO COMES TO A STUTTERING HALT, and I wonder if I've pushed too far. I clench my teeth together to stop them from chattering.

"Wanna repeat that?"

Though he looks almost angry, with his deeper tone of voice, his eyes flinty and hands anchored on his hips, I'm not afraid. It's the low, seductive tone of his voice. The way his chest expands, exposing his neck. The look of possession and intensity in his eyes.

I can't deny the tingling in my lower body, the anticipation of pleasure that make my breasts feel full and warm as wetness gathers between my thighs. I can hardly breathe.

"I said," swallowing before I continue, "you are full of shit." He heard that loud and clear.

"And what happens when you swear?"

I look away, withering under the heat of his glare. "I get punished," I whisper.

"What happens when you're disrespectful to me?" he asks, the same intense expression in his eyes.

I speak a little lower, casually. "Oh, I suppose… the same thing."

I bite my lip and look for a chance to escape. I haven't run from him yet, but I'm full of energy after a good night's sleep, and it sure is a nice day…

"Don't you even think about it," he says in a warning growl. I do. I definitely do think about it.

He crooks a finger at me. "Come here, now."

I SHAKE MY HEAD. Nope. Not gonna do it. He can't make me.

Actually, more accurately, he totally can, and I want him to.

"If you run from me..." He doesn't finish the sentence. I lick my lips and swallow, imagining what would happen if I do run from him.

I look at him, I look down at my feet, I look at those large, formidable hands of his, that can and will put me over his knee to spank my ass. And I make a dash for it.

I follow the path in the woods that leads to the beach, reasoning that pretty soon it will open up to a wide-open space and he's gonna have to really work to catch me. Of course he *will*, he's stronger and bigger, and I know I won't get away for good. But that's part of the fun of it.

I run down the embankment, and he curses behind me. "Thought you didn't like swears!" I yell over my shoulder. He curses again.

My feet hit sand, and I run faster. Running is the one thing I've always liked doing for exercise, and damn but it feels good to really let loose.

If this were any other beach on Earth, the sand would be peppered with colorful beach towels, huge umbrellas, beach chairs and swimmers, but there's nothing like that here. Nothing but a wide, bare beach with not a single footprint in the wet sand. I can hear the crash of waves and the distant cry of water birds, but other than that nothing but my panting and his heavy footsteps behind me. I actually think I'm giving him a good chase until I realize that the beach has already almost come to an end. He said it was small, and he wasn't joking.

I look wildly from side to side. My choices are to run deep into the woods, except there's nothing but a wall of leaves and branches to my left, or run into the wide-open ocean to my right that's freezing cold and probably full of fish. I don't have a lot of clothes to change into, and don't really feel like getting wet.

I think about my decisions way too long. With one quick motion, he gathers me up into his arms, tossing me over his shoulder before he gives my ass one hard, punishing smack to tell me what's coming.

Dammit. That was stupid.

"Oh, you naughty little thing," he says. Call it twisted, but I love the way he scolds. It's nothing like anything I've ever experienced before, none of the anger and belittling from my father, none of the harshness from my brothers. Though he definitely does fully expect me to obey him, there's a hint of amusement in his voice that tells me everything is going to be okay. That this is all part of the game.

But then I quickly change my mind, when he kneels right in the sand and hauls me over his knee.

Why did I do this?

I wanted attention.

Is this the kind of attention I want?

Yeah, I want any kind of attention.

You've been alone with him in a cabin in the woods for days, how much more attention do you need?

Ahem. *More.*

I'm over his lap, helpless to stop him, my hands flailing out in front of me, when I feel the first smack of his palm on my ass. I squeal and squirm, but he holds fast and gives me six more whacks before he speaks. My cheeks and chest grow feverish and hot, and even as I flinch in anticipation of the next blow, the throbbing between my legs intensifies.

I fucking love being spanked by Dario.

"Hey, stop!" I protest with such a futile attempt at sincerity and earnestness, I'm not even sure if he heard me, but it's part of the game.

"You know I like it when you're a good girl," he says, his heavy palm resting on my still-clothed ass. "And not when you disobey me like this." His touch is almost a gentle petting, making my body hypersensitive. I can hardly think beyond the desperate need for relief between my legs, how badly I need him to touch me.

I nod my head, feigning penitence. "I'm sorry," I whisper. "Not sure what got into me there."

I wriggle my butt a little. I want him either to smack me again and make it really hurt or make me come, but I'd die before I'd actually ask him for either of those things.

"Something you want to ask me?"

I shake my head, earning me another wicked smack of his palm. "Why don't we aim for the truth this time. Let's not forget it was dishonesty that brought you here in the beginning, wasn't it?"

Touché, big guy.

There's a lump in my throat preventing me from speaking. When I don't respond, he gives my ass another hard spank. I squeal.

"Answer me, Vivia."

I nod my head. "It was, yeah."

"Why did you goad me on?"

"Goad you on?"

I need more information from him.

"Yeah. You knew you'd end up here, so what was it? It's unlike you to talk back to me like that."

He's right, but I won't admit it that readily.

"You don't really know me well enough to say what's unlike me," I say reproachfully, but it's only a half-truth. In some weird way, I feel like Dario knows the real me better than anyone else.

"Ah, so we're playing *that* game," he says, almost to himself.

What game? Why does he always have to be one step ahead of me?

He adjusts me so he has even better access to my ass, and tugs at the waist of my yoga pants.

"Wait! Hey! I thought you were done?"

His voice is harder now, no longer amused. "You thought wrong."

I'm squirming now, real fear squirreling through me. "Then… why are you… Dario!"

I gasp when the hardest, most painful spank he's ever given me takes my breath away followed by another, then another, then another. "I want the truth. I'm not playing games. The truth, or you won't get up off my knee until I've blistered your ass."

This isn't a game anymore but very, very real.

"The truth about what?" I ask, stalling.

"Why you provoked me, knowing you'd end up here."

Fine, then. My cheeks burst into flame when I realize I'm going to tell him the truth that embarrasses me so badly I can't look at him. "Because I like being spanked."

"I know that. Tell me something I don't know."

Excuse me? He knows that?

I crane my neck to look up at him. "You knew that?"

His wicked eyes crinkle at the corners, his beautiful, handsome, completely masculine features stark and erotic against the backdrop of the bright blue sky behind him. "Of course I did."

"How?"

He shrugs a big, muscled shoulder, so sexy I want to lick every inch of him. "Easy. You get all aroused when I turn you on, and after a good spanking, you melt into me like you want to climb into my skin."

"I don't," I breathe, my cheeks flaming hot now.

"You do, though. There's nothing to be ashamed of, Vivia. It's normal and natural for a woman to enjoy being dominated."

I blame my uncomfortable position for the blood rushing to my cheeks.

"Dominated?" I whisper, imagining all sorts of things, like cuffs and clamps and the deliciously heavy weight of his body atop mine. "Yes."

Yes, I'll take some of that, and thank you.

He's quiet for a long minute, before he presses his hand to where my thighs press together.

"Spread your legs, lovely."

I obey. My eyes flutter closed and I can't stifle the moan that escapes my lips when he presses his fingers along my still-clothed slit. I throb against the pressure, heat, and dampness pooling between my legs. More, more, *more*.

"So we've established that you like a good spanking. You might not like a real discipline session, but there's something about discipline that appeals to you."

I don't reply. He's right, but I don't know if I'm really ready to admit that.

"So let's address that *first*. You don't have to play the brat to get a spanking. Just ask for one."

Just… ask for one. Like hi, I'm super thirsty and need some water and while you're at it, how about a good spanking session? Uh, no, too weird.

"Or you can provoke me like you did now, but that could prove dangerous."

I nod. It absolutely could, and I don't need him to explain how or why to me. It's a dangerous game, fraught with roadblocks and loopholes and pitfalls.

Glad we covered that.

"But you haven't really answered my question. You didn't just want a spanking just now, did you? There's far more to it."

I can't look at him. I can't think beyond the beating of my heart. I can't hear beyond the rush of blood pounding in my ears.

"Is there?" I ask, my voice husky and concerned. I know I'm on the edge of something dangerous, and I don't know how to respond. I've never been in a position like this before.

"I think that a part of you wants me to pay attention to you."

"What? No! Of course not. Why would I want that? I'd have to be a fool, since there's no one but the two of us for *miles*. I mean, I get plenty of *attention*."

"Not a fool, lovely," he corrects, smoothing his heavy, calloused palm over my ass. "But with what I know about your past…"

He doesn't finish the sentence. I need him to finish the sentence.

"What?" I whisper. "What do you know, then?" The blood's rushing to my face at this point.

"You lived a sheltered life. You gave your virginity to someone who betrayed you. You didn't deserve that. You deserve real love with a real man who can stand up to protect you, don't you?"

If he's implying what I think he's implying…

I don't respond, because I'm so caught up in my thoughts, I don't know what to say.

"I guess," I admit, my voice husky. I want to scream *Yes, yes, exactly that!* But manage to restrain myself. I squirm over his lap, eager to either be let up or spanked again. Anything to avoid this conversation that makes me feel too vulnerable, too needy, childish even.

"I think I know the kind of attention you want from me," he whispers, slowly dragging his palm down my ass.

"Do you?" I ask. I hope he does because I don't have the nerve to verbalize it. But maybe he's figured it out.

When he leans in, I'm momentarily floating at the smell of his clean, signature scent, rugged and masculine and woodsy.

He belongs here. I'm the one that doesn't.

"I've touched you. We've slept in the same bed. I've skirted the edge and brought you to climax, but we haven't had sex yet. And here you are, Vivia Montavio…"

He slides me off his lap and onto the sand where I land with a soft *oomph*. White sand cascades around my clothes and shoes.

"You want me to make love to you, don't you?"

Well since you put it that way…

I hold his gaze for long minutes, thinking over my response. I have no use for formalities or pussyfooting around and he *definitely* doesn't.

Instead of answering his question, I swallow the lump in my throat. "Why don't you?" I whisper.

He doesn't answer at first. I wait for his response, but he doesn't answer at all. He stands, helps me to my feet, and walks to the dock. "Let's get some food," he says.

Food. *Fish*. Ew.

My body's on fire, and I feel dejected. My belly drops, and a raw feeling of emptiness pervades me. I should know better than to get my hopes up. I should know better than to think anything matters beyond me being his captive and the families that rule us.

CHAPTER THIRTEEN

Vivia

I CARRY a towel and my soap with me to the water's edge, trying to make sense of it all. Trying to ignore the pain in my throat, determined to make the most of this situation. He hasn't proven the jailer I expected, not at all. We're almost... friendly.

Almost.

He might turn discipline into foreplay and I freely admit I enjoy that, but I'm also not dumb enough to pretend there isn't an element of *very real* punishment in his actions. If I were to defy him... really, truly defy him, like try to escape or refuse to obey, I know in my heart he'd be treating me very differently.

But when he loops his arm over me when we fall asleep... when he tucks a stray strand of hair behind my ear, or brings me a plate of food... when I catch him watching me when I wake or when I sit by the fire... I imagine I'm something more than a job to him.

We make it to the shore. He strips off his tee, revealing his tanned, masculine back, and tosses it far from the water. When he lifts the fishing rod he found in the cabin, I turn away. I do *not* enjoy the hook and bait part of things.

And it's time for me to take back what little control I have, anyway. I know I'm at a decided disadvantage as his prisoner, but that doesn't mean I can't take a roll of the die myself.

I step to the white sand shore. Water laps at my feet, surprisingly warm. We've had a bit of a warm spell, and the shallow water here in the little inlet where he fishes reflects that. Last night, we took a long bath, both of us, and I scrubbed every inch of my body and washed my hair. Today, I just need a good shave.

And he can fucking *watch me.*

I stand with my feet in the water and reach for my tee. Lift it over my naval, close my eyes, and go for broke. Tug it over my head and toss it behind me without looking at him. When the rest of my clothes except my panties follow, he makes a sort of strangled sound. I ignore him. I'd take the panties off, but I'm not interested in sitting bare-assed on the rock so I can shave. But those will come off, too.

"You gonna shave?" he asks. His voice is rougher and deeper than usual. He's following right along with me.

I nod, still not looking at him.

"I'd step over to the fresh water then."

Damn, he's right. I don't make eye contact but look to where he points to a small, shallow body of water.

"That's fresh?"

"Yeah. Tested it yesterday. Doesn't come from the ocean but from the stream in the woods, and it's running water so it's crystal clear."

"Why thank you, kind sir," I say, turning away and walking nearly stark naked past him, distinctly aware of his gaze following every movement.

Beside me, I hear the swish and *splash* of his fishing rod to my left. I step over and find a clean, bare rock. Sit on the edge with my back to him, lean over, and scoop warm water over my legs.

When my legs are damp, I uncap the shaving cream and lather them up good. I make sure to position my leg so that he can see all of me, my bare legs, my back, my ass... everything. I take my time shaving. It feels so damn *luxurious*. After the rustic living arrangements we've had here, this feels like nothing short of pure luxury. I sigh contentedly and ignore the grunts he's making.

One leg down, I rinse it, careful not to get the shaving lotion into the water. I lift my second leg, turn to give him another sidelong view, and shave from my calf to the top of my thigh. When I'm finished, I stand and remove my panties, place my razor beside the lotion, and begin to lather up between my legs.

"What the fuck are you doing?" he growls. At first, I ignore him. I begin shaving.

"Vivia," he snaps.

"Mmm?"

"I asked what the fuck are you *doing*."

"Thought it was obvious. Shaving."

"Don't you dare shave your pussy bare." I raise my eyebrows and finally bring my gaze to him. The fishing rod lays on the ground beside him, forgotten, and his fists are planted at his sides.

"Excuse me?"

"You heard me."

He's bending in the fresh water in front of me, washing his hands. Thoroughly. That's my only warning.

He's given up *fishing*.

"Uh, so I don't think that's your call?"

I underestimated how close we are. In three quick steps, he's caught me in his arms and hauled me up. My legs wrap around his torso and he smacks my ass, hard. I gasp and moan as he tangles his fingers in my hair and yanks my head back. When my lips part, he claims my mouth with a hard, punishing kiss that makes me melt. My eyes flutter closed. He's got the towel fisted in his hand. I didn't even see him pick it up.

"I'm the one that shaves that pussy. I told you, Vivia. You belong to me."

He… is the one… that *shaves me.*

Uhhhhh….

He sits on the sand and has me straddle his legs facing him, one on either side. "Lay back on the towel, head back," he orders. I obey. My legs part, and cool air kisses my private folds. He drags his thumb along my slit, and I moan, grinding myself against him.

"Beautiful," he growls. "Fucking *gorgeous.* Spread those legs for me, woman."

I spread them further apart. He lays me back, my legs on either side of him, and gives himself room. I tremble when he lifts the razor. "Stay still and don't move. I don't want to hurt you."

He could. He could so easily hurt me, it scares me.

I nod, my mouth dry, and watch as he carefully lowers himself and lathers me up. I don't breathe with the first stroke of the razor. In between swipes, he fingers me until I'm dripping wet and panting. I'm well aware of how precarious a situation I'm in, how dangerous it is to be shaven on a beach and *at the most sensitive parts of my body,* but he takes such utter care, I don't feel a thing but the gentle glide of the razor and the erotic pulse of his fingers rewarding me.

"Gorgeous," he groans. "Fucking gorgeous."

I look down to see him nearly worshipping my body, his eyes wide in adulation. His erection tents his shorts, and I bite my lip. Who'd have thought such a simple thing could be such a turn-on.

"I wanna taste that pussy," he growls, his eyes molten and concentrated on me. "Give me that pussy, baby."

He leans back on the towel so he's flat on the sand and quickly, deftly arranges me so I'm straddling his face, my knees on either side of him. My hands are planted on the towel on either side of him, bracing before he grabs my nipples and licks my pussy.

The first swipe of his tongue feels like heaven. My eyes flutter closed at the erotic feel of his warm, sensual mouth circling my clit. I grind against him and he slaps my ass appreciatively. The hard spank only excites me more. Over, and over, and over again he laps and sucks and worships my pussy. My pulse races and I can't speak, can't think beyond the next lick of his tongue, the next blissful wave of pleasure.

"Come," he grates against my thigh. "Come on my mouth." He accentuates his command with another sharp slap on my ass. It's all I need to soar into ecstasy.

My mouth opens in wonder before I pull in deep breaths. My body flushes with pleasure as spasms rock me. I moan and press my pussy to feel more. He grips my ass and holds me to him.

I ride my orgasm in a state of euphoria. I'm weightless and warm. I'm not here anymore but floating, soaring, somewhere far away from a world of pain and sadness. Enveloped in nothing but sheer, utter bliss.

I'm coming down from my high when he lifts me and drags me down his body. I slump over him just as he rolls and pins me beneath him. I sigh under the full weight of him, relishing the feel of his hard, masculine body over mine.

"Open your legs," he growls. "Open them for me, *now.*" He emphasizes the command with a hard smack to my hip. Desire spikes at the sharp command and hot feel of his palm. I quickly obey. I crave the feel of him inside me. I never knew I needed anything like this in my life before, but now I feel if he doesn't come inside me soon I'll wither and die.

I groan when he slides his length inside me, stretching me in all the right ways. Lightning bolts of pleasure erupt over my skin, and my nerves are on fire. My arms encircle his neck so I don't drown in ecstasy, but his own hands hold me to him as if to ease me into the rhythm of his nearly savage thrusts.

Oh my *God.* It's utterly perfect, so perfect I want to savor this moment forever, and I don't think anything could feel better than this moment until he thrusts.

I cry out loud at the perfect feel of his cock in me, lightning bolts of arousal skating under my skin, across my chest. My whole body's engulfed in flames.

"Fuck, Vivia," he moans in my ear. "You feel so damn good."

I kiss his cheek in response, helpless to speak right now. He responds with another perfect, savage thrust. My climax is building a second time, different than the first but somehow more intimate. He groans in pleasure at the height of his own bliss, and when he empties himself inside me, my own climax consumes me.

I've never felt anything like this before in my life. If anyone had asked me if I was a virgin I'd have told them no, it wasn't my first time… but I was wrong. There's a world of difference between what I did with Gray—it was painful and awkward and left me wondering how anyone really *enjoys* sex—and what just happened now.

"I take it all back," I groan. Our bodies are melded together. He rests his head on my shoulder in a rare moment of his own surrender. I run my fingers through his hair, needing to feel the closeness and savoring this moment. "I told you I wasn't a virgin."

"Mmm?" he murmurs, still drunk on his own arousal as he kisses my cheek. "How so?"

"But I feel like one. That was definitely the first time I've ever had sex."

His throaty laugh makes me smile.

"It's different when feelings are involved," he says softly, threading his fingers through mine.

That's putting it mildly.

"Ah, yeah. And it's also different when the… because you… well *you* know what you're doing."

He pushes up and braces himself so his eyes meet mine, a wicked, lopsided grin on his face. "Oh really?"

"Mhm," I say with a nod, then think twice. "But wait, I don't think it's okay for you to, like, get a big head or anything, okay?"

His grin widens, softening his rugged masculine features. Goddamn is he hot.

"I can make you scream when you climax and make you nearly go into orbit just from a spanking, but I'm not allowed to actually be proud of my accomplishments?"

"Well, I… guess maybe a *little*…"

I love the way his shoulders shake when he laughs. The way he drops his head to my chest and breathes me in, as if clearing his mind and his senses and drawing closer to me.

"Come back with me to the cabin," he whispers in my ear. "And I'll prove to you that I know *exactly* what I'm doing."

He doesn't have to ask me twice.

CHAPTER FOURTEEN

Dario

WE MAKE LOVE ALL AFTERNOON. Therein lies the difference between what's happening between us. Vivia had sex before. I've had sex before. The two of us coming together after everything we've been through is more than the meeting of two bodies and carnal pleasure. So, so much more.

We take our time making slow, sweet, lazy love. I bury my face between her thighs because I relish the way she comes against my tongue. I finger her to completion, and she makes me nearly lose my mind when she falls to her knees in front of me and takes my hard length in her own mouth. We lavish each other with affection, explore each other's bodies like two honeymooners with nothing better to do with their time.

If I bring her back to The Castle pregnant, she'll have a chance of surviving this.

We both will.

Maybe.

When the sun reaches its peak around midday, we lay in bed, weary from our sex fest and momentarily tired out. She lays on my chest, naked, her hair askew, her breathing so soft I wonder if she's asleep, when her stomach growls.

"Dammit, we forgot to eat," I mutter.

"Mhm. We had better things to do. And correction, sir. *You* didn't forget to eat."

I've eaten her out three times since the beach. I grin against the top of her head and tug her hair.

"Naughty little girl."

"Ah ah, don't start lecturing me because you know when you go all dominant on me it turns me on."

"Everything turns you on." I fucking love that about her.

She shrugs lazily and doesn't deny it. "Didn't know what I was missing."

I give her ass a good squeeze.

"Well, we'll need sustenance if we're going to continue this."

"True," she says with a nod. "So much for fish."

"I don't really like fish anyway," I tell her.

She grins at me. "I think I saw some noodles in there?"

"Noodles are fast. I like noodles."

Fifteen minutes later we're back in bed, our bellies full of pasta and ready for a nap.

She spreads her hand over my chest, playing with the sparse, curly hairs, and cautiously drags her fingernail over my nipple. I hiss out a breath.

"Do you like that?"

"Yeah, baby," I say on a laugh. "I like every fucking time you touch me."

With a teasing smile she pinches my nipple, which earns her a good, hard spank. "Hey!"

"Watch it."

"You said you liked it every time I touch you."

"I do."

"Then why'd you spank me just now?"

"Because I want to and *you* love to be spanked."

I love the way her cheeks flush pink. My hard length presses against her and she smiles up at me again. "Your stamina is impressive. Could you really go again?"

I groan when she strokes her hand along my length and show her that I can, absolutely, go again.

Finally, after three more sessions, it's growing dark outside. With a sigh, I sit up. This is the part of rustic living that really sucks. Ain't nobody gonna come in here to build us a fire to keep us warm, and even though it's warm here by the water, it's still cool enough at night that a fire's necessary.

We also need more to eat than a bowl of plain noodles.

"Alright, baby. Let's get something good to eat."

"I'd kill for a good shower."

We could take a shower outside, but it's grown colder. "Soon. For now, I can heat up some water for a bath?"

She pushes off me and nods. "Works for me."

I toss her my tee. "Put that on to keep the bugs away."

With a quick tug, she pulls my tee on. It hits her knees adorably, like a little girl playing dress-up, but the way it drapes over her ass and tits makes her all woman.

I tug on a pair of jeans to head outside to get us some wood. We exhausted the supply yesterday and today was supposed to be about replenishing our wood stock… but we made other plans instead.

I head out to get the wood while she sets water to boil. I haven't given her this much freedom since we got here, but she's almost built trust with me. She likely knows this is the safest place for her right now, and I don't think she's made up the way she enjoys being with me.

I never expected to actually have feelings for her. It's unexpected, but it makes what I have to do that much easier.

She needs to have a baby. There's no getting around the boldest way to save her. When whatever truth our brothers are searching for comes to light, bringing her to The Castle pregnant will be her only saving grace. It'll be a more powerful talisman against the vengeance her brothers will want to seek than any blows I could throw with my own two fists, and I'll be damn ready to throw down.

"Dario," she says over her shoulder. "I'm not gonna look, I promise. But it looks like you have some missed calls here on this phone?"

I left the phone out right where she could see it. I'm slipping.

Fuck. During our sex fest, Orlando probably tried to reach me.

"Alright, I'll be there in a minute. Don't touch it, Vivia."

She backs away as if it's a venomous snake, then shakes her head. "Not touching it. I don't know the password anyway. Just boiling water like a good girl over here."

I'm smiling to myself when I turn away.

Enamored with how adorable she looks in my T-shirt, and the plans I have for her for later, I miss the warning sounds behind me. I should goddamn know better, but when I finally hear the hiss and growl, it's too late.

I turn just in time to face a vicious howl and sharp, razor-like teeth. At first, I think someone's dog's got off leash, a wolf dog or husky ready to fight. I crouch, throw my arm up to defend myself, and just in time as the animal attacks. I scream as its teeth sink into my arm, tearing flesh with ease. This is no dog—the flatter forehead and sleeker physique, pointed snout and long, slender yet powerful legs, give it away as a coyote in the wild, common in these parts. What isn't common is for one to attack a human.

I kick at it, trying to prevent another slash of teeth, but it's bent on attacking and doesn't give up easily. I hear Vivia's pounding footsteps seconds before she yanks open the door. Dammit, I don't want her hurt.

"Go back inside!" I yell at her. "Shut the door!"

"Oh my God!" she screams, and reaches for one of the logs by the door, but when she throws it, she misses by a mile.

"Go inside!"

"It'll eat you!" she screams, and doesn't make a fucking move to go inside.

I roll and kick the beast, causing it to cry out and flinch, but it only attacks me with more vigor, doubling the snarls as it claws and bites at my bare flesh. I kick it again, and again, but I can't pry the relentless teeth from my body. Blood splashes on the ground, the coyote's gray fur splattered in crimson.

"I'll get the gun!" she says.

The pain is all-consuming. I've never had an adversary attack like this so relentlessly, as if it has a personal vendetta against me. I can't get a punch or kick in at this point. My only option is to wrestle it to the ground.

It's ferocious and strong, but I'm stronger. I throw my body weight on it, pinning it to the earth as Vivia comes running with my gun.

"Fucking wish I could shoot," she says on a sob. "Here!"

She could shoot me. She could run.

She holds it out to me. I try to reach for the gun but can't. As soon as I reach my hand out, I'm met with cruel teeth and another bite that sends pain radiating through every nerve in my body. I stifle my screams, not wanting to scare Vivia. The gun falls to the ground and goes off. Vivia screams.

"Are you okay?" I yell, over the snarls and turmoil.

"Oh my God, you're being attacked by a savage beast and you're worried about me? Kill it, Dario. Kill it!"

She lifts a huge branch from the ground, rears backs, and swings it with all she's got. The coyote whimpers and cries, falling to the ground. She whacks it again. It won't stay down for long, but I have just enough time to grab the gun and cock it.

"Hit it again!" I scream. She quickly swings the club and clocks it across the jaw. She isn't strong enough to really hurt it, so she's only managed to infuriate it. I can almost hear the creature think, hear the decision to attack and kill the woman that has the nerve to hit it. She's next.

I *never* miss.

I aim my gun, my hand shaking with the effort of holding my aim as I point it at the coyote's skull. Just as it lunges at Vivia and she trips, falling down, I pull the trigger. She screams as the bullet sinks deep into the eye socket.

I shoot it again, and again, until I'm confident it won't attack again. The beast falls, dead, on top of her.

"It's dead, Dario," Vivia says in a choked plea. "It's dead. Let it go. Please, let it go. We might need those bullets." She swallows as she pushes the animal off of her and gets to her feet. "It isn't going to hurt me or you anymore, Dario."

She's using a gentle tone, her voice tender as she reaches for me. "Now come inside with me and let's get you cleaned up."

I wonder at first why she's treating me with kid gloves, as if she's afraid that I'm going to run or do something drastic. Does she think I'm going to hurt her? But when I look down at myself, barely clothed, lacerations and open wounds oozing blood and gore all over my body, I realize she's in shock. She's seen me attacked and faced her own endangerment. She doesn't know how I'll respond this badly injured.

I sink to my knees, lightheaded.

"Please," she says on a whisper, her hand in mine. "Hold onto me. But I can't carry you, Dario. And I can't take care of you out here in the woods. I don't know what kinds of animals will come for the carcass, or if it was alone. Please," she says, her voice breaking. "You're too heavy for me to carry, or I would."

She would. This woman…

I push myself to my feet. I've faced worse than this. Even with my head swimming and my body aching, I manage to get myself to the doorway with Vivia's help. Poor girl bows under my weight, and I try to put as little on her as I can. I stagger through the doorway and collapse by the fire.

"Can you make it to the bed?" she whispers.

I shake my head. "Not yet." My voice sounds distant and hollow as my body teems with pain. I need to staunch some of these wounds fast before I lose too much blood. I'm baffled as to how one animal can cause such damage so quickly.

I close my eyes. I want to sleep.

"Don't you dare go to sleep on me," Vivia says sternly. "You listen to me. We have to get these wounds treated and I can't have you passing out on me. Stay with me. You know more about these things than I do, you have to help me through it."

I nod. "Hot water," I croak out. It's getting harder to talk, but I can still do it. My head throbs with pain. Jesus, I feel like a pussy for letting a fucking coyote get the better of me.

"On it." She leaps to her feet and fills the metal bucket we use for heating water and bathing. Thankfully she's now skilled at this, and soon the water sits over an open flame. It will take a while to heat, though.

"Can you find the first aid kit?"

She nods. It's then that I realize she's crying. Tears flow freely down her cheeks.

"Vivia," I ask, surprised. "You okay? What is it?"

She shakes her head and doesn't answer, as she walks to where we keep the first aid kid. I watch her pick it up then drop it because her hands tremble so badly.

"Vivia." My voice is sterner. I want to know what's going on.

"You could've died," she says, her voice wobbling. "It just… tore into you like you were meat. What if it had? What would I have done?"

"You'd have found your way out of here and called for help."

She gives me a curious look and doesn't respond, but opens the first aid kit and unzips it.

"You are strong and capable." I swallow, remembering how she does so well under my praise. "And you're my brave, brave girl, aren't you?"

She nods. "If I knew how to *shoot—*"

"We'll fix that."

"Promise me?" She holds my gaze. "I want you to promise me, Dario, that once we're out of here and find… some sort of… normal again, that you'll teach me how to shoot."

She reaches me and kneels beside me. I squeeze her hand. "I promise you, baby. *Promise.*"

Her eyes flutter shut and she kisses my bruised and bloodied fingers.

"Thank you."

The next few minutes are spent with me biting down to keep from screaming out loud and her pouring antiseptic on my open wounds. It hurts like a motherfucker, but I don't want her to feel any worse about it than she has to, so I make myself swallow down the need to scream.

She's a gentle and tender nurse. I close my eyes and let myself enjoy this brief moment of role reversal—me being the one in need of help, and her being the caretaker.

It's then that I realize for the second time that night… she could run. And easily. I'm in no position to give her chase or to even know where she went. If she took off now, she'd have the best chance of getting away with it she's had since we got here.

But she doesn't. She doesn't try to get away from me. She only doctors my wounds like a gentle nurse and stays right by my side.

In a short time, sleep overcomes me. She's bandaged every wound she could after disinfecting them as thoroughly as possible.

"Tell me," she whispers. "I don't know much about these things, but I've figured out a few things."

I close my eyes, drifting in and out of sleep.

"Mmmm?"

"So, for starters, I don't think coyotes normally attack humans?"

"Correct."

I take in a deep breath and release it slowly.

"What would make a coyote attack?"

"Few reasons," I whisper, my voice sounding strangely distant. "First, if you're on what they consider their terrain, they could get territorial. But we've been here for days and this is the first I've seen one, so I'm going to assume that wasn't the cause here."

"Okay. Go on."

"Second, they feel you've attacked their young."

She frowns. "Haven't seen any young, and that was a male coyote."

"How do you know?"

She rolls her eyes. "Because my mama taught me about the birds and the bees, and that was most definitely a male coyote displaying his wares."

"Greeeeaaaat," I mutter. "So that's probably out of the question."

"Right."

I blow out a breath. I feel as if I'm half-conscious, in and out of reality, as I talk "And finally," I say on a wheezy breath, "the coyote could be rabid. Rabid coyotes are much, much more likely to attack than for any other reason."

"*Shit.*"

"Yeah."

"So we need to get you some help."

I nod. I don't much care. All I want is some sleep right now. "Eventually."

She's on her feet, but she seems as if she's living on another planet. I can't reach her if I tried. I open my mouth to speak, but nothing comes out.

I close my eyes. I need a nap. The blanket of darkness falls over my eyes. Vivia's voice becomes distant. I wonder why she's troubled. I wonder why it sounds as if she's crying.

CHAPTER FIFTEEN

Vivia

DARIO'S in and out of consciousness. If he were bit by a rabid animal... I stare at the door to the cabin as if it will give me the answers I need, but all I hear is the lonely howl of wind.

I have to get help.

I don't know much about first aid, but I do know that if someone's bitten by a rabid animal, it's important to get emergency medical care. Crucial, even. If we don't, there's no telling what could happen to him.

I stare at the phone, unable to use it. I can't call out since I don't know the password, and I've been obviously blocked from making outbound calls. I try a few random passwords, but I'm only one try away from locking the phone for an hour, so that's useless.

I bite my lip and stare at Dario. His cheeks are flushed and his breathing's grown rapid. A deep, gnawing feeling of dread claws at my belly. Something is terribly wrong, and I have to help him, but I don't know how.

I can't run for help, because I don't know where we are or how to get there.

And then a little voice whispers at the back of my mind, tempting me. Beckoning me.

Run.

You could... run. Not for help, but to escape. It's what I planned on doing from the very beginning, but now that the option's upon me... I can't do it.

No. I can't leave him, sick and unable to do a damn thing to help himself, alone in the woods with no lifeline.

I can't run for help, either, for the same reason I can't run to escape.

We have to reach someone, and it has to be now.

I stare at the phone in my hand, trying to find a way around the facial recognition requirement that unlocks it. I draw in a breath and try to talk to him again.

"Dario?"

I need him awake.

"*Dario!*"

I need him here, with me, so I'm not alone with the coyotes and whatever other predators are outside that door. There's just… I can't. I can't go it alone here.

Or later, when I'm no longer a captive here. He's the only barrier I have between me and literally everyone else.

I hear him mumble in his sleep and bring him the phone. "Dario. Please. If you could just open your eyes for like one minute— just tell me the password…"

He doesn't open his eyes but lifts his hand, a barely perceptible little wiggle of his fingers.

What?

I stare at the phone for minutes before it dawns on me. It needs a thumbprint recognition. With a dry little sob, I quickly lift his heavy hand and press his thumb to the screen. *Error,* it flashes in red.

No. My heart sinks. How am I ever going to get the help that we need? I throw my head back and scream out the sheer frustration, anger, and helplessness I feel.

Goddamn my family.

Goddamn the Rossis.

Their ruthless and archaic laws have bound me worse than Dario ever has. I can't help him even when I need to.

Okay, alright.

I can do this. I'm not gonna go all helpless female, not now.

I'm not getting anywhere wallowing in my anger and self-pity. I need to figure out what the hell I'm doing and *now*.

I glance down at his hands, gently folded over his abdomen. He sleeps as if he's resting, but I know that's his body's way of conserving energy. And if I don't get him the help he needs, he may not wake up.

I know his fingerprint opens this phone.

But I only tried his thumb, and it was on his left hand. He's right-handed… could it be… that I need to try another way? He'd be holding his phone with his right hand, which means…

I reach for his hand and lift his thumb, slide his right thumb along the lock pad. The screen flashes to life, and the phone unlocks.

I almost sob in relief. I bring his hand to my lips and kiss each one of his fingers. With shaking fingers of my own, I swipe through the phone.

I could call a friend.

I could call the police.

I only think for seconds, before I pull up the last dialed numbers. I know this is only a burner phone, so there won't be any contacts saved. I'll hang up if it isn't Orlando.

Ring.

Ring.

Ring.

I close my eyes, squeezing them tight. "Please work," I whisper. "Please."

"Jesus, motherfucker, thought you'd never answer my call. Why didn't you—"

"Orlando?" I interrupt.

There's a brief pause, then, "Vivia? What the hell are you doing on this phone?"

Tears blur the screen in front of me. "It's an emergency," I say on a sob. "Send help, and quickly." I fill him in as rapidly as I can, though it takes longer between my half-sobs and shaking voice.

"Jesus, alright. Okay, I'm on it. Take a deep breath. You stay right there. If you try anything, Vivia—"

"Send help!" I shout. "If I were going to run, I'd have already done it! Send help *now*, or he won't make it!"

"On it."

I hang up the phone and stare at the screen. I've done my duty. Now's the time I could run. Orlando will take care of Dario, and I—I could just slip away. Just slip out that door and no one will know where I've gone or what I did.

I can take this phone and whatever cash I find...

I rifle through his bags until I find a wad of cash. I realize I'm barely wearing any clothes, so I quickly tug on a pair of jeans and shoes. I shove the money in my pocket.

His breath is coming in shallow gasps. I'll just... give him some water before I go.

I run to where we keep fresh water and a drinking cup and pour him some.

"Drink," I whisper, but he's out. I part his lips and dribble the water on them. He doesn't make a move until I tilt his head back and pour a tiny bit of water into his mouth. He instinctively swallows.

"Good," I whisper. "Just like that. Good job. Drink more."

I give him another sip, and he drinks that, too.

"Can you hear me, Dario? Squeeze my hand if you can hear me."

No response.

I close my eyes and think again of my plan to leave. With money and a phone, I could find my way out of here.

My brothers aren't the only ones with connections.

I could escape far away to the West Coast or Mexico, even. Find a place to stay where no one knows me. *No one.* I'll start from scratch, but I'll know that everything I earn is *mine*.

I could do it.

And I'll never see him again. I'll never feel those arms of his around me again. I'll never hear him say *good girl* in that deep, masculine voice of his, never kiss him, again.

I'll go the rest of my life and never know what it's like to be loved. Because no one, *no one,* will ever be Dario to me.

I stifle a sob. I hate that the only choices before me are dark and dismal.

I check every laceration on his body and make sure they're bandaged and disinfected, that he's comfortable and hydrated.

I remember the phone. I can look up what happens to someone bitten by a rabid animal, especially one who's experienced rapid blood loss. The amount of blood outside and in this cabin is staggering.

What would he have me do?

There's no way he'd want me to leave, not now, not after everything we've been through. Not when it's risky and dangerous for me to go.

Maybe he's prepared to tell my brothers what really happened.

Maybe Orlando has information that will let me off the hook.

Maybe…

Maybe I won't get a second chance.

Maybe… he *would* want me to take my one chance of escape, my one chance of getting away from my brothers.

Maybe he'd want me to start out on my own and make a new name for myself.

I don't know how far away we are from help or who Orlando called, but unless he was camping right outside this spot, which is doubtful, he won't be the one that comes. He could send EMTs, and they wouldn't know I was a captive.

Or… he could send someone else. Friends of his who know exactly who I am and exactly what they're supposed to do with me.

Sergio would give them the order to kill me.

I kneel in front of Dario. I hold his hand and kiss his fingers. I kiss his forehead and lean into his ear. He won't hear me, which is just as well, because I don't want him to be conflicted about what I need to tell him.

"I love you," I whisper in his ear. "Thank you…"

Thank you? I don't know why I feel the need to say that. He captured me, after all. But after everything we've been through... everything he's done. He's taken care of me, protected me, fed me. Listened to me. And keeping me here with him was only because of orders he himself got.

"I'm sorry," I whisper. "I'm sorry that I have to do this. I hope one day you'll understand."

I think I hear something in the woods. Someone's coming. If I know my cousin, and I like to think I do... he's sent someone local to come rescue Dario and take me into custody.

With trembling hands, I grab a scrap of paper from the table where we keep the board games. I find a tiny pencil we used for keeping track when we played Scrabble. I write him a hasty note, fold it, and tuck it into his pocket.

I don't take the gun. I can't do anything with it. I leave the phone because they could track me with it.

But I take the knife and the money.

I see headlights coming toward us. They're almost here. I can't leave through the door, but I know my way around this cabin, and I'm small and lithe. I leave the door ajar to give me more time, look once more at his body lying on the floor, bandaged and unconscious, and leap out the window to watch by the corner of the cabin. Here, behind the large propane tank, I'm hidden beneath a shade of pines.

They won't see me, and I know where I can hide until they're gone. I wait until I see who's come. A group of six, armed to the teeth. Paramedics race toward the cabin and find him on the cabin floor.

And once I know he's in good hands, I run.

CHAPTER SIXTEEN

Dario

I WAKE, the twittering of birds outside my window telling me it's early morning. I need to get up and get moving if I want to catch fish for today. I roll over and fling my arm on the bed, but only feel pillows. There's an ache in my arms and along my neck, and my body feels strangely tingly and lethargic. I try to open my eyes, but they're heavy as if I've been drugged.

What the hell?

With effort, I finally open my eyes and look around me. My heart sinks, as it all comes flooding back to me.

We're not in the cabin anymore. The last thing I remember... I was attacked, bitten by a coyote.

Vivia helped me by getting my gun and beating it off me. She... bandaged my wounds.

Did she call for help? How would she?

"Hello?" My lips are thick, my mouth dry. Jesus, what the hell happened to me? Where am I? I look around the room but no one's there.

"Vivia?" I whisper. There's no response.

I look out at the open window before me and see something I recognize. Crashing waves, water lapping at the shore...

I sit up, ignoring the pain that ricochets through my nerves like a ringing bell.

I'm at The Castle. I'm home.

If they found Vivia—

I throw off the covers and pat my body, looking for a weapon.

"Jesus, take it easy, brother."

The door flings open, and Romeo strides in.

"Where is she?" I ask. He doesn't need me to tell him who "she" is.

"Lay down, Dario. You're not ready to get up out of that bed."

Like hell I'm not. If they found her, if they hurt her—

"Lay. *Down*," he repeats, no longer friendly but my Don.

I have no choice but to obey. I lay back. "Tell me, Rome. What happened?"

He folds himself on a chair by my bed as Orlando walks into the room, sees I'm awake, and shuts the door firmly behind him. I watch as he spins the lock to the locked position, and when he turns to me, he puts his finger to his lips. "Shh," he whispers. "They're all here."

Romeo looks up at him and doesn't respond. Orlando sits on a chair next to Romeo.

"Why don't you fill him in," Romeo says, nodding to Orlando. Romeo, the eldest brother and leader of the Rossi family, dresses like he's about to dine at Boston's finest. He rarely raises his voice and leads with quiet confidence. His blue eyes are fixated on Orlando, who looks at me.

"How are you feeling?"

"I feel like shit, but I don't care about that right now," I tell him impatiently. "I wanna know—"

"Where Vivia is," he finishes. "I know, but you were pretty bad off, brother."

"And I want to know how you are, too," Romeo says seriously. I blow out a breath. Fine, then, we'll play it that way.

"I'm fine, I think. Head hurts, my body feels weirdly drugged and sluggish, but I think I'm alright. What the hell happened?"

"Patience," Orlando says, clucking his tongue. I'm about ready to come up out of this bed and strangle him. He must see I'm not fucking around, because he holds up his hand in surrender and chuckles. "Alright, alright. Easy, Dar. I'll tell you everything." He raises his eyebrows. "And fast, okay?"

I nod. Romeo hands me a glass of water. "Drink," he orders. I do what he says as I face Orlando.

"You were bitten, and badly, by a rabid coyote. I'm not sure how you escaped, but we found the body shot right outside the door to the cabin. Blood trail says you made it inside, or Vivia helped you. She called me. Must've used your thumbprint to open up the phone. The phone says she went through the records and called the last dialed."

Why is he talking about all this in the past tense? If he hurt her... if any of them did...

I take in a deep breath to steady myself, though it doesn't seem to be working that well.

"We had men in Rhode Island, sent an EMT crew to get you brought home and doctored and to bring Vivia into custody at The Castle. When they got there, she was gone."

Good girl.

I'm surprised at the sudden warmth that spreads across my chest.

She saw her chance, and she got away. Even as my heart splinters, even as I want to leap out of this bed and run to find her, pride sweeps through my chest at the knowledge that she not only saved my life, she saved her own as well. My strong, brave girl.

"She escaped," I whisper, looking at Romeo. "Jesus, I'm sorry." I had one job, and I failed it.

He shakes his head. "Come off it, Dario," Romeo says with a frown. "I'm not gonna take someone to task for nearly getting killed by a fuckin' coyote. You're strong and one of my most vicious fighters, but you're not goddamn Superman." He shrugs. "Plus, I'm not even sure she was guilty."

Orlando looks at the door. "Sergio, on the other hand…"

Before this all went down, I fuckin' liked Sergio.

"He ready to kill me?"

"I think if she'd come back here, he would have," Orlando says honestly. He frowns. "She looked guilty as fuck, brother. We've found nothing to vindicate her."

"After all that time," I begin, but Orlando cuts me off.

"It's only been a few days. We can't find anything but incriminating evidence, and we're no closer to finding out who took you into custody than we were before."

"That's bullshit," I tell him. My head feels like it'll split in two. Romeo puts his hand on my shoulder and pushes me back down.

"You're not in trouble for her getting away," Romeo tells me. "But you're gonna stay right fuckin' here until I know it's safe." He lowers his voice. "We've kept Sergio in the dark until now. He's fit to kill. Pissed. If I let him in here right now, he'd shoot you, no question, and that would get really fucking messy. You hear me?"

Jesus.

"Yeah." I swallow hard and remember who I'm talking to. "Sorry, Rome. Yeah, I do."

"Good." He pinches his lips together. "Based on your reaction, I'm gonna hazard a guess that you found Vivia innocent? Yeah?"

I nod. "She's innocent. She had nothing to do with the attempted assassination on Marialena."

"Got it. And furthermore, being alone with her, you've developed feelings for her."

Leave it to Romeo to put it all out in the open. I swallow, nod, and answer, "I did."

"Right." He runs his fingers through his hair. "It's best we don't tell Sergio all these details now, got it? You tell him she's innocent and we'll take it from there. I'll call him in, disarm him, and make sure he remembers that he's in our home. Got it?"

I nod.

"You do not provoke him. You do not fight him. You remember who you are and who he is. He's in the right to kill you if he wanted to, it's only respect for me that will stay his hand. You got that?"

I nod and release a sigh. "I do."

Romeo jerks his head at Orlando. "Call Sergio."

Orlando smirks. "No need. He's right outside the fucking door."

Romeo rolls his eyes and raises his voice. "Sergio, leave your weapons at the door. You come in here armed, I'll kick your motherfucking ass personally." He stands, as if ready to attack. "You get me?"

Sergio curses, and there's the sound of several weapons being dropped to the floor. Orlando shakes his head. A few seconds later, Sergio enters the room, his eyes on me.

"You," he says, shaking his head. "You're the motherfucker that faked your deaths and kept my sister in a cabin for days?"

I nod, sitting up in the bed. I don't care how much pain I'm in, I'll stand by what I did.

"Let's rephrase that," Romeo says coolly. "He's the motherfucker who obeyed his Don's commands to the letter. If you have a problem with any of that, *I'm* the one who you have an issue with, not him. You got that?"

But no, I'll take full blame. I stare Sergio right in the eye. Until all of this went down, we were fellow brothers-in-arms.

"I am. And yeah, I obeyed my Don's orders. I also fully interrogated your sister and would bet my life that she's innocent of all claims against her."

Sergio's gaze softens. I watch as his shoulders sag and he lets out an audible breath. "She is?" he whispers, his voice hoarse.

All this time, I've made him into a monster. I knew that he had a role to fulfill, and I knew that he'd kill Vivia if given the chance. But I see it now. He's as much a victim of his family's rules and regulations as any of them. He's so relieved she's innocent, he looks as if he might cry.

"I've got more to tell you, too," I say. I look to Rome. "You sure he's unarmed?"

I don't trust him.

Romeo frowns, stands, and snaps his fingers to Sergio to come to him. Sergio grunts but obeys. He has to on Romeo's turf. Romeo quickly frisks him, produces a short blade, shakes his head, and pockets it.

"Go on," he says. He fully expected Sergio to keep at least one on him.

"Your sister was with a guy by the name of Gray Mullet who used her to get at Marialena. We don't know whose payroll he was on, but she knew nothing about the attempted murder."

He nods, warily. He knows I have something else to tell him.

"And furthermore," I continue, holding his gaze. "Once I knew she was innocent... I took further steps to protect her."

"From who?" he snaps, his eyes flashing at me.

I push myself to sitting on the bed, ready to brace myself for an attack. I'm not going down without a fight.

"From *all of you*. From the rules she was bound by. I took her in that cabin. I claimed her as my own. I did everything in my power to put a baby in her. Your sister is mine, Sergio Montavio. And if we find her, we're having a wedding." I look to Romeo. "Whoever came after Marialena wants to prevent the union of the Rossis and Montavios. Well guess what, assholes. I just did the opposite."

Sergio blinks in surprise. "You fucked my sister," he repeats.

"I did," I reply unapologetically.

Orlando's low laugh fills the room. Romeo curses in Italian. Sergio stares at me as if he doesn't know what to do with me.

"You knock her up?" he asks.

"Not sure," I tell him honestly. "But I sure as hell plan on it if I haven't yet."

He looks to Romeo. "Can you believe the balls on this guy?"

Orlando laughs louder. "Why the fuck you think we recruited him?"

"You fucked my sister," Sergio says.

"No, brother. I fucked my future wife. Now you guys get me out of this goddamn bed so I can find her."

I push up, ignoring the pain that shoots through my body like liquid poison. Every goddamn cell of mine aches with pain. I don't fucking care. I want Vivia back. "I know I didn't get your permission. I know I did this backward. But I don't fucking care, Sergio. I made her mine because the sooner we join our two families, the better."

I don't know if she'll agree to go with me. If she's escaped to her freedom, I might never be able to bring her back, and I won't bring her here against her will. But if I find her…

Sergio opens his mouth then clamps it shut as if he doesn't know how to respond. I get it, I just dropped a few truth bombs on him.

A knock sounds at the door.

"Not now!" Romeo shouts.

"It's important." A woman's voice. My heart does a quick flip then settles. It isn't her. It couldn't be.

Romeo looks to Orlando and Sergio. Sergio nods. "Go on," he says. "Maybe it's the Easter Bunny. Wouldn't be surprised about anything at this point."

"Fine." Romeo sighs. "Come in."

Marialena enters the room holding three guns in her hands.

"Jesus, woman, put 'em down," Romeo growls.

"Those are mine!" Sergio takes a step toward her.

"Lena," Orlando growls. "This is not a good time."

"They were just sitting in the hall like a mob guy lost and found," she says with a shrug. "What's a girl to do?"

She makes like she's going to throw them to Sergio and all of the guys duck for cover. Her musical giggle fills the room. "Gotcha!"

"Oh my God," Orlando tells Romeo. "Thought you were sending her to Tuscany?"

"She talked me out of it but now I'm thinking…"

Marialena looks at me and clears her throat. "I'm sorry, I had to see Dario! I heard he was seriously fucked up."

Romeo growls at her. He hates when she swears. She hates when he tells her what to do.

"I was fucked up but I'm better."

"Good! Mama sent a message. She said all of you leave Dario to rest and go downstairs, Nonna's just pulled dinner out of the oven."

My stomach growls. I would eat literally anything Nonna made right now.

Orlando stretches. "Let's go. Sergio, you can interrogate the shit out of him later or whatever the fuck you wanna do."

"Bring me some food, brother?"

"You got it."

They leave. Marialena smiles and waits until the door shuts before she comes to my side of the bed and sits down in the chair Romeo just vacated. She talks in a low voice as she points out the window.

"Just look out the window," she whispers. "It's high tide, would you look at that."

I flick my gaze to the window, then back to her. She doesn't want anyone to overhear us. Fair enough.

She reaches into her bra and tugs out a little square of paper, stands and stretches. The paper flutters from her hand onto the bed beside me.

"I brought your clothes to be cleaned and found that," she says. "You're welcome." She turns to leave. "Oh, I was eavesdropping at the door, and I think you're brave and I hope we find Vivia because she deserves someone like you. I never thought she would actually try to kill me. She didn't even like taking my game pieces when we played checkers. Bye!"

She nearly runs out of the room and shuts the door behind her. She's a hot fucking ticket. I reach for the little square of paper.

It's a hasty note written on paper we used to keep score at the cabin. A lump forms in my throat. I spoke up to Sergio right now on the off chance that we find her, but more importantly to protect her if he does and I'm not there.

A part of me knows that loving her… if I really, truly love her… means letting her go. She doesn't deserve a life of misery and incarceration. She deserves her freedom.

I open the paper and read the words.

I HAVE TO GO.

I have no time to tell you any more than this...

I love you.

I CLOSE my eyes as the heat of emotion overwhelms me. When I open them again, my cheeks feel wet. I touch them, incredulously. I don't *cry*.

But God…

I didn't imagine it then. She left, because it was her time, and she may never come back. Finding one person in a sea of people is like finding a needle in a haystack, even with all the resources we have.

And I won't ever find another woman like her.

The door opens and Orlando comes in bearing a huge platter of food for me. The scent of Nonna's beef braciola fills the room and my mouth waters. It's a hearty, homestyle Italian dish, thin slices of beef with a savory sauce slow cooked and infused with wine. She usually doesn't make it unless it's cold outside, but she knows it's my favorite. It is, of course, served with a generous portion of Nonna's homemade pasta, wilted greens, and hearty slices of Mama's homemade bread. God, I've missed being here.

"I don't have to eat in bed like an invalid," I tell him. I want to get downstairs. I want to see all of them. I want to be at home.

"Tonight, you do," he says softly. "The doctor said you're in bed until he gives you permission to get out, but more importantly…" he clears his throat. "You've got shit to tell me."

I sit back on the sea of pillows, reach for a napkin, and nestle the tray on my lap.

And I tell him everything.

CHAPTER SEVENTEEN

Dario

THE DAYS PASS SO SLOWLY, it feels as if every minute drags its feet with dread.

I miss waking up beside her.

I miss the soft feel of her breath on my back when I sleep, and the way she snuggles up to me when she wakes.

I miss kissing her, holding her, and every damn way we touched each other.

I miss her wit and her smile, her generous laughter and simple honesty. The way she screamed when a bug skittered past her and the way she looked at me like I was her knight in shining armor when I rescued her.

The way she felt in my arms when I lifted her into the water, and the way she furrowed her brow when she was deciding on her next poker move. Vivia Montavio is the only woman I've ever loved, and being without her feels as if a part of my body is severed.

"You're mourning like your fuckin' dog died," Mario says three days after I've come home to The Castle. The youngest of the Rossi brothers, Mario's the most happy-go-lucky of the lot. "I would've thought you'd be happy to be home. I mean, the cabin's fun for a bachelor party, but—"

I give him a withering look. He blinks, then his eyebrows shoot upward and he stops. "Ooooh," he says, backing away. "So it's like that, is it?"

I turn away with a sigh. He married his Gloria but only after she was his captive as punishment. He's no stranger to how things sometimes work, how all's fair in love and war.

I quickly get my emotions under control so no one else sees. I trust Mario, though, and I haven't hidden my feelings for Vivia. Granted, my purpose was for a reason, but my feelings for her aren't a secret.

My phone beeps at the same time Mario's does. I glance down at the screen.

Romeo: *Shoot out. All men at The Castle report to the Great Hall immediately.*

Mario sets his jaw and turns to face me. I look at him and we stand in solidarity. I don't know any more about what this means than he does, but we had no warning of an impending attack. Wouldn't be surprised if this had something to do with the revelation that I wasn't killed in that car crash like others were led to believe.

And if people now know that I'm alive... they'll know that Vivia is, too.

So I drag my ass out of the pity party and focus on my job. It's all I can do now. Vivia is gone. I'm here, alone, and thankful I didn't lose my job or worse, my life, because I lost her.

The sound of people running fills The Castle as the men of the Rossi family join us. The kitchen door flies open and Mama tosses a hand towel over her shoulder.

"Who, Dario? Where? What's happening?"

"I don't know," I tell her honestly.

Romeo enters the Great Hall, dressed like usual in a suit and tie. His brother Tavi follows him, as well as fellow mob brother Santo. More of our men encircle us and we all look to Romeo.

"Orlando got caught in his restaurant," Romeo says with a look of grim determination. "Says they're heading this way."

My blood runs cold. "Is he okay?"

Romeo's jaw tightens. "He's on his way here."

"Did he say who it was?"

He shakes his head. "Doesn't fuckin' know who it was, just said they ambushed him and attacked. His bodyguards threw down for him. One gave his life."

Silence falls over us for a brief moment before Santo speaks up.

"You say they're coming here?"

He nods. "Orlando was sure of it. Said they came after him because they had footage of him rescuing Vivia and Dario."

Motherfucker.

"Who are you sending?" Mario asks.

Romeo shakes his head. "No use sending you to Boston, not after this happened. You guys stay here. We batten down these hatches and prepare for an attack."

I stand up straighter and remove my gun from its holster.

Vivia... where are you?

If they know that she's alive... she's in more danger now than ever.

She's gone, I tell myself. I hope for her sake she's far away, so far away that no one will ever be able to touch her or hurt her ever again. I ignore the rush of pain that stabs me at the thought, and focus.

Nearly silent, we all prepare. Reinforced metal bars on the windows go up. About a month ago, Romeo installed a privacy gate at the entrance after we'd been under attack. He says he feels safer with them up now that there are babies we have to protect.

The front door opens and Orlando strides in, looking ready to kill.

I watch as the large, wrought iron gate clicks into place and armed guards take their places. The more I watch, the angrier I grow. I scowl out the window and turn to Romeo.

"So we hide. Wait to be ambushed." I clench my teeth and remind myself that I'm talking to my Don and disrespect isn't tolerated. I want to grab him by the shirt and shake him until his teeth rattle.

Vivia's out there.

Romeo looks at me sharply. Guess I didn't hide that anger very well.

"No. We don't *hide*," he says, his own voice tight. "We protect the women and children and our home when we're attacked. What would you have us do instead, brother?"

"Keep your guard at the gate," I tell him. "Keep those security measures in place. Then you take your inner circle, your best gunmen, the bravest men you have and you fucking *ride out to meet them.* Meet them head on. Don't even let them come within shooting distance of this fucking *fortress.*"

Mario slow claps from behind me, meeting Romeo's gaze and not looking at me at all. Tavi blows out a breath and threads his fingers through his hair. He's got a family of his own here. Santo jerks his chin at me.

"He's right. And you know he's a good shot, Rome."

"Good shot?" Orlando mutters. "Best fuckin' shot we've got."

Romeo spins around and faces me. "You want to leave here because you think Vivia's out there."

"I don't think, brother," I say quietly. "Is she here? No. Then I *know* she's out there somewhere."

"Would you think differently if she *were* here?" he asks.

I think it over and shake my head. "No. No, I would not. I would want to ride out and ambush them. I wouldn't want them to get anywhere near The Castle so I don't have to worry about so much as a stray bullet whizzing by these walls or my kids or my wife seeing something they don't need to see."

"And if we head out, miss our mark, and they circumvent and come here? We've left our home unprotected."

"We *do not* miss our mark."

Romeo's eyebrows shoot upward and he nods slowly.

"Pull a team," he says to Orlando. "Take Dario in the lead. Sergio. Take our best guards and most efficient defense, so Santo and Mario go, too. Orlando, you stay here and call in what you hear to us."

Orlando's jaw tightens but he nods.

"Someone's gotta stay here," Romeo explains quietly, but I know him better than that. He's making Sergio leave and keeping Orlando here in case Vivia's got anything to do with this attack. If she does, he doesn't trust Sergio.

Adrenaline pumps through my veins when I gear up to go out. "Where are they?" There are a few routes someone could take to get to The Castle in Gloucester from Orlando's North End business.

"Not sure."

"Let's start there." I jerk my chin at Mario. "You could probably find them in seconds."

He shrugs. "A minute, anyway."

"Go. Do it," Romeo snaps. Mario runs to the office at the back of the main floor where he keeps his surveillance equipment and gear. We know we need to at least head south, and if Orlando's already made it back from the restaurant, they're not far behind him.

But I can't keep my mind off of her.

Vivia... where is Vivia?

Are you alright?

Are you safe?

I tell myself she left to save herself. It was the only choice she had. But it doesn't mean I don't think of her with every minute of the day that passes.

I may never see her again, and I have to be okay with that. I only had her for a short time. And in that space of time, she grew and sprouted wings, and flew away as she was meant to from the beginning.

Our phones all ding at the same time.

Mario: *located them. Three armored black SUVs ten minutes out.*

Another text follows of a picture of a map with a crudely drawn arrow. Fuck. That's more than I expected, and they're right up the street.

Who the hell *are* they?

I hear a soft chuckling sound beside me and look over to see Santo grinning. I always thought that motherfucker was a psychopath.

"Alright, dude, what the fuck's so funny?"

"They're coming at us with armored SUVs," he says, still laughing. "That particular model's easier to tip than just about any other car on wheels out there. Not only that, you have any fuckin' idea how much bigger *ours* are?"

I give him a curious look. Last I heard, Santo and Mario worked with race cars.

"Well maybe you should show us," Romeo says with forced patience. He looks like he wants to shake Santo, or maybe all of us.

Santo grins.

"With pleasure, boss." He winks at me and takes a remote out of his pocket. The next thing I know, I hear the grinding of metal. The garage doors beside the main entrance to The Castle are opening. Romeo opens the front door to get a better view and blows out a breath.

"I approved the budget on this. Knew you two were up to something but *shit*, Santo."

"Oh, he had a little help," Marialena says sweetly from the stairway. "Remember my friend Skylar?"

"The one whose brother runs a private detective agency."

"Mhm," she continues with a shit-eating grin. "He hooked them up."

"Hooked us up, and we went to town," Santo says. I look over Romeo's shoulder to see four heavy, death-defying armored trucks.

"A *little* harder to manage," Santo says. "They don't navigate the roads as easily as an SUV, but that's not why we got them. What do you get when you combine the strength and performance of a Hennessey VelociRaptor 600 with a bulletproof cocoon of protection?" His eyes shine with pride. "This baby right here."

"I'm driving!" Mario yells behind me.

"I got one, too," I say.

"And me," Santo says with a scowl.

"And me," Sergio says, claiming the last one.

"I'm riding with Dario," Romeo says.

We sprint to the trucks while Santo gives us the dummy's guide to shooting from one of these babies.

"Don't try to duck a shot. Trust that you're protected, cocooned. They won't get you. The most important thing to do is to focus on your aim, not your location or where *they're* aiming. Pretend like you're invisible and there's nothing but air between you and your target."

"Bring one of them in alive," Romeo growls. "You kill 'em all, we got no one left to interrogate."

I shut the door and get my gun ready. Feels good to be behind the wheel of a machine like this, and I don't fucking care that Romeo's beside me. He's one of the best shots in our company.

"Follow Santo," Romeo says, pointing his pistol at the wheels of Santo's ride going left. "As soon as you see them, tell me. I'll shoot."

"Why'd you come with me, boss?"

He grunts. "Because *you're* the one they're after, brother."

Jesus.

True, though.

"We're less than a minute out," Romeo says. "Anything else you need to tell me?" he asks quietly.

I shake my head. "No, I've told you everything."

He gives me the side-eye. "Everything?"

I swallow. "Yeah."

But it's a lie. Nothing I'd get punished for, though. I did tell him everything he needs to know. That I took her. I made her mine and that if I had the chance, I'd make her my wife.

But I didn't tell him how sweet she looks when she sleeps, her hands tucked under her chin. The way her hand felt in mine when I held it. How she melted into me when I dominated her. The way her voice grew soft and resonant when I told her how beautiful she was. Or how the slow, sweet smile spread across her face and she became putty in my hands when I praised her.

"You love her," he says with surprise. "Don't you? This isn't just about your role, or increasing your rank, or anything like that at all, is it?"

I shake my head and say earnestly, "It isn't. And yeah, I do."

He nods slowly, but then quickly draws his pistol to shoot. "There they are."

We're at the end of the road that leads to The Castle. With the four of us lined up like this, it's a goddamn fortress for them to have to get past. But I won't sit here and build a wall and wait.

"Dario," Romeo begins, but I ignore him. I crank the engine and roll in the front. Weapon drawn, I wish this was a real tank with real guns that would destroy the shit out of these motherfuckers. I know they're the ones that came after Vivia and me, and today they hurt Orlando.

They're coming at full speed toward us. The others pull back, but I hear gunfire all around me. Romeo shoots, and one car spins wildly out, the tire shredded. He shoots again, this time hitting the windshield but the armored glass only fractures and doesn't break. Again, and again, and again he strikes but he needs more lead. It isn't enough.

They came after Vivia.

I wrap my fingers around my M134 Minigun, a sweet, handheld machine gun designed for helicopters and armored vehicles.

"Take the wheel," I tell Romeo.

He sees what I'm holding, leans over and takes the wheel, slides into the driver's seat and starts to drive. I kneel on the leather seat beside him, take aim, and let loose a barrage of bullets toward the oncoming vehicles. Wheels explode. Even the armored glass splinters and shatters, and I don't let up. I shoot at the driver. Glass fragments into shards, blood splatters the window. Without a driver, the car spins wildly out, and a second crashes into it.

And still, I shoot. The bullets pump out, too many to count, a volley of fierce, impenetrable metal that does damage in a fraction of a second. One car's driver is gone. A second. A third spins wildly out and slumps over the seat.

"Wait! Jesus, we need someone alive to interrogate!" Romeo screams, but I've already pulled the trigger. I hit my target. Santo and the others quickly and efficiently round up the others.

"You should've saved one, brother," Romeo says quietly. "I'd have let you have him."

"Got one survivor!" Santo screams. He pulls the truck over and launches himself out of it.

"Santo, no!" I yell, but he's already gone. Gunshots pepper the air around us, making the lone survivor an easy target. Santo ducks, darts, then throws himself into the car. He comes out a second later with someone bleeding from the head. He's caught in a headlock.

"They've got your girl," the guy yells at me. I recognize him from the wharf. "Don't kill me and I'll tell you where she is."

"He's lying!"

A woman's voice.

A voice I know all too well.

I freeze. Santo holds tight, but the rest of us spin to look at the source of the voice.

Her hair is shorter, and she's dressed from top to bottom in sleek black leather, but I'd know those eyes and that defiant little chin anywhere.

Vivia.

"I'm right here," she says in a voice as clear as day. "They don't have me. And you don't need him to tell you who they are. I'll tell you everything. I don't care what you do to me but hear me out."

Santo pushes him to his knees. No need to interrogate him. I give him a nod to pull the trigger.

She sees me. Her jaw drops. I watch as her eyes soften, then she runs to me, just as Sergio cocks his gun.

CHAPTER EIGHTEEN

Vivia

HE'S HERE. *He's here.*

After all I've been through, after giving him up as lost forever, after *everything*, he's here.

I knew they'd come to The Castle, but I had no time to warn anyone and didn't think they'd listen to me if I did. I had no time to do anything but jump into my own car, a hijacked, stolen Yaris I swiped from a lot just south of here, and try to head them off.

Them being the group I targeted and have hunted for days.

But I don't think of them. I don't think of anything but Dario. He stares at me like I've come back from the dead, and when I turn to him, he does something I'll never forget for the rest of my life. He opens his arms.

So I run. My throat is tight, and my eyes burn, and even though I run as fast as I can, the ground between us swallowed up by my steps, it seems to take too long. When I reach him, I collapse against him. He catches me. He lifts me in his arms, his hands on my ass hiking me to his chest. My legs wrap around him, and I tuck my head into his shoulder. But the blissful reunion lasts only seconds before he pivots, spins, and falls to one knee.

I gasp in surprise as he lowers me to the ground behind one of the trucks and releases me. He lets me go. I blink, only to see him catapult himself forward. He crashes to the ground with Sergio beneath him, lifts his fist and slams it into my brother's jaw. His head snaps back and blood splashes across his face. Again, Dario punches and again, I flinch at the brutal slam of his fist against Sergio's jaw.

"How dare you pull a fucking gun on her," Dario growls, angrier than I've ever seen him. "How fucking dare you."

He lifts Sergio by the shoulders and slams him bodily on the concrete. I scream out loud and cover my face.

"Dario!" my cousin Romeo screams. "You'll kill him, brother."

Dario's fist is raised as if to strike again. He's vibrating with anger and brutality, fully unleashed. I've never seen my brother look so scared in his life. It's unnerving.

Dario pulls away with reluctance. He gives Sergio a look that dares him to make another move, while he yanks him to his feet and tugs his hands behind his back.

"We talked about her, didn't we?"

Sergio spits blood on the ground. "We did."

"I told you she's my future wife."

Someone's poured ice down my back. I stand, frozen in place.

His future wife?

Several things happen at once. Romeo unceremoniously grabs Sergio and jerks his chin at Santo. Together they lift, walk, and plunk Sergio into one of the huge, armored vehicles they were driving and lock the door. Romeo barks out orders for everyone but Dario to get rid of the bodies, then jerks his chin at Mario. "Any of these salvageable?"

Mario nods and jerks his head at the one closest to me. "The one near Vivia."

"Dario, take Vivia home. Castle." Romeo turns to me, sees something that makes his face soften, then drops to one knee. When he speaks, it's like he's talking to a small child he's trying to convince to take the meds she doesn't like. "You alright, kiddo?"

I nod, still shell shocked. "Dario's gonna take you home, Vivia. You two have some catching up to do. I'll give you that time. Then when you've told him everything it's time you tell *us* what you know. You get that?"

I nod again, thankful for his compassion right now. I feel like I'm coming apart. I can't now, though. Not after all I've survived and endured.

Dario's taking you home.

Home.

Home would be The Castle then.

Dario beat up Sergio.

Sergio's still mad at me.

I wonder what will happen when I tell them everything I've found. I'm fully prepared to be exiled. I'm honestly halfway there already.

The ride back to The Castle feels surreal. Dario reaches for my knee and gives me a squeeze, then rests his hand on my leg as if to remind me that I'm really here.

"I'm sorry," I whisper. "I hope when I tell you everything, you'll understand."

He lifts my hand and brings it to his lips, then kisses the palm and closes my fingers around it as if to remind me to hold his kiss in my hand and not to let it go.

"You don't need to. You did what you had to, and there's nothing to apologize for."

"I made sure you were safe before I left, I promise I did."

"Of course you did, baby," he says gently, kneading my knee beneath his strong, warm hand. "And thank you for that. It's because of you I'm still here."

I want to cry, but I swallow the need and only stroke the top of his hand on my leg. We ride like that back to The Castle.

"I found out who was after us. Who still is. I found the group that tried to attack Marialena and used me as the fall guy."

He nods. "I thought you would."

I have to ask him. I have to know. "Did you think I left you?" I ask quietly.

He swallows, and when he answers, his voice is gentle but firm. "I hoped you did."

My heart sinks. "You hoped I did?" I whisper. We aren't far from The Castle. I won't get the time alone with him that I crave. I still have to prove my innocence.

"I wanted you to have your freedom, Vivia. I didn't want you to have to stay with me, knowing what that might cost you."

"Oh." My voice is a whisper. I swallow hard. "Thank you."

He only nods. "Will what you have to tell us exonerate you?"

I nod. "It will."

My heart feels light again as hope blooms. I had to give up hope that we'd be united after everything we've been through, and it feels so damn good to be with him. I want to kiss him. I want him to hold me. I want to tell him everything I've done since I left and hear him tell me how proud he is. I want to condense the past few days into seconds so we can avoid the hard talk and skip right along to where we unite.

Without a word, he squeezes my hand again, then threads his fingers through mine and holds me like that as we pull up to The Castle. It's then that I look down and actually realize we're basically driving a tank.

"Uh… Dario? What are you *driving*?"

He grins, making my heart flip-flop in my chest. I missed that grin. A rare shining light amidst the darkness. He doesn't always smile or grin or give me any more than that lopsided upturn of his lips, but when he does, I feel like I come *alive*. Like I have purpose and that purpose is to keep that smile on his face.

"Some kinda armored truck the guys fixed up. Santo and Mario pulled their magic. You like it?"

"Like it?" I ask, dragging a reverent hand across the supple leather seat. "I'd… do dirty things in this truck if you asked me to."

His low, responding growl tells me he likes that answer very much.

"I've got a lot to tell you," I say as he pulls the huge truck into the garage beside the others. "But… before I do…"

I snap my seat belt open, and I'm in his lap straddling him before he can stop me. I frame his face between my hands. Tears fill my eyes as I look at him, at his handsome, rugged, honest face before I bend to kiss him.

When my lips meet his, I stifle a sob that rises in my throat. I've missed him so badly. I didn't know if I'd ever see him again, but I never gave up hope. Dario is mine. He belongs to me. He saved me when I was given up for lost, when my own family had turned their backs on me. And I won't ever let him forget what he's done for me.

I thread my fingers through his hair and moan into his mouth when his tongue licks mine and his teeth bite my lips. His hands span my ass and squeeze, pulling me closer, claiming me, and I'm instantly wet. He pulls away with reluctance.

"Fuck I missed you, baby," he says, giving me another, chaste kiss on the cheek. "Get your ass inside and tell them what they need to know so I can have you all to myself."

I give myself half a second to rest my head on his shoulder and nod. I have a job to do, but he will be next to me while I do it.

I slide off his lap with such reluctance I want to cry, but he eases the separation with his hand in mine. A firm squeeze reminds me that I'm not alone. I square my shoulders and head inside.

"Vivia!" I look up to see Aunt Tosca in the entrance. Her eyes light up and she opens her arms. I look to Dario. I expected that the Rossis would still think me a traitor. He only nods and smiles at me, gesturing for me to go see her.

"I heard what happened," she whispers in my ear while giving me a huge hug. "I never thought you were responsible for what they said you were. Never."

"Ah, cousin!" Marialena is on the steps. When she sees me, she smiles and gives me a tentative wave, as if waiting to see if I'll still want to say hello. She may also feel nervous given what she was told I tried to do to her, but Marialena and I have always been so close.

I pull away from Aunt Tosca and feel Dario's presence at my back. It will be okay. I know it will. We've come through the worst of it, now everything will be alright.

"Marialena." My voice is choked and cracks on the last syllable. "I—I didn't— I swear to you, I never—" I can't even get the words out before she envelops me in a hug and Aunt Tosca joins us.

"Our enemies may try to use us against each other," Tosca says, her eyes shining with tears. "And these men of ours might think they know better than we do sometimes, but *none* of them know how we stick together. None of them."

I feel the warmth in their embrace and let myself bask in the glow of forgiveness for a sin I never committed. "Thank you," is all I can say.

"Vivia." I hear Romeo's stern, no-nonsense voice from behind me. "I'd like you to come to the war room with us, please."

"Oh no you do not," Marialena says, glaring at him. She wags a well-manicured nail in his direction. "We know what you all do in that room and how *easy* it is for you to just *slip on down* to the dungeon if you feel it's necessary. Uh uh, brother. Anything she has to say to you she can say to us!"

Dario clears his throat. I look from him to Romeo to Marialena.

"Not true, Marialena," Dario says a bit more gently than Romeo. "We have business to discuss you're not included in. The intel Vivia will give us will be confined only to the inner sanctum. It isn't you we're excluding, but honestly everyone outside the smallest of the inner circle for the sake of all."

She opens her mouth to protest again when Romeo clears his throat. "That's enough. We need to have a talk, and soon, about your place in this family."

Here we go again with the high-handed bossiness. I'm tempted to roll my eyes but know better.

Marialena blanches. She's the only one left of the single women in both families, and we all know what that means. It's only a matter of time before she'll be married off in an arranged marriage. I recoil at the thought.

"What is that supposed to mean?" she whispers.

"Come, Lena," Aunt Tosca says, reaching for her. "Come help me get the food ready."

"Mama!" Marialena protests. "What is he—"

Aunt Tosca takes her more firmly by the arm. "Come, please."

I look to Dario, whose face is set in grim lines, his lips thinned. He puts his hand to my elbow and leads me past the entryway toward the back of The Castle.

I haven't been here in years, but I remember every room as if it were yesterday. It isn't often someone gets to play in a real, live castle, and this home is the stuff of dreams, with the courtyard and indoor pool, large Great Hall, library, pantry, and the pavilion overlooking the ocean. All food is made in the enormous kitchen by Aunt Tosca and Nonna, and we often all eat together, buffet-style, in the dining room, where there's an actual wall made of the Rossi family wine. My own mama used to scoff at that and say they were too rich to know what to do with themselves, but she is one to talk.

It still feels the same, still smells the same even, only now that I'm grown, it feels a bit... smaller.

When we arrive in the war room, I freeze in the doorway. There's only one person who's arrived ahead of us: Sergio.

"Go on," Dario says, his eyes fixed on Sergio. In my ear he whispers, "I won't let him hurt you." Still holding a paper towel to his bloodied lip, Sergio glares at me and Dario.

"Come in. Let's talk," he says. "I promise I won't hurt you. But you have some explaining to do, sister."

I nod and swallow hard. "I know I do. And I'll explain everything, I promise."

Oh, how I long to be forgiven by my family. And a part of me wishes I didn't care, that I could tell them to fuck off and not be bothered about it ever again. But when you're raised in a family as close-knit as mine, that's a lot easier said than done.

"I'll hold you to that promise," Sergio says. He looks at Dario again, then looks away. Footsteps approach outside, but he doesn't care. "So she's yours? You've made her yours? You've claimed her, brother?"

"I have."

"Without asking me."

"You wouldn't have given me your permission."

Sergio nods, then grins. "I absolutely would not have. But now you've forced my hand, haven't you?"

Dario blows out a breath, and shakes his head. "You left me no choice, brother."

Sergio's face is an unreadable mask as Romeo enters the war room followed by Mario, Santo, Orlando, Tavi, and Mario's wife Gloria.

"Timeo and Ricco can't be here, but they want to be conferenced in," Sergio says. I feel my body tighten. Timeo and Ricco are my other brothers, though Timeo has always been close with me, and Ricco is so preoccupied with his own family he's never given me shit about things like Sergio.

"Fair," Romeo says with a nod. "Since what Vivia will tell us impacts all of us." Romeo turns to me. "Is that right?"

I nod.

Romeo pulls out an enormous tablet and flicks a few buttons. "Here," he says to Sergio. "But before you call them, I want you to promise us that there will be no violence. No violence against one another again, Sergio. You're in my territory now. Are we clear?"

Sergio nods. "If what Dario tells us about Vivia is true, I have no need." He speaks with the conviction of a cold-blooded killer. I hate that he's assumed the worst of me. I want to be right again with him. Even though we've never been close, the chasm between us makes me ache inside.

He calls Timeo and Ricco, who are sitting together somewhere in Italy. I can tell by the vivid landscape behind them, the vineyard and walkway my family frequented when I was a child.

Timeo's brows rise when he sees me. Ricco waves. "Vivia. You're there, and you're in one piece. I can only assume what we thought about you isn't true, then?"

I give him a forced smile. "Right. I'm glad at least one of you has the good sense to make that assumption, but I thank you just the same."

Timeo chokes on his sip of wine and Sergio goes rigid in front of the tablet. Dario chuckles softly beside me.

Timeo leans in, his eyes earnest. "Are you alright, Vivia?" His voice hardens. "Did anyone hurt you?"

"I'm alright," I tell him. "And yes, many people have hurt me." I look involuntarily at Sergio who doesn't flinch or even blink.

Timeo's jaw tightens. "Give us their names, little sister."

I clear my throat. "Unless I'm mistaken, Timeo, that's why we're all here tonight. But I will say for the record that after my initial... questioning, Dario believed me. He kept me safe and protected me and made sure that no one hurt us."

Orlando smiles. Romeo nods. My brothers listen intently.

"We'll remember that, Dario," Timeo says to him. Dario responds by draping a casual arm over my shoulders, and my heart squeezes at the silent declaration.

I'm shaking. I have so much to tell them I hardly know where to begin, but I know that the truth starts here, with me, that I owe it to them. That none of this gets any better until the truth is out.

I clear my throat. "I'm going to start at the beginning."

Dario squeezes my shoulder. Mario opens up a tablet and turns to a fresh page, as if taking notes. His monitors blink and buzz behind him as he prepares to do his job. Orlando sits up straighter. Tavi's eyes are straight on me, as are Santo's.

"Several months ago, I had an affair with Gray Mullet. I did it behind your backs. I blackmailed and bribed my bodyguards so they wouldn't rat me out."

"Names," Sergio grinds out. "Timeo, find their names."

"Already on it," Mario says. "Both were recently killed."

My heart tightens. I didn't know that. I have to continue.

"I didn't know that Gray was involved with a fledgling group, headed by José Sanchez of Columbia. I found this out two days ago by digging through transactions they made with Gray. They aren't organized yet. They've pulled members together, united as forces in the Columbian Army. They began as a quasi-military group but have gone on to form a rough mob of sorts. They want a foothold here in New England."

"Okay, so... no offense or anything, Vivia?" Timeo says gently. "But you're... a mafia princess. Where did you get all that information? How did you find this out?"

I swallow the lump in my throat and force my voice to stay strong. "I had to. Dario put his life on the line for me. You all gave me up for dead. The only reason I left Dario to go find out what I needed to know was because it was so important for me to clear my name." I sigh before I draw in another deep breath. "And come back to Dario. So I left, and when I left, I thought about what Gray had access to. My phone. A bank account. So, I had to do whatever investigation I could with the limited time and resources I had."

I pull out a notebook and a cell phone. "I hacked into Gray's bank account and traced payments made from his account. I emptied my bank account and used cash to bribe people at the wharf. They were happy to talk for money. I cut off my hair and tried to keep my identity secret, which didn't prove to be that hard. " My voice wobbles. "The first payment hit his account the day after we had our first date."

"You went back to the wharf where they took you," Gloria says quietly, as if in awe of my boldness. I'm not surprised at all. No one's ever given me much credit for anything.

"And you did this behind our backs," Sergio clarifies. "The dating. This...man."

"Obviously." I don't bother to frame my words politely. A muscle clenches in Sergio's jaw, and Dario straightens beside me. Sergio sits back.

"You slept with him," Timeo says quietly.

I nod. "I did. But for crying out loud, guys, there's a lot more to this story than my deflowering, so may I continue?"

My brothers and cousins listen in silence. "I didn't know Gray was involved with them. He paid attention to me. I thought I loved him. He used me. Asked for information about the Rossis, which should've been a warning to me, but I— I thought that it was sort of a celebrity thing, like he looked up to you guys and wanted to know what it was like being related." I feel sheepish telling them, but it's all the truth. "Like you're all celebrities or something. I mean, people in school or work would ask questions all the time."

"Of course they do," Mario says with a smug grin. Gloria smacks him.

"I remembered that Dario said these people had money. He and Orlando thought they were trying to prevent the union of our family, the Montavios and yours, the Rossis. You all know that if we join forces and align ourselves with one another, we'll be unstoppable. The most powerful organized crime family in the entire United States, if not the world."

Sergio and Romeo look at each other and don't respond, but Dario squeezes my shoulder again. We all know it to be true.

"Gray had us meet at a club in Boston. The very same one where Gloria and Mario caught us the night they took me into custody. I didn't think much of it. I thought it was only a meeting place, but later I began thinking that it was more than that. So much more, because how would a group of out-of-state men even know a secret club like that existed? So I investigated."

"When was that?" Dario asks me.

"Two nights ago."

"You went into that club alone," he says, his voice holding a dangerous tone.

"I had to."

"Footage of the club," Mario says, and all eyes go to his screen. I'm pretty confident he's distracting them for me. Dario leans in and whispers in my ear, "Don't you ever, *ever*, do anything like that again. It was way too dangerous for you to go in there alone. You'll answer to me for that."

A responding tingle vibrates through my body at the promise of a punishment from him. I swallow hard and pretend he hasn't just lit my body on fire.

"Go on," Romeo says.

"I asked around in the club and got some answers. Not only is that group dangerous and threatening, I also have it on good authority that their purpose here is to establish a new crime ring from Boston to Maine, for the direct purposes of drug trafficking and money laundering."

"Right," Orlando says tightly. "Got it."

"So I did even more investigating. Found their headquarters on the wharf. Those boats were transporting more drugs than you can even imagine. And then I knew, I put it all together. They came after me and Gray because they knew if they framed me for attempting to assassinate Marialena I'd be ostracized from my family, and that no one would be looking beyond me as the target. And that if *I* were found guilty of attempting murder, there would be no way our two families would unite and strengthen."

Santo whistles. Tavi nods his head. Mario shakes his from side to side.

"Makes sense."

"Evidence?" Sergio asks sternly.

I nod and pull out my phone. I swipe it on and show the pictures, the documents, the transfers, the guilty faces of those who might've made an attempt on all our lives.

"How many survivors?" Romeo grinds out. Then, for an explanation, he turns to Sergio.

Sergio's counting. "None from today's attack. Not sure if there are any at the wharf." We had one survivor until we left him with Santo. Now there are none.

Romeo makes a phone call. "We'll know soon. Anything more, Vivia?"

I give him every boring, mundane detail that seemed irrelevant but now looks so clear after all that's happened. I show him pictures and names, reveal everything I know.

"Excellent," Romeo says with a smile, then smiles at Gloria. "She should work with you."

Gloria grins at me. "She could. And I apologize I suspected you were guilty, Vivia. That's eaten me up terribly, knowing everything you went through. And I pointed the finger at you."

"But they set you up," I say, instantly forgiving her. She smiles softly at me, accepting my forgiveness. Aunt Tosca is right. We women have to stick together.

"Anything else?" Romeo asks.

I shake my head, completely spent. "That's all I know," I whisper. "We still have some investigating to do but now we know the names and source, I think the rest will show."

Dario stands. "She's done her job. You promised her, Sergio. Now, give her to me as we discussed."

Everyone looks at Sergio. He nods and gives me a slow smile. "Go with Dario, Vivia." He turns to Romeo. "We marry them as soon as possible. We join forces and all this becomes obsolete."

Dario clears his throat. "You're forgetting something."

"What's that?" Sergio asks, but there's real fear in his eyes at Dario's formidable stature as he stands.

"You owe your sister an apology. That's my future wife you tried to hurt after I warned you not to. It's only out of respect for her and Romeo that I haven't slit your throat."

Well, that might not be the best way for in-laws to start a relationship, but…

Sergio nods and turns to me, the picture of repentance. "I'm sorry, Vivia. I truly am. I was convinced you were in the wrong and that you went behind my back to undermine our family. That you were trying to tear apart everything our family has built. Will you forgive me?"

I do. *I do.*

I give him a huge hug, my arms going around his shoulders and squeezing. "Don't hold your breath with me naming any of my children after you, but yes, I forgive you."

"Tomorrow, I'll call the priest," Romeo says, giving me a big smile. "Vivia, let's give Mama the news. We have some preparations to make."

CHAPTER NINETEEN

Vivia

THE REST of the meeting goes off without a hitch. Timeo and Ricco leave abruptly, because they're taking a red-eye flight home tonight to witness the wedding tomorrow. But before Ricco hangs up the call he leans in and says to Sergio, in front of everyone, "You have some work to do to make it up to her, and I won't let you forget that."

Sergio, to his credit, is the picture of repentance. "I won't forget," he says in front of everyone before he gives Dario the side-eye. "Pretty sure Dario will be on top of that anyway."

"The word is *grovel*, I believe," Dario says, rising and stretching his arms, as we disconnect the conference call with my brothers in Italy.

"And let the record show, Sergio, that one of the trademarks of true leadership is the ability to show humbleness. We do the work no one else wants to do, and the payoff is that we have more power and authority than others. But by the same token, our jobs require us to admit when we're wrong." Romeo scowls, lifting a stack of papers that are already straight before he tidies them even further. "Otherwise, we become nothing more than tyrants like our fathers before us."

Sergio nods. I love my cousin Romeo, who looks up at me before we leave. "Vivia, a word please before you go prepare for your wedding tomorrow." He holds a finger up to Dario. "And you. You both may have done this backward through no fault of your own, but we have traditions we uphold here. You two will sleep in separate quarters tonight." Dario opens his mouth to protest, but Romeo holds up a hand. "I'll give you some time together, but then you separate until you take your vows tomorrow." His face softens. "And when you do take your vows tomorrow, you'll relish being together again even more."

Dario grumbles and frowns, and if I didn't know any better, I think if I were Romeo I'd be taking an involuntary step back for cover, but Dario respects him.

"Got it," he says. "Will do."

"Wait outside for us, will you, Dario? It will only be a minute."

Dario nods as the room vacates. Soon, it's only me and Romeo left.

"Have a seat, little cousin," Romeo says with a soft smile. He looks older than the last time I saw him, his hair graying around his temples and his face lined with the weight of responsibility. I do as he says and sit. Though both Sergio and Romeo are heads of their respective groups, I know that Romeo is more powerful. He has a much larger family to lead, and the majority of the men in his family are married with children, which gives him a decided advantage.

Romeo strokes his chin while he looks thoughtfully at the wall behind me. "Are you alright, Vivia?" he asks. "You've gone straight from a traumatic experience to being wed. And even though that was bound to happen, and the only smart choice next is for us to join the Montavios and Rossis this way, I want to check on you."

I take a deep breath and let it out slowly. Am I okay? I can't remember the last time anyone asked me that. "I don't really know how to answer that." He doesn't push me or ask any more questions but has the decency to let me think before I speak. "I... it was hard. Running. Learning what I did about Gray. Somehow, I think I knew that it wasn't going to work out with him. That my brothers would find out."

"But you never thought it would work out quite the way it did," Romeo finishes.

I give a little tired laugh. "Yeah, you could say that."

He clears his throat. "Are you pregnant?"

I shrug. "There's a chance, but I can't deny or confirm that yet."

He nods again. "Fair. Things have happened rapidly, haven't they?"

"Yeah," I say on a sigh.

"I'm going to make you a proposition, Vivia. And there's no need to answer right away. Given everything that's happened, and since you'll be married to Dario, I think you two should stay here, right at The Castle, for the next year or two. While you've made amends with Sergio, that might be…"

"Uncomfortable?" I finish for him.

He nods. "Tavi and his wife are often in Tuscany, as are Santo and Rosa. Vittoria and I live here primarily, and Orlando and his family are here often as well, though lately he's been spending more time in the North End. Mama likes this castle filled with people, but as our families grow, we've sprouted…"

"I understand. Romeo, I'd love to live here."

He smiles. "Excellent. And I wasn't joking when I said you could work with Gloria. She was a police detective before she joined us, and there's none better. She could use an assistant."

"I'd like that."

"Good, then it's settled," he says, rising. He reaches for my hands before he pulls me in to kiss both cheeks. "Welcome home, cousin."

Dario's waiting for me outside. I can't wait to see him, even though I know I won't have the comforting warmth and weight of his body next to mine tonight. I agree with Romeo, that when we finally do have the benefit of being together tomorrow, it will only be that much sweeter.

That doesn't mean I don't reach for his hand and allow myself to feel that sense of protection in his rough, warm touch, or that I don't long to burrow myself against his chest and feel his arms around me, to drink in the firm strength of him and remind myself that I'm safe and secure in the shelter of his arms.

Either he longs for the same thing I do, or he knows how badly I want the assurance of his physical presence, because as soon as we're out of the war room, he tugs my hand and leads me down the narrow hallway past the pantry, past the dining room, and into the circular library at the furthest end of the estate.

The library hosts wall upon wall of leather-bound books, plush armchairs, and a fireplace. It's huge, with ladders that lead to shelves and thick, wall-to-wall lush carpet underfoot.

"I'm told when the Rossis were young they felt like kings and queens living in this place."

"I think some," I say softly, fingering the gilded edge of a book, "still do."

I love the sound of his throaty chuckle as he pulls me to him.

"Tell me how you really feel."

"Romeo is king of *this* castle, and he's invited me to stay here. After we've married, he thinks it's best we reside at The Castle for a while."

"Mmm," he says. "We discussed it briefly earlier and I'm in agreement."

"Oh, are you?" I ask teasingly as he bends and kisses my cheek.

"I am. I think if I were to be anywhere near Sergio I'd kick his ass, apology be damned, and that could make things a little complicated. I'm not the politest around assholes, so I'm not sure how I'd treat your mama. Maybe if I get laid a few dozen times, I'll soften up."

I curl my fingers around his warm, sturdy body and smile up at his face. His eyes are so intent they feel like lasers as I trace a finger along the rough stubble at his jaw. "I like to imagine I'm the only one who'll soften you up. And some day, our child."

"Our child?" he asks hopefully.

"Soon," I whisper, as I bend to kiss his cheek. But a part of me hopes it's a while yet before we have children. Though I know children are the Crown

Jewels in our families, after everything we've been through, I'd like some time to get myself together before I prepare to be a mama myself.

"Penny for your thoughts?" he whispers as he tugs a lock of my hair.

"I want to be a mother, Dario. And I can't wait to see you as a daddy. I know that's the expectation here, that as soon as we get married, which has to happen now… they'll want babies." It's way more than the standard expectation of children with regular families. With our families, it's almost mandatory. "I'm just not… ready yet. I mean I've hardly gotten used to the idea of even being your *wife*."

"I understand," he says, as he holds me. And I think that might be what I love best about him. He really does.

"Romeo wants us apart tonight," I whisper in his ear. "But that doesn't mean…"

I crave him so badly I feel like I'm in withdrawal. I want to feel him, touch him, wrap my arms around him and lay beneath him, feel the heavy weight of his body atop mine and the perfect fullness of him inside me.

"Say no more," he growls. I squeal as he lifts me straight in the air and into his arms, carrying me as if I weigh nothing at all. When we reach the furthest corner of the room, he lays me down on one of the huge sofas. "Stay right there."

I give him a wicked grin. "Yes, *sir*."

That earns me another groan that does wicked, wanton things to every nerve in my body. I shiver.

I watch as he pulls the shade on each window before he goes to the door and flicks the heavy metal lock. He takes out his phone and slides it onto the desk, then stalks over to me. We hold each other's eyes for a long moment. I arch my back in anticipation, and a crazy grin spreads across my face. There's a lightness in my chest as my pulse quickens. After everything we've been through…

My insides vibrate, my nerves are on fire.

"I love you," I whisper, surprising myself with the sudden need to make this declaration.

He kneels beside me, then over me, his huge body dwarfing mine and casting it into shadow. "And I love you," he whispers. "I'll never forget what you've done. I'll make it my life's work to make you happy, to give you everything you deserve and more. You're everything to me, Vivia. Everything."

I run a hand down his thick, muscled arm and back up again, memorizing the corded muscles while he holds himself over me and slides one giant hand under my ass and lifts me to him. My gaze is drawn to his lips and my breathing grows faster. "Kiss me," I whisper, my voice trembling in anticipation.

"Is that an order?" he asks in a husky whisper. If he had a tie, I'd grab it, but he's only wearing a stupid

T-shirt. I satisfy my need to drag him closer to me by running my palm over his chest, his pecs, then squeezing his forearms. I love, love, *love* the feel of him.

"Yes, sir," I respond. Let him guess who's the one giving commands here.

His lips meet mine, and he strokes the back of my neck. I taste him eagerly, desperately, and my body thrums with desperate need when he deepens the kiss. With a gentle stroke of my tongue against his, I tell him how badly I want him.

My hands explore more as I run them down the length of his body. They shake when I reach the button of his pants. It takes two hands to unfasten them and to reach inside to stroke him.

He groans into my mouth, his hips jerk at the feel of my touch, and I feel his length harden in response to me when I lick his tongue again. Oooh. He likes some tongue action.

That makes two of us.

I stroke him and groan into his mouth, imagining how it will feel with his fullness inside me again. I want him so badly I could cry.

His grip grows more possessive, more intense, and I stifle a groan when he tucks himself back inside his pants.

"Not yet," he whispers in my ear while his lips sample my neck, my shoulders, the tops of my breasts and the valley between them. He tugs my top down and reveals my breasts. When his lips close over one of my nipples, I stifle a scream from the intensity.

"Please, oh God, please, I want you," I moan. My sex clenches as a warm, sensual wetness grows between my thighs. The pressure builds along with aching desire that erases all thoughts and only allows me to feel.

"I want you," I whisper. "Dario…"

Our bodies press up closer to one another, on the very edge of becoming one. He laps at my nipple while he grabs my ass cheek and gives me a hard squeeze. I moan and grind myself unabashedly against him.

My mouth falls open on a gasp as he begins to undress me, his fingers and tongue and teeth and palms ravaging my body as he yanks off clothing. It rips and tears, but I don't care. I want to feel my naked body against his. I want to feel us becoming one.

I reach for his tee, and he lets me tug it off him, even as I mourn the loss of his mouth on me for that fraction of a second.

I rub and stroke and grope him as he fumbles to remove his own jeans. His huge, hardened length springs free and I stifle a little moan.

"I've missed you," I say, addressing his cock. He gives it a languid stroke.

"He missed you, too."

I grin as he bends to kiss me again, then close my eyes so I can focus on the intensity of the sensations that ravage my body. I whimper with agonizing need as his thick cock slides through my folds and circles my throbbing clit.

I grow hot, my whole body one throbbing mass of need and want, as he finds my entrance. With a savage, perfect, claiming thrust, he impales himself inside me. I cry out in ecstasy at the feel of him inside me. I've missed him. I've missed him so much. There's nothing that I want more than to be joined like this in shared ecstasy.

He lifts his hips and thrusts.

I scream out as the first spasm of pleasure rocks my body, tingling awareness in every nerve. I lift my hips to meet the tempo of his thrusts, harder and faster, some slow, some long as he takes himself nearly fully out of me, only to slam himself inside to the hilt again. Pleasure erupts over my skin with the first echo of an orgasm, and still, I ride it out with him, savoring every time he drives himself in me. It's perfect, so damn perfect.

My skin flushes and tears trickle down my cheeks. He kisses the tears away and sucks them into his mouth, making my emotions a part of him. My mind goes blank as he impales me again, and again, every movement of his hips sending me closer to climax.

"Come, baby," he orders against my ear. I try to let go, try to release, but I'm so caught up in desire I'm on the cusp, unable to fully relax.

Finally, he brings his mouth to my ear. "Give it to me, baby," he growls. "That's my angel. Such a good girl for me. Look at you. Look at how hard you've worked, how beautiful you are. You make me so proud. So proud, baby."

At the sound of his praise, I fly into ecstasy. I scream his name. I writhe in the throes of euphoria as he groans in pleasure and empties himself inside me. I'm dizzy with the power of my climax, paralyzed beneath him, and it feels as if he's the same. The weight of his body on mine doesn't ease, and I welcome the feel of him on me.

"I can't believe you're mine, Vivia. All mine," he says in awe. I smile, running lazy fingers through his hair, before I release a sigh.

"Yours," I repeat, closing my eyes and just *feeling* for a little while. "All yours."

He bends and kisses my cheek, then touches his forehead to mine. He breathes me in. Holds me to him.

Tomorrow we'll take our vows before everyone else, but I know as well as he does —we've already taken them before each other.

CHAPTER TWENTY

Dario

THE CASTLE always feels as if it's alive and teeming with people, but nothing comes even close to matching the excitement of a *wedding*.

I thought I would sleep better last night, knowing she was safe. But all I did was roll around in bed wishing she was with me. I know why Romeo declared what he did and had us spend the night apart from each other. It was partly to appease Sergio and partly to appease Mama, but it was also to hold onto at least some of their tradition.

I'm also not supposed to see her in her dress. We've had no time to shop so I'm sure that her dress is borrowed from one of the girls, or brought in from a local designer, since the Rossis have lots of different connections.

Whatever she wears, she will be stunning.

My tux has been laid out, my clothes ready, when a knock comes at my door. "Come in, it's open."

Orlando strolls in, dressed in a tux, his hair still damp from the shower and slicked back. "Romeo arranged a surprise for you," he says with a smile.

I can't imagine what it is. Can't really say I care that much either, because there's only one thing I worry about, and that's my ring on her finger.

"Oh yeah?"

He opens the blinds and gestures to where I can see the pavilion outside the window. Romeo's insisting we have the wedding inside, for safety reasons. He still half expects an ambush at any moment, before we take our vows, and has arranged for *all* members of our mob—from the newest recruits to the inner sanctum—to be present and armed.

I squint to see what he's pointing at, a handicapped accessible van with flashing lights.

"Aw, is that my grandmother?" I ask. I'm surprised when my throat tightens. I didn't think this would really be a "wedding" but more of a precautionary measure.

"Yeah, brother. Got permission to bring her here for the day. She's downstairs waiting for you, cracking Mama up with her questions. 'Is that a real chandelier? Is this a real castle? Did knights ever live here?'" He grins. "Mama says knights still live here."

I smile to myself and finish getting ready. The tie is crooked, but Orlando comes over and straightens it.

He's the brother I never had.

"Thanks for everything, man. I knew that you'd take the hit from Sergio when he found out."

"Eh," he says. "Sergio can kiss my ass. I love the guy like a brother, but he needed to be taken down a peg or two."

"Or ten," I say with a shrug.

He grins at me. "Something tells me he won't pull anything fast once you two are married."

I nod in the mirror at Orlando. "He'd better not." And I mean it. It would cause a feud between the families, but once we take our vows, Vivia is mine. *Fully.*

"I understand," he says with feeling. "Anyone tried to fuck my wife around, they'd deal with me."

"Of course." That's how it is. That's who we are. Some say we're ruthless and don't have any emotions at all, but they're wrong.

We absolutely do. We just have different priorities than other people do.

"You ready?" he asks. I nod. I'm ready.

I never really allowed myself to imagine what this day would look like. I knew when I took vows to the Rossi family that my future wedding vows would be to whomever Romeo saw fit for me to marry. I had more of a say in it than many others, but in the end, we all know a joining of our two families would be best.

But here I am. Ready to take vows to a woman I really, truly love. A woman I look forward to spending the rest of my life with. A woman I want to raise children with and grow old with, and this is a gift I never thought I'd have.

"You gonna cry, brother?"

I give him a fake punch to the gut, and he obliges me with a duck and groan.

"I don't cry," I tell him, even though it's a lie. I do cry. I'm just selective about who sees me.

But when I stand in front of the priest downstairs and see my future wife turn the corner toward the Great Hall, Orlando chuckles beside me.

"Don't cry, my ass," he says, while I swipe at my eyes and try to get my shit together. Because God, is she *beautiful.*

She wears a dress that is so pretty she looks like she stepped out of a fashion catalog. It isn't the dress, though. It's *her.*

The short-sleeved dress has a sheer floral lace overlay and a plunging neckline trimmed with flowers. The back is a deep V. The little cap sleeves make her look fetching and feminine, and the slim waist of the dress cinches and flares to a long skirt that hugs her body before it flourishes downward and graces the floor with pretty embroidered panels. She looks like a princess. *Princess.* The first little argument we ever had was when I called her princess.

I can only see the tops of her satin shoes, and her pretty honey-colored hair cascades around her face in waves, pinned in place with a pearl clip.

When she sees me, she smiles, clasps the bouquet of fresh flowers from the garden to her chest, then walks toward me on Sergio's arm.

He gives me a look as he walks toward me, almost surprised, definitely resigned, and a little bit wary. This decision will be in his family's best interest, we know that. But he doesn't know what to expect from me.

When they reach us, I kiss her cheek and take her arm.

"Take good care of her," Sergio says warmly.

"You have my word," I promise him. And I mean it. Taking care of Vivia and the family we create together will be my life's work.

"You look stunning," I whisper to her.

"You look like Prince Charming," she whispers to me.

Grinning, we face the altar, the priest.

And the rest of our lives.

EPILOGUE
VIVIA

"Keep those hands steady."

His voice in my ear vibrates with command, and my body, as always, responds. "It's hard to keep my hands steady," I grate out through gritted teeth, my eyes focused on my target ahead of me, "When *someone* has his big, hot, manly body all pressed up next to *mine*." And my ass still stings from the retroactive punishment he gave me for heading into Boston without a guard.

Bossy.

"Is my girl needy?" he whispers.

"Dario. I'm never going to learn how to shoot if you use every single lesson as an opportunity to flirt with me."

He sighs and releases me. "Go on, then," he says. "Do it without me touching you."

But I miss the warmth of him next to me and pout a little. "No. Come back here."

With that manly chuckle that does wicked things to my insides, he comes back, wraps his arms around me, and squeezes. He kisses my neck and holds me to him.

"You've done an awesome job for today. Let's put this down for now and get something to eat."

He doesn't have to tell me twice. I've already taken off my ear muffs because we were just practicing stance, which is why he took decided advantage of the situation to whisper in my ear and damn near grope me.

Naturally.

"I'll grab your things while you put those away. Sound good?"

I nod. "Yep."

We leave for Maui tomorrow, and I cannot *wait*. While others have gone to Italy or stayed right here in Boston for their honeymoons, Dario and I have good reason to want out of here for a little while. We both need some space. We want time alone, without interference from any family, where we can get to know each other more, and enjoy things like *room service* and white sand beaches where we don't have to fish for our own dinner. I will pay top dollar for a drink with a little umbrella in it.

I take our ear muffs and weapons to put them away, when two other men stride in. Normally, we like to shoot at the private range, but Dario wants me to practice at different places so I can get more of a broad spectrum for practice.

"Not every day you see a beautiful woman a shooting range." I blink in surprise. Is he talking about me? I've been so smothered under Dario, it never dawned on me that anyone would even attempt to hit on me. I look up to see the most piercing pair of blue, blue eyes I've ever seen. I'm around hot men all the time, but this guy's… breathtaking. He exudes raw masculinity, power, and danger. He's got three other men with him, all armed, all hot, but there's something about all of them that makes me want to find Dario, and now.

I give him a forced smile. "My husband's teaching me," I say sweetly, just as Dario turns the corner and sees the two of us. *My husband.* It feels nice to say it aloud, and I like the way this guy cools his jets a little.

"Gentlemen," Dario says. I don't miss the way he casually turns his arm to reveal the rose tattoo on his forearm, and I definitely don't miss the way they all step back, all but blue-eyes. Dario takes my hand. "Everything alright, Vivia?"

"Of course," I say, but I'm still happy to walk out with Dario.

"Who were they?" I whisper, when we're no longer in ear shot.

He shakes his head. "I'm not sure, but they weren't here accidentally. Nothing to worry about, though. The only thing I want you to worry about right now is how many bathing suits you're gonna pack that I can strip off you when we get to Maui."

I grin. "One for every day of the week, of course," I say, my heart soaring as we walk to his truck that's waiting nearby. I cannot *wait* to be alone with him, just the two of us.

It's all happened in such a whirlwind of events, I still haven't really wrapped my brain around any of it. But I do know one thing. Having him beside me — solid and dependable, loyal and protective — feels different than anything else I've ever felt before. I don't feel suffocated, like I have in the past. I feel… *cherished.* And that's a world of difference.

"Dario," I say thoughtfully, when he opens the door for me to get in.

He nods, walking to his side of the truck and sliding into the driver's seat. "Yes?"

"What if we don't have babies right away?"

He shrugs. "Then we don't."

"Won't that affect your rank, though?"

"I'm not worried about that, not at all, babe. I like who I am. I like who you are. And when and if the time comes for us to have children, we will." He reaches for my hand and squeezes it. "But I'm content knowing that you're *mine*. And that no one can take that away from us."

I stroke my thumb along the top of his hand and nod slowly. "Thank you."

He kisses my fingers in response.

"Anything else on your mind?"

Now that we're no longer in danger —for now, anyway, I'm not naïve enough to think that things are always sunshine and roses in our world — I feel like I can *breathe*. Probably for the first time in my life.

"There is."

"And what's that?" He takes a sharp turn, heading back to The Castle. We're not far, and I have some packing to do. Marialena is helping, and she said that Rosa and Rosa's little daughter Natalia are coming to help.

I have nieces now, and nephews, and *sisters*. It's all still so surreal.

I clear my throat, draw in a breath, and square my shoulders. I have no idea how he'll react to what I want to tell him next. I know very well how my father reacted, and how Sergio did, but Dario... Dario's another kind of man than they were.

"I want a job."

His brows draw together and he doesn't respond at first. When he does, he seems a bit incredulous. "A job, Vivia? Why? You don't need money."

"All my life, I've relied on the money I've been given that belonged to someone else. I want money of my own, that I've earned with my own hard work." I want to do things like donate to charity with money that's all mine.

"That's fair. Of course. We'll have to make sure it's safe and you have bodyguards with you."

"I know, yes."

"Then I see no problem with that." My heart expands and I feel a silly smile creep across my face.

He gives me a sidelong glance. "I'm getting rewarded for that, aren't I?"

I wink at him. "I think you should pull over right this minute so I can answer that question."

His low, growling, *all male* response makes me shiver in anticipation while he does, indeed, pull the truck over to an abandoned side of the road where no one can see us. I slide off my seat and straddle him, kiss him until I feel his hardened length press into my ass, then push myself to the floor between his legs.

"Vivia," he groans at the first feel of my tongue along the velvet heat of his skin. "We have to go pack — *fuck*." I suckle while I knead his balls and he throws his head back with a groan.

We'll have plenty of time to pack.

"Fucking perfection," he says with a contented sigh a few minutes later, fully sated and relaxed as I slide into my seat beside him and buckle my belt. I *love* pleasing him. I love the taste of him on my tongue. I love the way his hands slide into my hair as if to anchor himself to me right before he chases his own climax.

I'm all tingly and warm from our brief but incredibly hot encounter.

"I guess you're thankful," he says with a teasing smile as we pull down the long drive toward The Castle.

"I guess I am," I say with a sigh.

He makes me feel like a *queen*.

Dusk falls, as the lights around The Castle spring to life.

It looks like there are visitors.

"Evening, sir," the guard at the gate greets us.

"Evening," Dario responds. "Looks like company?"

The young guard, a new recruit barely out of college, gives Dario a half-smile. "Marialena's up to something. That's all I know," he says.

"She's always up to something," I tell Dario.

He chuckles. "She's the last of the sisters to marry," I tell him thoughtfully.

"And *that* might happen sooner than later," he responds.

"Oh, she'll be such a beautiful bride," I say wistfully, while a part of me mourns the loss of her freedom. I sigh. It happens to all of us.

We head to the second guard who does our second security check, then sends us off with a nod.

"Welcome home," he says. "Both of you."

I smile, leaning my head on Dario's shoulder as we park the car.

Welcome home, I think to myself.

My home is wherever I'm by his side.

PREVIEW - OATH OF SUBMISSION

CHAPTER ONE

Marialena

I finger the sparkling amethyst crystal before I place it in the palm of my hand and hold it to the light. A ray of sunshine hits a facet, and it feels as if it glows in my hands. At its very core, the gem is a deep, transparent shade of lavender.

"It's beautiful," someone breathes beside me. "What is it?"

I answer without looking at first, I'm so mesmerized by the crystal. "Amethyst. It's a violet-colored quartz. It's a semi-precious stone, but so powerful."

"Powerful?"

I finally turn and look into the curious eyes of a young, pretty blonde with pale blue eyes, her hair cut into a short but stylish cut. Waif-like and thin, I can see the pale blue veins at her throat. She's a full foot shorter than I am and looks like she probably has to shop in the children's section of the store for her clothes.

"Yes, powerful," I respond. "It gives protection and security and used to be recognized as a symbol of royalty. It calms the mind and spirit and protects against nightmares. I keep a large one by my bed to help me sleep."

She gives me a skeptical look. "A *rock* can do that?"

I smile and look back at the stone. "Why not?" I ask. "Sodium chloride is a rock, and we all widely accept the beneficial qualities of salt, don't we?"

I don't hear a response. I continue.

"But you don't have to take my word for it." I've long since given up trying to convince people to believe what they can't see with their eyes or touch with their hands. And I don't need others to believe what I do. I know who I am. I know what I believe.

She only gives me a thoughtful look and nods. "Thank you," she says softly, but I'm not sure why. She walks to the back of the store.

I breathe in the cleansing air, permeated with burning incense. I exhale my stress. *Namaste* is one of my favorite stores in Boston. Just wandering in here seems to make me calmer, more centered. Wind chimes softly tinkle above us, hanging from circular hooks from the ceiling. Large glass domes filled with crystals of every shape, size, and color line shelves upon shelves. Silken, hand-crafted meditation pillows with satin covers and hand-embroidered details are scattered throughout the store, beckoning customers to rest a while and let inspiration and intuition guide them to their next purchase. And Murry, Namaste's resident golden doodle, peacefully wags her tail in the corner of the store.

I love it here.

My bodyguard *does not.*

"Hmph," he grunted under his breath when I told him I was heading to Namaste. He was half a second away from rolling his eyes when I scowled at him.

"Why do you hate that place so much?" Amadeo's one of our most seasoned guards, having been with us since before my father passed away.

He pursed his lips. "I don't hate the place," he said curtly. "Literally, go have a séance or whatever the fuck it is you do in there. It's that the store's design makes it impossible to keep a good eye on you. It's all narrow and dark with only one entryway." He grunted. "Fire hazard if you ask me, especially with all that incense burning."

"Ugh, *hello,* incense is the smoke that comes *after* you blow out the fire. And you people are ridiculous," I protested. "I'm a grown woman who doesn't need *a good eye* on her. When are you going to realize that?" He fixed me with that no-nonsense look I know all too well, like he learned it from the manual on *how to be in the mafia*.

"The day your brother gives the order to lift my instruction to guard you."

I rolled my eyes and scratched my forehead with my middle finger, casually flipping him the bird. "*Of course*. Right. Romeo says *jump* and you ask how high."

Cue another eye roll.

And here we are. I may be Marialena Rossi, mafia princess under the thumb of the Rossi family hierarchy, but if I want to go to Namaste, I go to Namaste.

He only purses his lips tighter and tries to get an angle where he can stand and keep me safe, but his monitoring doesn't last long. I am an expert at losing my bodyguards, much to my big brothers' chagrin. The second I catch him looking away, I duck behind a velvet curtain meant to give privacy for palm readings. Make him look a little harder. Maybe it's juvenile, but I am *so done* with the overbearing protection bullshit.

My sister-in-law Elise once fell in love with her bodyguard. I cannot even *imagine.* It would be like kissing one of my brothers. *Ew.*

The scent of incense is nearly cloying behind the curtain, and I swear it's ten degrees hotter in here than outside. Maybe they think air conditioning interferes with an accurate reading or something. Considering the fact that it's July in New England, it is not super comfy.

I sit on one of the two fabric-covered stools in here and flap my hands at my armpits so I don't sweat through my thin white peasant top. Should've worn the tank top.

A row of unlit but well-used candles sits on a tiny table between the two stools. Tacked in the center of the table is the bright picture of a full moon, and on the wall right near the entrance is a picture of an open-palm, but it's drawn like a map. I know the image well. I've studied palmistry for years.

A horizontal line at the top, near the base of the fingers. *Heart line.* Right below it, curving more downward. *Head line.* The vertical line through the center of the palm. *Fate line.* And my favorite, the curved line that traces the muscle below the thumb: *Life Line.*

I hear the jingle of the shop door open, and the general buzz of conversation in the front come to a halt. I hold my breath. I've been born and raised in the Rossi family, and I know all too well the signs that someone dangerous has entered a room.

"Can I help you?" Someone asks, their tone guarded and concerned.

"Blonde." The voice is curt and deep, husky and unnerving as if the speaker hasn't had the need to speak in a very long while but when he does, he speaks as little as necessary. "Little pixie girl. Blue eyes. Pink dress. She's hiding in here. You seen her?"

"No, sir, I'm sorry I haven't."

Hiding in here? She was just wandering around shopping like a normal person a minute ago.

I listen for more people entering the store. I tuck my feet further up on the stool and hold my breath. I close my eyes so I can concentrate

The voice continues. "Amadeo. Fancy meeting you here." My bodyguard. He must be frantic looking for me. I can't help but feel a little twinge of smugness at that. *Good.* Let him sweat it. Serves him right, like he's the smothering *boss* of me.

Who would enter the store who knows Amadeo?

I look around me frantically, as if I can find a place to escape, but I don't see a way out. This is only a small, cramped hole of a place where people go to reveal secrets and lift the fog of the future. It isn't meant as a hiding place.

As footsteps draw nearer, something catches my eye — a worn rug covering the center of the floor that's been pushed to the side in my haste. There's a small golden handle on the floor that should be covered under the little throw rug I've kicked out of place.

A handle?

Why is there a handle on the floor?

My mama tells stories of when I was a child, how I would hide in the large family room in our home aptly dubbed The Castle, for a glimpse of Santa Clause, the Easter Bunny, or The Tooth Fairy. I knew I was supposed to be in bed. I knew I wasn't supposed to be downstairs after bedtime, and that I risked punishment. My father punished us all harshly, and often without much provocation, but I could grin and bear it like the rest of my siblings.

I was never afraid of getting caught. I was afraid of being conned.

They say curiosity killed the cat. In other words, better to be alive and remain curious. I'd rather be dead and know who's behind the damn curtain already.

I hear the jingle of beaded curtains being moved, the clang of glass jars filled with candles being pushed aside.

"Sir, you can't—" She comes to abrupt halt. I wonder why. As a woman born and raised in the mafia, I can hazard a guess.

Whoever "sir" is has just proven he *can.*

I have no time to waste. That little golden handle might be my ticket out of here. I don't have a second to waste. My heart beats frantically as I reach for the handle. I lift it. I stifle a little squeal of delight with the handle quickly gives way and the entire floor rises on a hinge. It's a door. I cover my mouth with my hand. Beneath the floor, I see her, crouched and hiding, the little pixie blonde with wide, terrified eyes, holding a finger to her lips. Her eyes plead with me.

Those heavy footsteps came to carry her away. I nod, a promise that I'll protect her, or, at the very least, *hide* her, as footsteps draw so near to me I feel the vibration of the heavy footfall landing. I silently put the trap door back down, tug the rug back over it, and sit back on my perch. I grab a worn copy of *Palmistry through The Ages* as the heavy curtain's pushed aside.

I gasp, but it's a faint sound. I knew they were opening that damn curtain.

But there is no *they*.

There's only him. One person. And given the air of authority that surrounds him, I'm confident he doesn't need back-up.

If I thought this little room was small before, I know better now. It isn't even a room but a nook, as this man's entire presence fills every inch. So tall he hides every filament of light behind him. His hulking frame looms in front of me. Black-brown hair cut shorter on the sides and longer on top. A scruffy beard covers a strong jaw and sturdy chin. I watch as a flare of recognition lights his eyes — he knows me? — but just as quickly, the look disappears and I wonder if I've imagined it, as his dark eyebrows slant in a frown.

I quickly glance at his clothes. Nice, well-made, probably custom work. But it isn't the cut of his pants or the way his white polo reveals cut, bulging biceps and shoulders too large to fit in here comfortably that catches my attention. It isn't the faint fragrance of cologne that makes me want to sniff his neck and moan, or the commanding air of authority. No.

It's those... *eyes.* I've never seen eyes so blue. They remind me of the blueness of the hot springs in Tuscany, deep cerulean eyes almost too pretty for a man. Almost. The stern, ruthless cruelty embedded in those eyes erase anything that even smacks of femininity. No. He's all male, every inch of him, and my body doesn't miss the memo.

I swallow, finding it hard to breathe, and I'm glad I'm sitting down. He catches me in that gaze and I lose the ability to speak. I open my mouth but nothing comes out.

His eyes flick from me to the palmistry chart and the book in my hand. I hope it's obvious. I'm an employee, prepared to read some palms, not a mafia princess hiding from her bodyguard and sitting nearly on the head of the nameless woman I'm protecting, the very same he's looking for.

I finally find my voice.

"Why, hello there," I say pleasantly, leveling the full wattage of my flirtation card at him. "Are you my two o'clock?" I'm stunned at how nonchalant I sound, but Marialena Rossi's been here a time or two. You don't have to *be* nonchalant. You just need to fake it.

He glances at his watch. "It's three twenty," he says suspiciously. "And I'm never late."

Fuck.

I smile and I really, *really* hope it's the dazzling one.

"Oh, right. I get so lost in my head sometimes I don't pay attention to the time. Time *is* so capricious, isn't it? My three-thirty, then?"

I pretend like I'm going to rise from my chair and offer the other for him to sit on. Maybe if I'm casual about getting up off this chair he won't even think I'm hiding a full *human* beneath these floorboards.

"No." He shakes his head. "I'm looking for a woman."

I give him a coy smile. "Are you, then? Just any woman, or do you have a type in mind?" I wave my hand suggestively as if to say, *yoohoo, woman here.*

His eyes narrow dangerously. Calculating. *Heated.* I stifle a gasp as an erotic pulse of need shoots between my legs when his look grows stern. *Mamma mia.*

When the corner of his lips quirks up showing a flash of white, I know he isn't amused. It's the look of a predator baring his teeth.

I quickly glance at his clothes. Nice, well-made, probably custom work. But it isn't the cut of his pants or the way his white polo reveals cut, bulging biceps and shoulders too large to fit in here comfortably that catches my attention. It isn't the faint fragrance of cologne that makes me want to sniff his neck and moan, or the commanding air of authority. No.

It's those... *eyes.* I've never seen eyes so blue. They remind me of the blueness of the hot springs in Tuscany, deep cerulean eyes almost too pretty for a man. Almost. The stern, ruthless cruelty embedded in those eyes erase anything that even smacks of femininity. No. He's all male, every inch of him, and my body doesn't miss the memo.

I swallow, finding it hard to breathe, and I'm glad I'm sitting down. He catches me in that gaze and I lose the ability to speak. I open my mouth but nothing comes out.

His eyes flick from me to the palmistry chart and the book in my hand. I hope it's obvious. I'm an employee, prepared to read some palms, not a mafia princess hiding from her bodyguard and sitting nearly on the head of the nameless woman I'm protecting, the very same he's looking for.

I finally find my voice.

"Why, hello there," I say pleasantly, leveling the full wattage of my flirtation card at him. "Are you my two o'clock?" I'm stunned at how nonchalant I sound, but Marialena Rossi's been here a time or two. You don't have to *be* nonchalant. You just need to fake it.

He glances at his watch. "It's three twenty," he says suspiciously. "And I'm never late."

Fuck.

I smile and I really, *really* hope it's the dazzling one.

"Oh, right. I get so lost in my head sometimes I don't pay attention to the time. Time *is* so capricious, isn't it? My three-thirty, then?"

I pretend like I'm going to rise from my chair and offer the other for him to sit on. Maybe if I'm casual about getting up off this chair he won't even think I'm hiding a full *human* beneath these floorboards.

"No." He shakes his head. "I'm looking for a woman."

I give him a coy smile. "Are you, then? Just any woman, or do you have a type in mind?" I wave my hand suggestively as if to say, *yoohoo, woman here.*

His eyes narrow dangerously. Calculating. *Heated.* I stifle a gasp as an erotic pulse of need shoots between my legs when his look grows stern. *Mamma mia.*

When the corner of his lips quirks up showing a flash of white, I know he isn't amused. It's the look of a predator baring his teeth.

"Looking for a blonde who came in here. Smallish woman."

"Oh, the one with a little pixie cut?"

"Yes. Have you seen her?"

The best way to lie to someone is give them a few threads of truth.

"Yes, she and I were admiring the amethyst before I came in here." I sigh as if sad. "But I'm so sorry, I didn't see where she'd gone to."

He turns to leave. *Please, go.*

"Leaving so soon, sir? I'm happy to give you a reading."

And I'm not fully lying this time. What I want to do is hold that heavy, massive palm in my hand and feast my eyes on the tendons in his forearms, the corded muscle that I could imagine wrapped around me, while I—

But no, it's only part of the innocent act.

"Maybe some other time," he lies, as the curtain falls heavily behind him and he leaves.

I stand as soon as he leaves, unsure of the air quality in the little hidden passageway. What if she's smothering to death in there? But I can't risk opening the door quite yet.

After a full sixty seconds I count silently, I pull aside the curtain and look to see if he's gone. Instead, I catch Amadeo's furious eyes but no other customers. I hold up a finger to tell him I need just one more minute, but of course he doesn't care about that. No respect. He marches straight toward me, then grabs my wrists as if to physically pull me out of the store.

"Let me go, or I'll tell on you to Romeo!" My oldest brother doesn't like any man to put his hand on me, which is decidedly in my favor right about now.

"Oh, good," Amadeo says. "How convenient. That's exactly who I'm going to."

I stomp on his foot. He releases my wrists, and I run back into the little room.

"They don't pay me enough for this. They *do not* pay me enough for this!" Amadeo grunts.

"I'll tell Romeo to give you a raise," I say as I open the door. It's then that I realize it isn't a storage place, but a *ladder*.

"You okay?" I ask her.

She nods, her eyes wide and terrified and whispers two words that are impossible for me to ignore. "Help me!"

PREORDER 'OATH OF SUBMISSION'

Jane Henry

USA Today bestselling author Jane Henry pens stern but loving alpha heroes, feisty heroines, and emotion-driven happily-ever-afters. She writes what she loves to read: kink with a tender touch. Jane is a hopeless romantic who lives on the East Coast with a houseful of children and her very own Prince Charming.

You can find Jane here:

Jane Henry's Newsletter

Jane Henry's Facebook Reader Group

Jane's Website

- bookbub.com/profile/jane-henry
- facebook.com/janehenryromance
- instagram.com/janehenryauthor
- amazon.com/Jane-Henry/e/B01BYAQYYK
- tiktok.com/@janehenryauthor

Printed in Great Britain
by Amazon